Obligations

Cheryce Clayton

I write for a market of one, my husband, though you are welcome to read along.

Chapter One - Wergol - 1998

"Nobody panic, now," Morgan heard Greg say from behind her. "I don't know what Tim was going to say, but take a lesson from my people. Do whatever it takes to survive, and plan your freedom carefully."

Morgan twisted around to look up at the black man who now loomed over her. Twenty-eight years old, and the closest thing to an adult their make-believe family ever had, Greg was talking. As much to keep himself from panicking as anyone else, Morgan thought, with a glance about the room.

It was an auditorium, larger than her school's, but less than half-filled. They were on a raised circular stage fifteen feet wide. Several of the gray robed aliens Greg had described from their capture were also on the stage, standing about the edges. Many other species could be seen scattered throughout the room, including several humans.

"I hear you, man, pride slaughtered my ancestors," Sam said from above Morgan.

As Sam helped her to stand, Morgan looked into his midnight eyes and remembered the television westerns she loved watching when he wasn't around. The memory of feathers and war paint threatened to block out his face, and she blinked her eyes to clear her conscience.

"Human female. Step forward."

Morgan held her breath, thinking they meant her.

One of the robed aliens moved a step closer to them and flicked a whip at the dazed and still sitting Denise. The teen screamed in pain as the pink flesh on her bare arm went white and blossomed into a vivid red welt.

"Damn you!" Tim shouted and lunged for the alien. He never

got close; a whip hit him hard to the chest, and he staggered backwards, to be caught by Sam.

"You okay, man?" Greg whispered, his deep black face gone gray as he eyed the robed aliens.

"Yeah," Tim said, with a brisk shrug to shed Sam's hands, and moved to stand beside Morgan.

Morgan tipped her head back to look up at him, and ignored everything around her as she tried to memorize Tim's face. Brown skin; not black, not white, just dark, even with his tan beginning to fade. His eyes were a green no contact lens could fake, rimmed with thick, black lashes. His mustache had grown thicker, and a faint beard now outlined his thin chapped lips. Morgan refused to drop her gaze from his mouth as she blinked tears away. The room's silence brought her attention back to Denise.

"Female friend. Sold."

The whip again moved toward the crying Denise, but this time did not connect. Denise looked at Tim and then the others, in panic, before she stepped forward one very small step.

"What, what do you want?" Denise cried out in a high-pitched whine.

One member of the auditorium crowd moved up the stairs to the stage. Her buyer was human: a very tall man with Middle Eastern clothing. He smiled in answer to her question and threw a small pouch at the robed alien auctioneer.

"I don't understand, Tim. Tim?" Denise turned her frightened gaze back to her friends.

"World's oldest profession, baby," Greg called to her when it became evident that Tim was not going to answer her.

The buyer put his arm around her shoulder and gently forced her to the steps.

Morgan closed her eyes as she grasped the older girl's situation.

"I can't, I won't." Denise resisted her buyer, and stared from Tim who refused to meet her gaze, to Greg who just shrugged without further comment.

Her half-formed protests were stilled when her purchaser paused. He stroked his hand along her cheek before he pulled her dirty, bleached blonde hair from one side of her face, and pinned it in place. Denise pulled the pin from her hair. It was shaped like a snowflake that was crafted of white metal and brilliant gemstones. The man smiled one last time before he placed his arm around her shoulders and directed Denise down the stairs.

"Woo-ee. Looks like she fell into a pampered pet position. Let's hope we all do as well." Greg didn't smile when he spoke.

Morgan felt Tim move to hold her in response, his large hands over her small shoulders; thumbs circling the top of her neck, his hands encasing her chest with an external set of ribs, but this one made of fingers.

"Humans. Males, step forward."

Once more the whip flicked out, this time catching Tim on the wrist, and Morgan's ear burned as the whip retracted.

Tim clenched her shoulders tight but did not move.

"Humans, separate. Child pain."

Tim stepped to the side of Morgan when their keeper pulled back to strike again.

"I love you," Morgan whispered, staring at his back as he stepped forward to join Greg and Sam.

"Man, we are popular," Greg said as the sound level in the room increased. Where one had bid for Denise, nearly every person in the room was bidding now.

"I love you too," Tim said, but never turned to look at Morgan.

She thought he might be afraid of what would happen if his resolve broke. Afraid he would get them all killed.

"Mercenaries sold. The House Medori. Bow."

"At least we know where we stand," Greg said to the room, which had grown silent as four short, orange aliens moved towards the stage.

Only one climbed the stairs. It was of a fur bearing species, with visibly pointed teeth. "Yes, you do. Follow me," their buyer said in accented English as it handed a large pouch to the auctioneer.

"Wait, buy Morgan," Tim called out and moved towards his new owner. "Please."

Morgan saw no hesitation in his step even when a whip caught him hard across the cheek.

"The infant? I think not."

Tim lunged halfway down the stairs at this pronouncement.

Repeated applications of the whips prevented him from reaching their new owner.

Morgan bit her lip as Tim fell the rest of the way down the steps.

"Carry him." Their owner made eye contact with Greg before turning and walking away. "Next time he dies," was said over a retreating shoulder.

"Come on." Greg moved past the still-silent Sam and bent to pick up the unconscious Tim.

Neither looked to meet Morgan's gaze.

"Human, child. Step forward."

Morgan moved to the edge of the stage and watched Greg and Sam carry Tim from the room. She continued to stare at the door they exited without noticing the silence in the room.

"Ship rat. Sold."

Morgan pried her eyes from the door and stared at the creature that moved towards her up the stairs. It was short, maybe half a foot taller than her own four feet. But there the similarity ended. Morgan gasped in horror as a rancid odor reached her; even the robed slavers kept their distance from the obese, filthy alien, allowing its pouch of money to fall to the floor untouched.

Chapter Two - Bystocc – 2011

"Was it really necessary?" Morgan asked from where she stood framed by broken glass. She stared down out of the window at the carnage and destruction just beginning to be repaired.

Two young Sansheren could be seen studying a pile of rubble across the street, and Morgan squinted to see the bright green danger flag they placed before walking to the next pile. It was the symbol for unexploded ordnance, she realized without surprise. Her eyes followed the road and the warning signs, so many that they reminded her of prayer flags waving in the breeze, and she closed her eyes to block the memory of Earth.

"Two months since the cease-fire, and not a single hospital in operation for the natives," Neavillii said, forcing Morgan's attention to her friend and aide. A mature Sansheren, Neavillii was short, orange, and every bit a bored predator.

"The sewers and water are still out in every major city, half of a continent has been reduced to glowing craters, and the Ouosin's own people whisper of torture and brutality. I guarantee their beloved Twelve will not risk another House's neutrality," Neavillii finished in a soft voice that soothed Morgan's own nervous fear as she stared out at the city once more.

Below on the street, new flags marked a buried body, unexploded ordinance, and radioactive debris. The rules of war had not been broken, they had been ignored, and Morgan wondered if memories of her human childhood were coloring her mood.

"And yet, I find myself unready for this confrontation," Morgan said, and turned from the window to eye the large dining room where she had been left to await Tadesde, a Twelfth level Sansadee, leader of the conquering force. As a new Ninth level

Sansadee, Morgan's own party numbered ten: eight security, her aide, and herself. The Sansheren in the room were orange with hints of green, a muscular people who trusted to their own fur for warmth. Morgan wore a long black scarf draped across her shoulders and wished for thicker material. Her security stood in a cluster between her and the platforms where the meal would be served. The Arbitration papers lay ignored beside an empty seat in the center of the largest platform.

"My adopted father, Neadesto, should have sent her beautiful daughter Iedonea. At least with the rank of an Eleventh she could have pretended peerage with Tadesde. As Neadesto's adopted –"

"You are Tadesde's equal," Neavillii insisted. "It matters not your species."

Morgan tilted her head toward her aide, Neavillii, in question. "I know the stories of Tadesde's inception, but dare I call her an Ouosin and discover the rumors false?"

Neavillii moved nearer, and reached up with her claws sheathed to begin massaging Morgan's tense shoulders. "Her own people claim peerage to her, and few are even your rank. I am honored to attend this meal, and I will hold my head high," Neavillii said, and Morgan twisted around to smile.

More than thirty retainers swept into the room; at their lead was a bannerless Sansheren who was so young that Morgan was startled by the green fur that still dominated the other's adult orange. "Tadesde?" Morgan whispered, and knew she must be wrong. Tadesde's archetype was marked by a reddish coloring and narrow features, and the other did not match any of the descriptions of the young leader Morgan was waiting for.

"Have you any questions for our Lady?" asked a voice from the crowd as Morgan motioned her people to approach the platforms.

"I find the extent of the damage appalling," Morgan said while studying the cluster of Sansheren in front of her. "Can there be a reason for such brutality?" None present bore the banner of Sansadee, and she knew insult was intended as those facing her sat without waiting for her bow. Herself a Ninth-ranked Sansadee, Morgan was an independent leader and by her own choice Neadesto's servant. The fact that none facing her across the platform could claim even her own rank was apparent in the banners they wore.

"There was resistance, even after the cease-fire was

negotiated. The alien mercenaries refused to surrender for ransom, your Ladyship. Their species has no sense of honor or peerage," a new voice said, but Morgan could see no one bow.

"Perhaps you set the ransom too high," Morgan replied, not quite ignoring the second insult, being as human as the slandered mercenaries.

"But if our House is to gain any profit from this experience we must demand full restoration and reconstruction of the prize," another Sansheren said, and this time Morgan spotted the speaker. The woman was not the youngest present, and yet she was still far too young to wear the banners that proclaimed her rank of Twelfth in the order of Gulardee, a soldier. She was the same soldier who escorted Morgan on her recent tour as Arbitrator for the devastated planet, and Morgan paused to collect her thoughts as she noted the scar on the woman's shoulder and stain on her House banner that proved that she had jumped from Tenth ranked to Twelfth overnight and wasn't a sister or cousin.

"Traditionally, a mercenary's ransom does not exceed twenty percent of the time involved in the original conflict. Your own demands are in excess of one hundred and thirty percent," Morgan said with a smile. She knew she was toying with the powerful young soldier. "Why?" she asked, and retainers on both sides of the room tensed as the military leader stood and flexed her fingers, unsheathing her claws.

"As my wonderful friend said," the first voice interjected, "there was resistance after the cease-fire. We should be reimbursed at one hundred percent for this time. We also feel that we should be granted a bonus of half of the traditional time to discourage such dishonorable actions in the future." The woman who stood to calm the Gulardee was old and nearing retirement.

Morgan blinked when she noticed that the other's chest banners betrayed her as a Tamsatel, and little more than the head of Tadesde's House's domestic pyramid. "No, the traditional ransom was set to discourage such destruction of the prize as we see here," Morgan replied. "Your House acted against the better interests of this planet in pursuing the battle after the original cease-fire was negotiated. The new nuclear bombardment of the Western Continent only proves my-"

"But, most honorable Arbitrator, we have already informed you that the mercenary Captain, Timone, was responsible for all of the nuclear weapons that ravaged the Western Continent," the Gulardee leader challenged.

Morgan was distracted for a moment by the Sansheren's pronunciation of the mercenary leader's name, Tim-o-nee, and how her name always became Mor-gan-aye. She remembered Neavillii once telling her that a one-or two–syllable name was as unnatural as a one- or two-sided triangle.

"You cannot plan to penalize our wonderful and benevolent leader Tadesde, she who holds the Twelfth rank in the order of the Sansadee? It is Timone you should punish!" the Tamsatel shouted her disbelief as the others in the party sat glaring at Morgan.

"Am I to be forced into accepting your honor as to what occurred?" Morgan asked, and allowed her growing disgust at Tadesde's treatment of the planet to surface in her voice. "How convenient Timone did not survive. Ransom will stand at twenty percent of the time involved. Mercenaries will be provided the option to purchase their debt, and medical care will be provided for any who need it, native or mercenary. As punishment for the use of nuclear weapons, I insist that any mercenary or native found to be dying by radiation contamination or exotic poison can expect full family benefits for the length of their lives, plus family status for up to ten whom they choose to record," Morgan finished, and felt guilty at the amount of pleasure she received from handing down such a harsh judgment. Watching the two standing, Morgan saw the young Gulardee's look of protest shift to one of fear and hatred. Glancing around the room, she noted that none of Tadesde's retainers would accept eye contact. Among her own people, Neavillii was smiling at her, and Morgan almost laughed when she realized the very human smile that played on her own face.

"Will you sign the judgment papers for your mistress?" Morgan used an intimate inflection on the traditional compliment to return the insults offered earlier with a twist. The young soldier was too far beneath her, regardless of rank, but Tadesde was not and Morgan enjoyed the look of irritation that crossed the other woman's face at the childish slur.

"It is said that the House of Sheresuan is the most neutral and honorable, this is why we asked your own love, Neadesto of the

Twelfth and highest rank of Sansadee, to send us one of her daughters to arbitrate the ransom. Dare we risk another House deciding worse? I will send for my most loved Sansadee of the House Dejymo, Tadesde. She will have the honor of signing the papers herself. I look forward to dining with you when she arrives," the young Gulardee said, and without a bow, turned and stalked out of the room.

Morgan waited a minute and watched as Tadesde's retainers shifted in their seats before moving to reclaim her own.

"Tadesde," Neavillii said.

Her whisper caught Morgan half-way beginning to sit. The rapidness with which the other leader appeared surprised Morgan as she shifted to bow.

"Do not bow to me, child," Tadesde said with a smile. "We are equals, you and I."

Morgan had a difficult time covering her surprise at the undeserved compliment. "You jest at my expense," Morgan said in a soft whisper meant for the other woman and finished her bow. "You have obtained the Twelfth rank of Sansadee, and I am new to the Ninth; surely the only equality between us would be found in a bedroom?"

"A proposal, Arbitrator?" Tadesde asked with a smile and took her place opposite Morgan on the large platform, moving the Arbitration papers aside without reading them.

"Only truth," Morgan replied and sat.

"A compliment, then," Tadesde said, her smile fading. "I had heard that you boiled your meat and served it in broth as a toothless old woman would prefer. I did not believe this rumor, but, as my dear wife Meshari of the Twelfth rank of Gulardee reminded me, you are alien," Tadesde said, and shared a smile with the young soldier who had represented her. "I ordered my chef to fix such a dish especially for you. You do put vegetables in this dish, do you not?" Tadesde - leader of the conquering forces, Twelfth rank Sansadee, and ruler of two planets - asked as she offered a feral grin to Morgan. The Arbitration papers sat ignored as native servants placed deep plates of liquid before each diner.

"I eat your food as an invited guest," Morgan said. "Why do you bare your teeth?"

Neavillii placed her hand on Morgan's leg, sharp claws penetrating silk pants by way of warning, and Morgan remembered Neadesto's advice before leaving on the mission: "Do not allow her to anger you. You can only lose from such emotion. She will try to establish a case for bias."

Morgan sampled the soup before her. "This is the best hot and sour broth I have tasted since leaving my first planet." Morgan smiled without showing her teeth as the soup's spices burned their way down her throat. "I must ask your chef for the recipe."

Neavillii leaned away and picked up her own spoon. The small ladle was awkward in her grasp.

"No," Morgan whispered. "It's too hot". She could see the other leader smiling, watching their exchange, and not sampling her own broth.

"I prefer more traditional fare, myself," Neavillii said as she looked at the spoon and set it back down with a sneer.

"And I as well," Tadesde said as the tall, native servants stooped to place platters of meat and breads before each diner. The planet's natives stood more than seven feet tall, and the dining platforms were less than two feet high, forcing the natives to bend both sets of knees and their back as they worked.

Morgan watched as Tadesde picked up a large bone-in piece of meat and began to laugh while eating. The meat's cooking juices ran down her bare chin, soiling her banners of House and order, and matting the thick orange fur that covered her midriff.

Morgan eyed the conquered natives with a bitter sympathy as she ate the soup. Their feathers were frayed and faded, their metal garments pitted with rust and worse. Morgan dropped her gaze to her plate to keep from making eye contact with one. She didn't want to bring anyone to Tadesde's personal attention, and while enslaving the natives was allowed, the custom had lapsed into disrepute long ago. And the reports of brutality were still sharp in Morgan's mind.

The meal passed in silent agony, and by its end Morgan was glad she had eaten the soup. The meats were tough and chewy, the rancid smelling breads were gummy, and Tadesde's manners were not the worst at the dinner. The only pleasant part of the meal was seeing Tadesde's irritation when Morgan accepted Neavillii's bowl of soup to eat.

"I would appreciate the recipe for the delicious broth you

honored me with," Morgan said, and hoped her smile didn't show.

Tadesde leaned back from her food as the servants began to remove the dishes, and met Morgan's eye with a fierce scowl that betrayed a growing rage. "Yes, I would take this moment to speak with the cook myself," Tadesde said and nodded to one of her aides. Then, grinning, she used a claw-tip to pick pieces of dinner from between her sharpened teeth. Probing at a spot of decay that was visible to all, Tadesde grinned toward Morgan once more.

"The broth was delicious," Morgan said when the aide returned trailed by the reluctant cook. "It was just as my grandmother used to make. Tell me, was there red root or just spice berries?" Morgan asked of the ancient woman who stood at the end of the platform wearing a soiled apron over her new banner of House and faded banner of order.

"Oh! Both, definitely both," the old Sansheren muttered. "I was uncomfortable that you would not enjoy it. I am glad that my most benevolent Lady was right about people of your unusual species receiving pleasure from consuming painful foods. Should I have my aide bring you the recipe?"

"Yes, do have your aide bring out the recipe," Tadesde said in a voice as soft as the cook's. "Tell me, is this the same aide who requisitioned the ingredients for this feast?"

"Oh, yes, your Ladyship, yes," the cook stuttered, bowing and backing up.

"Then I would definitely speak with her," Tadesde said, the grin now etched upon her face as she paced to the window and back without sitting.

Morgan and Neavillii exchanged a look as they watched Tadesde's people and the natives avoided eye contact.

"You sent for me, most kind and beautiful Lady?" The cook's aide was young enough to be mistaken for an apprentice, her fur showing more than a few traces of green throughout her orange and red stripes of maturity.

"What foul plot have you hatched against me?" Tadesde interrupted, and moved to stand beside the platform. "Did you deliberately set to cause me shame? Surely there was acceptable fare upon this worthless planet? Am I to be convinced that nothing of quality could be found? What of the animals we saw grazing in the fields as we approached this forgettable city?" Tadesde demanded, her voice harsh as she swept her gaze across the room to meet Morgan's eyes.

"But my most wonderful and intelligent Lady, surely your own personal aides have informed you of the radioactive granules that the vile Mercenaries spread upon this city not one year ago?" The younger cook's voice was calm, but her large eyes were wide with fear. "I dared not expose your most sensuous body to the minutest risk of radiation, so I was forced to resort to foods packaged before the onset of hostilities."

"Could this be the truth?" Tadesde demanded of those seated on her side of a large platform. "Were the Mercenaries so utterly without honor to use such a vile and unforgiving poison? And why are we meeting here then, if this city is so very dangerous? I have no desire to be so vulnerable before such a ruthless and unemotional a tyrant as radium." Tadesde's flamboyance was not missed by those present as she jumped back onto the platform.

"Did your aides not tell you?" Morgan asked from where she still sat. "We meet here because the radioactive granules present the least of the poisonings this planet has endured. The Western Continent is destroyed, and the prevailing winds have forced the depopulation of entire latitudes. The desert regions of the Southeastern Continent were subject to a scorched retreat policy, I am told by the Mercenaries before they could secure a route to safety," she said. Her own voice mirrored the sarcastic tone Tadesde had affected. "I do not understand how Mercenaries with such a reckless and dishonorable Captain could succeed in holding your family forces at bay for seven years. Luck must have followed their every escape." Morgan made no move to sit but offered her comments as if it were a joke between friends.

"Luck?" Tadesde shouted. "I have long suspected other Houses of supplying this vile planet. My intelligence informed me of the financial weakness of this miserable rock when I decided to make it mine. There is no way that the pathetic creatures born here could have afforded to pay for their defense beyond the first year!" She punctuated her sentence by picking up the writing pen from atop the Arbitration papers, and throwing it at a native servant across the room. The pen skidded to a stop as Tadesde slammed her fist against the top of the platform, and spun to face Morgan once more.

"I know a House must have plotted against me, using this puny planet as cover. They did not succeed! I am triumphant! My enemies will feel true terror when they realize that I will build my armies anew to challenge them in their beds. I pledge my honor: those who plot to destroy me will feed my children!" The room was silent as Tadesde, teeth bared, finished speaking with a pant.

Morgan thought of the intelligence information concerning several of the older Houses and hired mercenaries she alone had been given before leaving on her mission. "Indeed, then, I am glad my chosen father, Neadesto of the ancient House Sheresuan, took a vow of neutrality so long ago." Morgan turned her face away from Tadesde and met Neavillii's gaze before asking her aide: "Do you have any evidence that would implicate an individual House or species?"

"I do not need evidence!" Tadesde said in a near-shout before appearing to calm herself. "The circumstances bear me witness. A battle that should have taken months has only been ended after years of pain. The planet is no longer habitable by any civilized person, and now you, my lovely alien Arbitrator, have ruled that I shall see no profit from this venture. I begin to suspect that even you are against me, for why else would you rule so harshly when it was the mercenaries who caused this destruction?" Tadesde asked as she forced her lips to cover her teeth.

Morgan tensed until Tadesde looked away to drink from a glass. The retainers from each party shifted about, and Morgan felt Neavillii's hand once more upon her leg.

"I will not bankrupt my House trying to make this world profitable, and I will not sign your ruling," Tadesde said, and her anger faded. "I would instead honor you with a gift. I would hope you do not take offense at the presumptuousness of my present. Some, less honorable than we, will consider it a gift to the order of Ouosin. You shall be recorded as the only Sansadee of the Ninth rank to obtain your own planet," Tadesde said with a soft laugh, before swallowing the last of her wine. "I give to you, the Arbitrator Morganea, the ruins of the planet Bystocc and all who dwell upon it. And I will include all of the captured mercenaries and natives; for you will need all the help you can find in restoring this cinder. I do not know what possessed me to think it was a prize worth taking," and with that said, Tadesde threw her empty glass at an unsuspecting servant, and swept toward the exit.

Tadesde's entourage were slow to follow, leaving a stunned Morgan with her own people. Sansheren history gave few examples of refused arbitrations, ancient history from the First Houses' Wars. And when arbitration was refused, history spoke most often of the renewal of war and rarely of defaulting to the arbitrator. Morgan knew that she was now expected to honor all of the terms in her own harsh arbitration; she just didn't know how she would do it.

Chapter Three - Bystocc – 2012

"Who's that?" an old man, human, asked from the doorway of a large tent. "Isaac Meyers, Combat Medic – Tansea Isaac, Doctor" was painted above the door in several languages, including Sansheren. The blood of several species stained the front of his apron.

The person he stared at was also human. Oriental, he thought despite thick orange make-up, but he could not decide on a gender. She, he decided on a hunch, but knew he could be wrong, was taller than anyone else walking on the crowded street, five foot, five inches, and wearing rich quilted banners that he thought marked her as a high ranking member of the Sansheren family government House Sheresuan. The other human's black hair was very long, straight, and pulled back to be tied in a severe knot at the base of the neck. Her skin was a deep cream, almost almond that betrayed no wrinkles beneath the garish make-up, and Isaac wondered at her age.

Isaac watched as she straightened the banners that crossed her chest, again.

"Our new owner, I'm told. Name's Morganea," a red-haired alien exited the tent and answered Isaac's forgotten question. The alien was small and thin, the size of a small chimpanzee, and her voice sounded very old and tired as she leaned her head against Isaac's hip and slid her arm around his thigh. Isaac looked down to the alien woman he loved. She looked up at him, and her reptilian tongue tasted the air before she smiled at him.

Isaac looked back to the street and watched Morganea raise an edge of her rich, black scarf to shield her face from the dust and wind that blew through the city's ruins. The scarf dropped away from her right shoulder as she walked, and Isaac wondered at the clean, straight scar that could be seen on her stomach, low, drifting below the waist of her pants. She wore no shirt, Sansheren style, and he watched her hunch her shoulders down. Sucking in her chest like a teenage girl, Isaac thought and puzzled over her lack of development. She could not be thirty, Isaac decided, with a sigh for her youth.

"Tadesde's House is bugging out. That illegitimate spawn of a dead animal was forced to realize how badly he screwed this rock and gave the problem to the Arbitrator. I told you Sansheren Arbitrators were honorable." The small alien's anger did not disguise the intimate familiarity between her and Isaac as he massaged the top of her head.

A deep hum slowed the people walking on the street, and Isaac watched as Morganea moved to put her back to the wall of a nearly-destroyed mural directly across from his tent. The art had depicted a group of dancing Bystocc natives throwing crumbs of copper to small gilded birdlike creatures while rays of sunlight made halos around them in silver, all of the valuable metals were picked out soon after Isaac and Tansea set their tent up two years ago, and he still remembered the night when the drunken Gulardee shot the heads off each of the dancers while screaming obscenities in the rain the day the cease fire was announced. All that remained was faded paint on a pitted wall.

They made eye-contact as Morganea's people stopped in the street and assumed defensive positions around her. Isaac watched Morganea stare at him as the blast of a landing shuttle craft almost deafened them both. The street traffic came to a complete halt until the echoes of the craft died away. Isaac nodded to Morganea as she turned to speak with a companion and then continued down the street.

"Tansea, I know you've worked with Sansheren before, and they were basically good and honest with you. But I can only go by what I've seen, and if Tadesde's just one bad fruit, he sure has a hell of a lot of seeds sprouting up around him," Isaac said as he knelt to lean his forehead against hers.

He tried not to tense as two Sansheren wearing Tadesde's livid purple banner paused to read the sign above his head before moving forward.

"You are Isaacke? A medical technician? The father of our children has been injured. You will come see him now," The speaker's voice was blunt, and Isaac knew it could be considered an insult.

Tansea squeezed his hand as he stood before she moved to retrieve his carry bag from inside their tent.

"I charge a Faldebbian Croat, in gold, for visiting; it would be cheaper if you brought him to me." Isaac's voice was just as cold and distant as he set his price high enough to discourage them.

"Our beloved mate ranks Sixth in the order of the Gulardee. She asks for a human medic, we must pay your ransom." The second Sansheren made a shallow bow to Isaac and opened a small pouch to dig for an appropriate coin.

Isaac held it in his hand, trying to decide if it was more than a quarter of an ounce. Shrugging, he handed it to Tansea and gestured toward the street. "I will do my honorable best to attend to your beloved husband," Isaac said in less than perfect Sansheren, but he was confident that they understood him.

"I have no doubt," one of the Sansheren said as they started walking.

"I'm the only human medic around," Isaac said with a sigh; an inability to distinguish one from the other forced him to address them as a single unit. "Have you met many of my species?" It was a polite question often asked at any mixed-species gathering. Isaac, like most humans he knew, used it with a desperate sincerity.

"I must admit that our experience with humans is limited to the mercenary captain Timone, and to the Arbitrator Morganea of the House Sheresuan. I find myself grudgingly impressed by the personal strength of these two; I believe this is why my love suggested we contract your person for her care." The speaker wore bright blue cloth pants with a red banner crossing Tadesde's purple House banner.

The other wore a cold, angry expression that told Isaac she did not agree.

"I met Captain Tim when he brought some of his men to me during the war. But I have never met the Arbitrator Morganea. How did she come to be a member of the House Sheresuan?" Isaac asked. Every human he had met since leaving Earth was a slave or former slave; to see a human interacting with such a powerful species on an equal footing intrigued him.

"I am told she was taken in as an apprentice by the most benevolent Neadesto herself, she who is loved for her neutrality. Come, we approach the dwelling of the father of my children," the Sansheren said.

Isaac paused as he puzzled over his difficulty in understanding gender in the Sansheren language. He shrugged; even Tansea became confused on occasion, and she had been speaking the language longer than he had been alive.

#

"I am saddened," Isaac said, choosing his words with care. "The pellet that struck you is highly radioactive. The damage is done." Isaac knelt on the edge of the patient's sleeping platform and indulged in a few silent curses to the Sansheren medic who decided to leave the shot pellet in place. "I am sorry."

The Sansheren lying on the bed was young, and might once have been healthy, but now there were bare patches of skin randomly exposed where the pale, orange fur had sloughed off, and a red and black ulcerated sore on the upper right arm. Ugly, green lines traveled away from the wound, and Isaac suspected that removing the pellet lodged deep in the bone would allow the poison's instant access to the patient's blood-stream.

"So I am to die a wasting death, you think?" the patient asked, and held his good hand out to the wife that Isaac knew did not like him.

"How will the radiation affect our yet born child?" the hostile wife asked.

Isaac paused to stare at the oldest of the three aliens as he worked at understanding their language. "You should be safe; just have someone else change his bandages," he tried to reassure her with an unfelt smile.

"My children have long been born and are late into their apprenticeships. I was asking after my beloved's now-to-be-born children," the hostile spouse said, and Isaac knew he had missed something vital.

And again, he wished that all species had easy to distinguish sexual indicators. The first five years he and Tansea had worked together they had both been wrong about the other's gender, it had taken a drunken depression to straighten things out. Now he found himself sitting beside a patient who was not only female, but also nearing the full-term of pregnancy.

"Well, I would not risk removing the pellet for fear the poison would spread through your bloodstream and endanger your yet to be born," Isaac said. "Perhaps you should contact a doctor of your own species; I would not even consider removing a child from your body," Isaac finished. Marsupial? he thought and glanced at the patient's bare chest and waist looking for a clue. That would explain a few things.

"If the arm were removed, would my love's child be free of the danger of radiation poisoning?" The friendlier and younger wife now moved forward to speak, and Isaac looked up to see her pain.

"Removing the arm would gain time, a week, no more. As long as the child is within the mother, it will be exposed to radiation," Isaac said with careful enunciation, trying to hide the blow behind his difficulty with the language.

The trio accepted his statement without pause.

"I am dying, Doctor, you have said so," the patient said with equal slowness. "Is one week so wonderful a gift if it means I leave no child to bear my honor? I would ask you to remove my arm, now, and leave the father's responsibilities to my beloved wives."

Isaac thought the woman in the bed appeared untroubled by her impending death. He saw the love between the three, and nodded as he reached for his bag. "This will render you unconscious. I have used it on your species before, and I do not believe it will affect the infant." Isaac placed a pressure capsule against the inside of the woman's unaffected arm.

"Not yet, anyway," the patient said with an almost smile.

With a look to the other two, Isaac triggered the capsule and watched as the alien lost consciousness.

Isaac laid out his surgical tools on the edge of the platform and UV-wanded the spread, his hands, and the patient's arm. Attempting to work quickly and efficiently, Isaac twisted a strip of cloth around the highest point he could reach on the arm. He doubted the tourniquet would be necessary; previous experience with Sansheren taught him that they did not bleed profusely. Tourniquet secured, he placed an absorbing cloth under the arm and gave a silent curse at his lack of proper sterilizers. His one justification for not taking the patient to his makeshift hospital was his own diagnosis. He began the operation by inserting a drain tube into a small vein. He watched as the greenish-black blood dripped into a bowl placed on the floor.

"If someone would hold the arm, I will begin." He felt bad at asking the two spouses, but he could not perform the operation without assistance.

"I would be honored."

The one Isaac was beginning to like moved to the bed and grasped the arm firmly at the joint. "Thank you," Isaac said as he began to cut the flesh with a scalpel. With the bare bone exposed, Isaac moved the skin and muscle tissue up higher, and began the long task of sawing through. He noted that Sansheren had by far the thickest and strongest bones of the many species he had become proficient at treating. He had never seen a broken bone on one and would be surprised if he ever did.

"They're all surface veins," he realized with a start as the saw blade reached the bone's internal artery. Pressurized blood squirted past the blade to strike him in the face.

"There is an artery supplying this, correct?" he half shouted as he wiped the hot, green blood out of his eyes.

"The arteries connect through each joint. You have to work quickly and seal the end when you are done," the one assisting said, with a startled glance to the older wife.

"I thought so," he muttered as he began sawing again. The hollow spot in the bone was surprisingly small, and he cut a wedge out of the bone to expose it. He shoved his finger into the gap to slow the bleeding as he tried to think of some way to seal the bone end. The realization came to him that the other half of the bone must contain the return vein.

"Hand up the blue box," he said, gesturing to his plaster cast kit. "Now open it, okay, green jar, put a large spoonful of the powder – that is a half a Faldebbian Croat's weight worth – into the silver bowl. Yeah that thing. Okay, open the bottle and pour out just enough liquid to make a thick paste. Do not get it on your skin! Good, now mix it well. Now scoop it into that canister and connect the canister to the nozzle. Very good, hand it here. I will need a small circle of metal as well; perhaps a coin?" With his finger still in the hole, Isaac reached awkwardly for the canister.

"How do I clean this?" the hostile spouse held out a small gold coin, cousin to the one he had been paid, and Isaac wondered if he should have charged them more.

"The white canister contains a pressurized sterilization solution. Do not get it on yourself!" Isaac said, and realized he was shouting. "Your delicate skin would blister. Put the coin on that tray and I will pick it up after you spray it." He could not turn far enough to see if the other was in danger of getting the spray on her-his skin.

Isaac gave up on the gender issue and tried to devote his full attention to the patient.

"I am surprised with your concern for me. Here is the coin."

The tray was held within his reach, yet Isaac had to pause at the softness of the voice. Shit, he thought, delicate – deleecate. For food or for sex. Damn language. He forced his internal monologue quiet as he prepared to shift his finger and put the coin in its place.

"Hold the arm absolutely still! This has to work the first time." He made eye contact with his drafted assistant and then moved quickly. The coin slid into the slot he cut and he began spraying the quickset cast solution over it. Within a moment, the coin was anchored, and Isaac was sawing feverishly at the bone. When the blood began to spurt anew from the cut, Isaac dropped the saw, grasped the arm lower down, and struggled to snap the bone against the platform rather than take the time to finish sawing through it.

"I need another coin," he said impatiently as he placed his thumb over the ragged hole.

"My apologies; I should have foreseen your need and had one ready. My only excuse is that I was entranced by watching your efficient work."

Isaac was astounded as the formerly hostile woman appeared to flirt with him. It dawned on him that he still did not know who the husband among the three was. He knew he must be mistaken about the gender of at least one of them.

"I, myself should have told you of my need. Your apology is unnecessary, though appreciated." Watching the woman's pleased blush, a greening as unmistakable as his own species' reddening, he reminded himself to pay more attention the next time he and Tansea worked on language skills.

Then he devoted his attention to finishing the operation without flattering either of the two again.

Chapter Four - Earth - 1995

"Turn it back on," Morgan said when the strange guy turned off the movie she was watching. She knew he wasn't supposed to be there; he had climbed in the window and then straightened the bookshelf and picked up her pen before turning to stare at her. The blaring commercial interruption caused him to walk over and unplug the small TV.

"You're awake?" Tim turned away from the television.

"He's going to kiss her soon. Turn it back on. Please." Morgan's voice was soft, and she decided she should be afraid, but the hollow spot inside of her didn't care.

"You shouldn't be watching that shit anyway. It rots your brain. What are you doing up so late on a school night, anyway? Your parents out or something?" Tim plugged the TV in, turned it on again and moved toward the couch.

"I'm waiting for my roommate to get home. Are you hungry?" Morgan opened the pizza box beside her, and heard his stomach grumble as he stared at the large, barely touched, pizza.

"Thanks," Tim said and shoved a piece of pizza into his mouth. "Roommate?" he mumbled around a second bite and reached for another piece.

"My parents are at home. Taiwan. I live here with a guy named Greg." Morgan nervously turned her gaze to the TV, in time to see the kiss she anticipated.

"He your brother or something?" Tim said, and Morgan felt the terror and pain flash across her face.

"No." Morgan tried to focus on the TV and block out the part of herself that still wanted to cry at night.

And she watched his face. As he studied her, there was a quick flash of anger - not pity - before he closed his eyes for a moment. He moved to put his arm around her.

"No," Morgan said pulling away from him. She tried to keep herself facing him, watching him, and she saw the look of concern and tears in his eyes.

Tim moved towards her slowly and held her in his arms.

It took her a long time to begin crying.

"It's okay, I'm here. He hurt you, didn't he? It's okay; I promise. I won't let him hurt you again," Tim said, and Morgan allowed the youth she had just met to hold her as she sobbed against his chest. An hour later, before her roommate returned, Tim coaxed her into telling him about her first night in America.

And Morgan fought the dream.

Chapter Five - Bystocc - 2012

"Hush, my Lady." Neavillii's attempts at reassurance penetrated.

Morgan realized she was screaming aloud. She took a ragged breath and tried to smile at her friend. The smile died unborn, and she turned her eyes away, not wanting Tim's face to fade away again, to be replaced by the older Sansheren beside her bed, but, even as she realized her reason for looking away, only Neavillii's face remained.

"I am okay," Morgan said while still struggling for air. "I am."

Neavillii moved to sit beside her, and Morgan looked up into the Sansheren's large brown and green eyes. Over an inch across, there was no clear delineation between their green pupils and brown iris.

Morgan found herself falling into their dark green center and shook her head to clear the sensation.

"Indeed. It would appear that you are better at least" Neavillii said, and smiled from the edge of the bed.

Morgan forced herself to return the expression. "Thank you. I...," Morgan paused, trying to release the emotions that choked her. "Thank you," she ended with a feeling of bitter loss.

"I will be in the next room should you want me, my Lady." Neavillii patted Morgan's bare arm once and stood to leave.

"Wait!" Morgan found herself reaching out, capturing Neavillii's hand. "I... I do not want to be alone. Stay, tonight." Morgan held Neavillii's hand tight as she spoke, but refused to meet the other woman's gaze.

"Tonight is almost over, my Lady. Perhaps it would be best if you rose now? We could feed early and begin your tour anew before the sun finishes rising," Neavillii said and resisted her desperate pull.

"Or we could sleep in and resume the tour when the afternoon heat has faded," Morgan offered and again tried to smile as she finally met Neavillii's larger eyes.

"Indeed?" Neavillii answered, and resumed her seat on the side of the bed.

"It is your decision, my love," Morgan said as she reached out to stroke the soft orange fur on her friend's shoulder. "I would not pressure you."

"'My love,' she says. 'Not wanting to pressure,' she claims. I would enjoy this night, my Lady." Neavillii laughed as she slid into the bed beside Morgan.

"I did not mean to, that is, I did, but…"

Neavillii silenced Morgan the way any lover should, with fingertips against her lips and a distraction somewhere else.

#

"I can still feel my fingers," Isaac's patient said in a bemused voice.

Isaac moved past the other two and stood beside the bed. "Phantom nerves are common among many species after amputations," he said. "It will fade with time…" his voice died as he looked away from the stained bandages and remembered his own diagnosis.

"My wives tell me you worked with courage and skill," the patient said sleepily. "Do not feel distressed for me. Eat with us and sleep with us; I would be very happy if you could take my place this night. I am very tired and do not feel up to my responsibility. Please, give me this honor."

Isaac thought about his Hippocratic Oath for a moment, but Earth was a lifetime away, and Tansea insisted that, with the Sansheren, the offer was literal. "It is I who am honored, though I, too, am exhausted and fear I would not do your lovely wives justice tonight." The entire time he was talking, Isaac could see Tansea laughing at him in the morning.

"You will want to send a message to your companion. I will take care of that and the meal." The one who was friendly to him from the start bowed briefly and moved out of the room.

"And I will arrange our bedroom for tonight, my strange alien doctor," the second said with a shy bow of her head to Isaac, and left the room.

"Aldera is enamored with you. Strange, I thought it would be Yolunu who courted you." The tired amusement in his patient's voice was contagious, and Isaac found himself having to fight a hysterical laugh. He sat on the bed, beside his patient, instead.

"They never gave their names. Or yours, my friend." Isaac leaned against the wall, and was hard-pressed not to show his surprise when his patient twisted to place her remaining hand on top of his thigh.

"I am Numane." The small hand stroked at his pant leg in an almost casual manner. "And I truly regret not being able to consummate our friendship."

Isaac found himself captivated by the claw fingers as they slid across his leg. "A regret we share." Isaac leaned over the woman and kissed her bald forehead. The skin was soft, and he couldn't see the orange coloring with his eyes closed. "Sleep now. You need to rest if you are to bear a strong child." Isaac pulled the cover up and sat up as Yolunu entered the room.

"She sleeps?" Yolunu asked, and Isaac looked again at his patient's relaxed expression, before answering.

"Yes. The rest will help strengthen her and her child," he whispered, and shifted the limp hand off of his thigh and onto the bed. With a nodded bow, he stood and moved toward the door, indicating they should leave.

"Aldera is still preparing our sleeping room. I have sent a message to your tent stating we are honored that you are joining us for the evening. I hope you will not find it presumptuous that I included another gold piece so that your companion could replace you tonight. It was our desire that caused her to miss your presence; we should pay, not you," Yolunu said, and once more Isaac was forced to control his facial expression, using a second nodded bow to imply acceptance. "It shames me that we cannot provide you with an elegant meal, but you must be familiar with the difficulties involved in finding edible food."

Isaac thought about the planet they were on. "I am confident that your food will be more elegant than anything I have tasted in years. If I may be so bold as to inquire, what is your ranking in the withdrawal?" Isaac followed Yolunu from the hallway into another room.

This one was empty of furniture; Aldera knelt in the middle rearranging a mound of pillows and blankets. Beside the makeshift bed was a cloth, on which were ten or twelve plates heaped with breads and dry meats. There were also several dirty glass bottles, whose contents he hoped were fermented.

"When our beloved gifts us with her children, we will be placed at the head of the list. Undoubtedly we will leave within an hour of the parenthood," Aldera said before she stood and bowed to both Isaac and Yolunu.

Isaac found himself wondering about the structure of Sansheren families. Aldera seemed to be the junior member of this family even though she appeared to be much older than either spouse.

"I was born of the House Sheresuan, and I think perhaps we will seek to claim kinship with the lovely arbitrator Morganea," Yolunu said, and Isaac tried to ignore Aldera's obvious surprise at Yolunu's plans for their future. "Would you care to begin the meal with an intoxicant? I am pleased to hint at a surprise I have accomplished."

"I would love an intoxicant," he said as he chose to sit beside Aldera.

Yolunu moved to sit on Isaac's other side. "The surprise I mentioned, a human drink, distilled wine I am told. A bit much for our metabolism, it was found in the ruins of Captain Timone's bunker. I hope it is to your liking," Yolunu said with a gesture to one of the bottles.

Aldera lifted the bottle and poured a small, narrow glass full before handing it to Isaac.

"Brandy!" Isaac gasped after taking a very satisfying swallow that drained half of the glass.

"If it is not to your liking, I am sure we can find something else for you," Aldera said as she reached toward his glass.

Isaac shifted to place his entire body between her and his prize. "Oh, it is to my liking," Isaac muttered as he felt the alcohol entering his bloodstream and he forced his concentration to translating from English to Sansheren via Tansea's Grec-based language lessons. "I have not tasted anything this good since Earth. My final graduation to be exact; Becky Johnson and I got drunk in the music room and discovered the difference between um, fathers and daughters. That's not right; between husbands and wives. The next morning I left to travel to military training with the worst hangover I ever had, before or since. I am afraid you will have to kill me to get this glass back." Isaac took another large drink, emptying the glass, and felt the liquor burn all the way down. He knew he should eat something, so he reached out to pick up a piece of meat.

Aldera reached forward and took the meat from his hand. "I would be most happy to see to all of your needs tonight," she said, piling bits of meats and breads onto a small plate before placing it in his hand. "There is no need for you to serve yourself."

"I had heard that humans were two separate species, and that reproduction was symbiotic. Would it be impolite for me to ask about the differences you mentioned?" Yolunu's question caught him taking a large bite of sliced meat, and she waited for his response.

Aldera refilled his glass, and Isaac realized that he was getting drunker than he had been since leaving Earth. He took a second bite of food and hoped he wouldn't alienate his hosts.

"Well, humans show their teeth as a sign of pleasure, so I apologize in advance if this happens during the evening," he said with exaggerated care in his inflections. "The physical difference between husbands and wives is that one carries the seed for an infant and the other carries the infant. No, that is not quite right. Each contains half of the pattern for an infant, and after the two halves are joined, one, the mother, carries the infant inside of her until delivery. That is not right either." Isaac made a sandwich of meats and breads while resisting the urge to drink more.

"How do the two halves combine, and which spouse decides who will bear the child?" Yolunu seemed interested in the puzzle.

"Only a wife can carry an infant and only a husband can cause an infant. Um, a mother cannot become a father," Isaac said, and tried to wish the first glass of brandy away. The conversation was almost shedding light on his difficulty with pronouns.

"Strange, to be so limited. But how does one cause the other inception?" Yolunu asked, staring at him.

"The husband has a longish, um, limb that he places within a hole in the wife, and then he places the seed, or his half of the genetic code, into her. If everything works right, she grows a child." He needed another drink, he decided, and drained his second full glass.

Aldera interrupted Yolunu's gaze by reaching for the almost empty bottle of brandy, and filling the once-again empty glass.

"I see no extra limb on you, have you many children?" Yolunu asked.

"I do have an extra limb, it is just, ah, discreet." Isaac could feel his face getting hot. Never too old to blush, he thought with amused disgust.

"Very discreet it would seem. Enough of reproduction, what do humans do for pleasure?" Yolunu asked, and pushed Aldera back out of her way.

Aldera moved to kneel behind him, and Isaac felt her begin to stroke his shoulders and back.

"We make infants. Or at least pretend to. Contact friction is at the center of our pleasure," he said and gulped down the last of the brandy. For a moment, he couldn't distinguish the heat of his embarrassment from the blush of the alcohol.

"I would see this discreet limb that concentrates your pleasure. If it would not seem too forward." Yolunu moved toward him and touched his stomach, pressing; her hand began to move upward.

"I would have to take my clothes off, and it can be rather messy. I mean, when the seed comes out. It is not very appealing by itself, you know." Isaac found himself lying back as Aldera unfastened his shirt and Yolunu's firm hand hunted in circles around his chest. Tansea will definitely tease me tomorrow, he thought.

"Of course," Yolunu said, sliding her hand down and off of his stomach. She nodded to Aldera, and they each unfastened crossed banners.

The silken pants favored by most Sansheren were untied, and joined his own shirt and pants beside their makeshift bed. Isaac stared up at the square, muscular bodies, and reminded himself that they were female, before stripping off the last of his clothing. "Unless," a small voice whispered. "Regardless," he decided, "they're not human, it doesn't matter." Isaac allowed himself to surrender to the sexual feelings and drifted on the cloud of alcohol within his system.

#

"I would bear your children," Morgan heard Neavillii say from above in a voice muted by exhaustion.

And took a long time finding an answer. "I love you," was Morgan's final response.

"Indeed," Neavillii said without inflection. "You are correct, my Lady; perhaps it would be best if no one parented on this rock." Neavillii untangled her small hand from Morgan's hair.

Morgan twisted about to bring her face close to Neavillii's. "I did not say no," she said with a reproachful sigh.

"You did not say yes," Neavillii answered after her own pause.

"I was thinking of the dangers. Especially here." Morgan gestured toward the room's window, but she thought Neavillii had already considered the war-devastated planet they were in the middle of resurveying.

"House Sheresuan's nursery will be fine. I can wait until we return to Our Lady Neadesto," Neavillii said.

"I can wait, can you?" Morgan asked with a smile, and slid her hand from Neavillii's shoulder, down her back, and around onto her thigh as she leaned back onto her pillow.

"Oh, to have children you meant," Neavillii said and laughed outright.

Morgan joined her new spouse in laughter as Neavillii's hand disappeared beneath the blankets once more.

#

"Tell me, why was this missed during our initial assessment tour?" Morgan asked. She stood beside an all-terrain ground vehicle.

They were parked just inside a broken gate. Twenty foot tall steel walls stretched out to enclose the long, narrow valley. Cloth tents in clusters of fifty or more covered the valley with no pattern to be found. She glanced up at the guard tower that was situated just outside the gate. It was as empty as the camp, and Morgan scanned the tents again for any sign of movement or life.

"I assure you that this camp was not on any list I was provided with," Neavillii said with unconcealed irritation. "One of Tadesde's people, begging kinship, told me of it. No one has entered, and little movement has been seen within. It could be a trap, my most lovely wife." Neavillii moved to stand beside Morgan while the other retainers milled about their own vehicles. A few heard Neavillii's comments and turned to stare in surprise.

"Your only wife, as yet," Morgan said, and placed her hand on Neavillii's shoulder to soften the warning. "I would give my newfound kin the honor of walking beside me. Come, let us begin." Morgan moved forward, barely giving Neavillii time to summon security personnel.

"The smell of death is rampant, and yet I see no carrion eaters," Neavillii said with a puzzled glance as they approached the first scattered clump of tents.

"Look closer, friend, between the tents, there, and over there as well," Morgan said, and pointed to the small, dead and bloated bodies that lay amid the refuse piles.

"I trust we have done a complete radiation scan of the valley?" Neavillii asked of an aide.

"Oh yes…, my…, Lady," the aide replied, stumbling through the honorific with several timid glances at Morgan who was greeting a new arrival to their team. "The background radiation is definitely elevated, and there are a few hot spots as we noted on the map, but overall there is no indication of anything strong enough to kill quickly," the aide said, and a second aide moved forward to offer a hard copy of the aerial map of the camp.

"And what of the subtler toxins? Did Tadesde, I mean the mercenary Captain Timone, use anything exotic?" Morgan asked with another glance at the scavenger's carcasses that clustered around garbage piles.

Those present laughed nervously at Morgan's deliberate slip in placing blame.

"Not that anyone has named. It might be wise if we withdrew and allowed a security team to survey the area further," Neavillii replied with a forced nonchalance. Her words echoed the growing discomfort felt among many of the twenty or so people who were following Morgan through the cluster of tents. When Morgan shrugged her response, Neavillii paused to speak with an aide before turning back to Morgan.

"My newfound kin tells me that there were over thirty thousand mercenaries here when she was stationed at this camp less than one year ago. Surely Tadesde did not kill them before abandoning the planet," Morgan said with a nod to the very young Sansheren who had arrived earlier, and now walked beside her.

The youth's fur was still almost entirely green, with an occasional stripe of the red to attest to maturity. "Oh most beautiful and caring Morganea, it is true that there were over thirty thousand mercenaries, compromising every species imaginable, but it is also regrettably true that I personally saw over twenty-five thousand buried in the year I was stationed here. As I have reported to your kind and generous wife, this was a destination for those who could not work. In the year I was here, she never sent supplies for the prisoners, only for her guards and that barely enough to survive on. Many children were born of the guards, but few survived of either generation," the youth said with head bowed, and none present could doubt the rage and despair in her voice.

"I wonder if Tadesde ever considered the day her war would be over. No Arbitrator would condone such actions. What did she hope to profit?" Morgan threw the question out as she moved forward and opened the flap of the tent before them. The odor that wafted outward was enough to prevent her from a closer inspection.

"But she did profit!" The young woman said with her head still bowed. "Please excuse me for so rudely pointing out an obviously unimportant and rightly overlooked fact, but she did!"

Morgan placed her hand under the young woman's chin and lifted. "I like to see the eyes of those I speak with, child. What is your name? Tell me how Tadesde profited."

"I, um... Nealoie. She took the art. Bystocc has always been known for its art treasures. She stole them all."

Morgan shot a puzzled look to Neavillii who shrugged and turned to speak to one of her own aides.

"I toured the vaults in every major city before the Arbitration. I assure you there is no way Tadesde could have looted them before her people left," Morgan said, her hand forgotten on Nealoie's shoulder as she continued to watch Neavillii.

"But, the first year I was apprenticed to Tadesde, I worked the shuttle docks on Shere. I saw the boxes come in stamped with her House emblem. They were transferred to a Faldebbian trader. When I was transferred to this forgettable planet, I heard the other Gulardee boast among themselves of the riches they had acquired. Could the artworks you saw be forgeries?"

Morgan nodded and put her arm across the troubled woman's shoulders as they continued walking toward the next group of tents.

"I have contacted our base camp on the Eastern Continent. Zimsasha is looking into it. If they are forgeries it will be difficult to find a native artisan to prove it," Neavillii said, and moved to open the tent flap before Morgan. "The carrion eaters were butchered."

"By?" Morgan asked, but did not wait for a response. "Tell me child, how many years out of apprenticeship are you, and why did you choose to wear Tadesde's banner if you suspect her of crimes?" Morgan moved on toward the next group of tents, trusting a member of her entourage to check the tents she passed.

"A knife," Neavillii answered Morgan's first question.

"I was to graduate from my apprenticeship the year after I was transferred here," Nealoie said. "I have been here two years, and yet my sponsor insisted I am not qualified in many of the traditional skills. I was sent to this camp when I asked to write the one who fathered me."

Morgan stopped walking and pulled the young woman into her embrace. "I would name you as my daughter and declare you complete of apprenticeship. Would you do me the honor of coming to my banner?" Morgan said, and looked up to smile at Neavillii's startled expression.

Before Nealoie could respond to Morgan's generosity, a soft moan was heard coming from a tent to the left of them. Neavillii moved to stand beside Morgan, hands outstretched, and prevented her from moving toward the tent as three of her security members drew weapons and approached the tent.

"This is not necessary," Morgan muttered, with more amusement than annoyance.

"But it is, my most wonderful father. It is!" Nealoie gave Morgan one long, beseeching look and ran forward through the tent flap.

No one moved.

Morgan stormed toward the closest member of her security

detachment. "You did not even attempt to stop her!" she yelled.

Neavillii shifted to stand directly in front of the tent flap, but nothing could be heard from within.

"I am determined to protect you, my Lady. I knew you would enter that tent. She did first what I was planning. Your House is honored by her courage and devotion." The security officer was an old soldier wearing a single banner of the Eleventh rank of Gulardee and nothing where Tadesde's House banner used to be; she stood firm and did not step from Morgan's way.

"Honor to an unborn House is not a very kind epitaph," Morgan said abruptly. "Assist her or move aside."

Again no one moved, and in the uncomfortable silence that built, she considered the complement the officer had paid her. Standing in front of the tent, she thought of the interviews she had granted in the week since Tadesde began her pull out. Nearly two hundred of Tadesde's people had contacted her camp about defecting. If all requests were granted, her own retainers ranks would swell to over a thousand, families included. Even the Gulardee that stood before her was of Tadesde's blood family, and yet the loyalty in her eyes could not be doubted.

Every Sansheren dreamed of becoming a Twelfth ranked Sansadee and establishing her own House. A power pyramid with her at the top and a planet or more in dominion. A long lived species, most never considered the possibility until well beyond their first century, so Morgan dismissed the dream. But now, as she stood in the silence of the death camp, with her people refusing her orders out of love and respect, Morgan saw the dream bloom.

Nealoie moved the tent flap aside with her shoulder and carried out an emaciated human. Morgan could not tell if was a man or a woman, and she winced in sympathy as a moan escaped the body.

"She needs water. There are two others inside, dead," Nealoie said as she placed the human on the ground beside Morgan and then bowed her head.

"No apologies. I have been told I am not acting in the best interest of my family. Let me look at her." Morgan placed her hand on Nealoie's shoulder, and knelt in the filth to examine the survivor.

A teen, Morgan decided as she stared at the prone frame. The youth had browned skin and black hair, knife cut with long bangs that tangled over her face, and Morgan brushed the matted hair away to find the beginnings of a mustache darkening the teen's upper lip. Morgan pulled her hand away in shock.

"I have sent for a stretcher. Will she live?" Neavillii moved to kneel beside Morgan.

"He is young and needs a doctor," Morgan said after a long pause. "The leg is badly broken; I think it will need to be removed. He is also dehydrated and starving. Who was helping him?" Morgan asked to herself as she brushed the teen's matted hair off of his face again.

He opened his eyes and moaned before his eyes focused on her face.

"Where are the others?" Morgan asked in a near whisper. "Tadesde has left, we are here to help. You must tell me where the others are."

The youth stared at her with distrust in his face visible to any proficient at reading human expressions.

"Such fear and hatred," Neavillii said, and Morgan recognized the expression. "Why do you think there are others?" Neavillii asked, and Morgan heard her curiosity.

"Humans cannot live long without water, and this camp has been deserted for months. There must be others. Why does he fear me so?" Morgan again tried to stroke the youth's forehead, but he wrenched his head away in panic and then lay still, looking exhausted and frightened.

"If he is a child, perhaps he cannot yet speak or understand," Neavillii said as she accepted a bottle of water from an aide.

"How stupid of me," Morgan said without a laugh. "Can you understand me?" she asked in slow and careful English.

The youth stared at her, and Morgan thought that he understood that she was trying to communicate.

"Yo no hablo Engles." His voice was hoarse as he worked to sit up to accept water from Neavillii.

"And I don't speak Spanish," she said in English. "He is from a different House than I, and his accent is thick," Morgan explained in Sansheren.

"¿Yo no soy norte Americana?" he took another drink of water, and Morgan noted with interest that he knew better than to drink a lot of water fast. He had been a long time between drinks of water before.

"My name is Morgan, they work for me," she said, using a wide gesture that incorporated everyone within sight before ending at her chest. "I was Asian. American. You are from Mexico?" Morgan found that speaking slow came natural; it had been fifteen years since last she spoke a sentence in English outside of her dreams, and she found it difficult to remember the words she wanted to say.

"Yo soy Mexicano, si'. Me llamo Enrico. Tengo hambre, por favor," the youth blurted out and then brought his fingers to his mouth in a gesture most humans would recognize.

"Yes, I have food." Morgan turned to Neavillii and requested fruit for him to eat. "Where are your friends? Um, Enrico amigos?" and again Morgan used a sweeping gesture to encompass the entire camp.

"Tengo un amigo. Su nombre es Sam, es Norte Americano. No he visto a mi amigo desde hace cinco dias. Por favor encuentrenlo!" Enrico fell back as he finished his impassioned plea.

Using her full reserve of self-control, she patted Enrico's hand before standing to give orders to her security people. "We are looking for one person," Morgan said in Sansheren. "Get more people in here and have them begin searching. They need to shout "American". Can you say that?" Morgan clenched her teeth together as the name Sam continued to echo through her.

"There is a live human in this tent!" shouted one of the security people before Morgan could hear if the officer could imitate the word.

Old dreams surfaced with memories long suppressed, and she wanted the fantasy to be over, but she was unwilling to make the effort to dispel it herself. She made no attempt to enter the tent and see the other human.

"And this one." Another security officer stood in the doorway of a different tent, and Morgan knew she didn't want to see, to have her false hope destroyed.

"Spread out. And remember, "American"!" Morgan leaned against Neavillii as her people began searching the thirty or so nearby tents. She felt strangely alert as more calls of discovery echoed around her. Ten, then twelve, then twenty humans were discovered alive in the immediate area. But it soon became obvious that there were no survivors beyond the first ring of tents. And the mystery remained, because none of those found was even remotely ambulatory.

"Do not move anyone; they might have a bone injury. Send for my personal doctor," Morgan said, and had to struggle for the proper Sansheren inflections. "We are still missing one," she said to Enrico as she sat holding his hand. The hours passed, and Morgan found herself feeling guilty for his physical state, as well as uneasy toward the other humans who were in the tents. She made no attempt to see the humans, but instead waited to hear that the one who kept them alive was himself alive. The sky darkened, and, with the light, hope of finding him dimmed, but Morgan insisted her people continue looking and ordered her aircar to light the ground for the searchers.

#

Neavillii watched as Morgan drifted to sleep with the rising of the sun. Neavillii called for a blanket to cover Morgan.

"We have found another human," a voice echoed over Neavillii's communication unit, and she nodded to Enrico as she stood.

"Have the aircar pick me up," she said to an aide and made no move toward Morgan.

"Yes, my Lady," the aide replied.

"I would join you, Lady," the old soldier from before said.

"Your name?" Neavillii asked as they walked toward an open area of ground beyond the tents.

"Banessa," was the reply.

"I will speak with my spouse on your behalf," Neavillii said, and placed a hand on the other's shoulder as the aircar landed.

"I sought no such generosity, my Lady," Banessa said. "But I accept it with honor."

"I made no promise," Neavillii cautioned the Houseless soldier as they climbed into the back of the aircar.

"And I asked no commitment," Banessa replied with a smile as the craft rose above the camp.

"Where is she?" Neavillii asked as she climbed from the aircar and spoke with those already on the ground. The aircar rose up, its spotlight rivaling the dim sun.

"Up the hill to your left, and then down behind the rocks," the pilot of the aircar answered from above, and Neavillii wondered who's communication unit was broadcasting. She watched with amusement as the older soldier discreetly thumbed her unit off. There was no static click to indicate a closed line.

"I see the rocks, we are on our way. Any sign of movement since you spotted her?" Neavillii asked and thumbed her unit off with a click. She and Banessa began climbing the steep hill with the other searchers.

"None," the pilot said from above. "Banessa, you will want to move farther left."

Neavillii did not respond, saving her breath for climbing.

"This is no hill," muttered one of the climbers.

"I see her body." Banessa was the first up the hill.

"Look at her legs!" Neavillii stood and stared at the body below them. What may once have been a strong human was skeletally thin with both legs missing just below the knee. The exposed stumps were bloated and black. Two small cans were tied to a rope that was clenched in one hand, and farther down the hill a small stream could be seen glinting in the aircar's light.

"The amputations were not sealed," Banessa whispered in agreement.

"Here, contact camp," Neavillii said and handed her communication units to another searcher. "We will need a stretcher and a medic; we will risk moving her." It was over fifty feet to the ledge that the human lay sprawled upon, and Neavillii felt herself age as she climbed down the nearly sheer rock wall.

"She cannot be alive," the mutterer from before said.

Chapter Six - Sheresuan - 2004

"Please!" Morgan tried to stand perfectly still. She was nearing the day when the group she apprenticed with would have to choose their career line and find a Sponsor: Sansadee, Tamsatel, or Gulardee.

The Gulardee were soldiers, medics, and mechanics; they were also the spaceship pilots and crew. Fierce and loyal with little room for debate, they followed orders and risked their lives without pause. They were everything Morgan wanted to be and was afraid she would never be. The Tamsatel were cooks and maids, seamstresses and nannies, and even though Morgan knew they were vital members of society, she feared being labeled as one. Feared the dead-end life with little imagination and no hope of real independence. The Sansadee were the politicians, rulers, and elite. Everyone wanted to achieve at least one rank within the Sansadee, to prove themselves capable of leadership. To be of the Ninth rank was to have self-determination, to be of the Tenth was to be desired, few held the Eleventh rank, and fewer still the Twelfth. Morgan knew she was not born Sansheren, and would never be a leader; she held her breath and focused on the dream of space ships and finding Earth.

Representatives from each of the major trades of Tamsatel and Gulardee were in attendance at Neadesto's court, watching as the twenty youths demonstrated their skills in fighting, cooking, medicine, repair work, and carpentry. If one of the apprentices showed a flash of brilliance in a given field, the representative would motion the apprenticed to sit beside her.

Morgan offered her selection of food and was awaiting her mentor, Neadesto's, opinion. With fists clenched tight, Morgan resisted the urge to rub at the face makeup her teacher, Neavillii, had given her that morning. "So no one will question your maturity," Morgan remembered the former spacer saying.

"What, dear, do you call this dish?" Neadesto asked from where she stood beside the platform with a puzzled look upon her face. She poured liquid from a spoon back into a serving bowl.

Morgan took a deep breath and stepped forward to try and explain. "It is from my first House, my father. There, it is called soup." Morgan, nineteen years old and on an alien planet, wanted nothing more than to please the Sansheren leader who had saved her life and adopted her.

"Soup," the Sansheren repeated in phonetic English. "The miniature bowls and spoons you made for your carpentry exhibit. Very unusual and creative, we thought," Neadesto nodded to a representative sitting on one side of the court as if to conclude a previous conversation. "Now we understand the nature of them. But what meat did you use that required such a strenuous boiling? Surely it has enough flavor to be served on its own?" and with the same puzzled look as before, Neadesto began ladling out the bits of meat and noodles she could locate.

"Soup is to be drunk as well as chewed. This one is called Chicken Noodle," Morgan said, and hoped Neadesto did not see her hand shake as she took the serving spoon to add liquid to the bowl.

"This is but one recipe you have recreated from memory, intriguing. What are the noodles frightened of, drowning?" Neadesto politely ignored Morgan's nervousness as she poked around the bowl, still unwilling to sample the fare.

"Chicken is also the name of an easily frightened bird on my first planet. I substituted Alkefro," Morgan explained. "It is customary to add a few biscuits at a time and then eat them with the meat and noodles. This adjusts the amount of liquid to taste." Morgan took another deep breath and proffered a plate of hard, dry yellow wafers.

"Then there was a reason for these, I am relieved," Neadesto said with a smile. "When I saw them I feared that you were unsuccessful in learning the art of cooking. They crumble easily enough, and the odor of this soup is quite pleasing, like something a father would offer a sick child. Very well, I will not be frightened of a bird, I will taste it." Neadesto brought a spoonful of cracker, noodle, and broth to her mouth and sucked the liquid off.

"Perhaps a little less liquid," Neadesto said, and added several more crackers. "But a most soothing treat. Everyone, come and try this soup my lovely apprentice has made for us." Neadesto gestured her court to the platform.

Morgan watched with relief as the others begin sampling the soup. She forced her face still as she realized that the thin lips and sharpened teeth of the Sansheren Court made it impossible to sip delicately.

Chapter Seven - Bystocc - 2012

"But I have already told your most beautiful person, I have no skill to operate on the most wonderful Morganea's species. And these I am not even sure are the same species. They have differences…"

The medic's voice roused Morgan, and she sat up where she lay on the ground. She stretched to release the lingering aches in her back and was left with a dull throbbing headache. Lack of sleep or lack of food, and neither soon available. She paused to hand Enrico the blanket that covered her as she pulled her shoes back on.

"They are of my species, I assure you, my good doctor Fanlelo," Morgan called out as she stood. "The differences are not superficial, but they should not matter." Morgan walked toward the group whose argument her awakening interrupted.

"My lovely and patient Morganea, I fear I will kill any I attempt to cure. Especially this valiant mercenary. Her injuries –"

"You found him! " Morgan cut off the medic. "What are his injuries?" Morgan asked when Fanlelo waved towards a stretcher set aside from the clump of human survivors.

"Oh most loving Morganea, I fear she is beyond help," Fanlelo said and bowed almost to the ground. "The legs were amputated, but a seal was not established on either bone. The blood has been pooling for some time, and I am afraid it is now rotten. To raise the amputations to the hip joints is beyond my small skill," Fanlelo said as she moved toward the cot, and Morgan felt forced to follow.

"I do not believe human bones have veins within; remember when I broke my arm? Everyone was so afraid, and I kept saying my veins were outside the bone? Neadesto made me stay in bed for nearly two months," Morgan said and smiled at the memory. "I think that is gangrene. You should be able to raise the amputation to the mid-thigh. There will be large veins that can be pinched."

Morgan forced herself to look at the injured man's face. "He looks familiar," she whispered to herself. Hearing the gasps around her, she realized that for the first time in many years she had misplaced an inflection.

"I am extremely sorry, my most loving Lady," Fanlelo cried out. "I do not think I could do the operation you suggest. If your father dies, I will not be able to live with my shame and incompetence. Would you be so generous as to raise my children?"

Morgan looked up from the man to her physician, who was weeping. Others stood with various looks of shock and sorrow on their faces.

"Bring me water, I would better see his face," Morgan said without addressing the doctor's request, and then used her banner of order to clean the man's face.

A human man. The sun had burned him, and his lips were split and bleeding. His hair was deep, straight black and his chest bare except for a small leather pouch on a twisted cord. His nose was prominent in his gaunt face, and Morgan was certain of his identification even before he opened his eyes in response to the water she dribbled between his lips.

"Rest, you are safe now," was all she could think to say in English as she stared down at the ghost from her childhood.

Neavillii moved away from Morgan and ran to the aircar, which powered up and was gone.

"He saved my life, I was only eleven years old," Morgan whispered in Sansheren, not looking about to see who was listening. Her entire entourage was silent, in shock.

"They would have raped me, he saved my life," Morgan said, and paused for a moment when she realized her words would be misunderstood. But she was staring into Sam's black eyes, and she knew she did not care.

"They shot him; here, you can see the scar, and he still fought them off. I took him to the hospital, I could not just leave him," and again she paused and dripped more water into Sam's mouth.

"They told us to wait; we had no money so they would get to

us when they could. I called my… I called my.., the older child of my father. I asked him for help. He laughed at me. I explained that Sam had saved my life and my…sibling just laughed." Morgan held the tears in, and wet her banner in a bowl of water Nealoie placed beside Sam.   She gently wiped more dirt off of Sam's blistered face as she continued to speak her memories out loud.

"I called my father's House. It was so far away I could barely hear. My mother was home; I told her he had saved my life, and I asked her to ask my father for help. For money. My mother parent laughed, and then said of course. It was a matter of honor, she said."

Sam closed his eyes without ever focusing, and Morgan groped at his throat for the pulse. His heart was still beating, fast but weak.

"I sat down next to him and the medic came back out," Morgan whispered as her hand fell from his throat. "She said he was next. He was in a lot of pain, even after they sewed him up, but they said he would not have died. They said he did not need to stay there and to go home. They gave him a shot for the pain and some pills for later. The police.., The Gulardee never came to talk to us, we waited a long time," Morgan whispered, and Nealoie traded the dirty banner in Morgan's hand for a clean, damp one without her noticing.

"I could not just leave him, I took him home. He saved my life, they would have raped me." Morgan was sitting on the side of the cot, wiping Sam's sun blistered chest with the new banner, staring at his face without focusing. All activity in the camp came to a complete halt as everyone watched their employer and Lady.

#

"Relax. You're going to be fine," a man said in English from beside the bed Sam found himself in. The gravity was light, and the room was small, free of any decoration.

Sam woke up thinking he was dreaming, that this was a pirate ship; his panic was mildly abated at the other's words. "Where? Who? What happened?" his voice was hoarse to his own ears, and the memory of lying on the ledge as the sun crept across the sky became superimposed over the reality of the moment.

"You are an honored guest on the good ship Sheresuan, flagship of the most benevolent Neadesto," the old man said, and Sam forced himself to focus on the room.

"You talk like an orangutan. You one of their frogs?" Sam struggled to sit up as he studied the man's reaction.

"Not by far. I am Isaac Meyers, head surgeon of the hospital for surviving human mercenaries. Newly established. I'm also your personal physician, and personal physician to her most beautiful personage, Morganea, Arbitrator and now owner of the planet Bystocc. Tadesde abandoned the planet," Isaac ended with a flourish and sat in a chair facing Sam. He reached into his frock pocket and pulled out a small flat bottle.

"Tadesde left? Morganea is human? How many of my people survived?" Sam asked, but he no longer watched Isaac as the memories overwhelmed him and he was lost again.

"Sixteen from the camp, counting you. Here, it's brandy, Doc's orders." Isaac held out the flask and waited a long time before Sam took it.

"Tim had some brandy." Sam did not offer to return the liquor.

"I know. This was found in his bunker. A patient of mine's wives gave me seven bottles." Isaac leaned forward to retrieve the bottle from Sam.

"The patient die?" Sam demanded, and felt his eyes fill with tears as he stared straight at Isaac.

"Yes." Isaac offered the bottle back, and Sam felt the man watch as he tipped it back for the last swallow.

"Good stuff. You ever see one give birth?" he asked, and saw confusion on Isaac's face.

Isaac appeared to consider the question before answering. "No." Isaac walked to the door. "Tansea, bring us a bottle, okay?"

"There was a crippled guard left behind. I tried to help her; I brought her as much as I could bring anyone else. She made me burn her alive. She told me why, and talked the Drecos into helping. That was when the Faldebbians went into withdrawal, and I didn't have to worry about them anymore. And then the Drecos started committing ritual suicide. They asked me to attend and record their last moments. The notes are in my tent, I need to send them to their families. Did anyone find the Faldebbians yet?" Sam asked as Tansea walked into the room with a bottle held in both of her tiny hands.

"Yes, they were found several days ago," she answered in English. "And you remember the last time you got drunk." Tansea aimed her last comment at Isaac before turning to leave.

Sam stared at her small form with no hostility, only curiosity as she walked out of the door. "Have you ever seen a Dreco warrior fight?" Sam asked, still staring at the closing door. "They won't surrender. That group was captured when their transport craft was intercepted. They travel in some kind of suspension for the shift. Thanks," Sam said as he accepted the new bottle and took a large drink.

"I've never met a Dreco. How did you save everyone? You're a hero, you know." Isaac took the bottle from Sam's limp fingers. Sam was silent for a long time, his eyes closed against the glare of the sun he could still feel beating down from the desert sky.

#

"Sixteen survived? I'm not a hero," Sam said, and Isaac watched as the other man got drunk. "I held the rear; Tim had the best chance of getting the men out. I thought I was dying, so I demanded Tim run for it, and I took the rear. You know? I don't even know if Tim escaped. I dreamed about a girl named Morgan, dreamed that she was a Sansheren, that she stopped the war and rescued us. Isn't that crazy? Dreaming about a dead kid."

Isaac wanted to tell the soldier that it wasn't a dream, but Sam was far enough into the alcohol that Isaac doubted he could hear the responses he was waiting for.

"The Drecos dried their dead for meat," Sam continued. "I would have buried them but their Captain or priest, I don't know, he insisted I use the meat. I never told anyone. I told them it was game I had trapped. There were three thousand Drecos and they just killed themselves, twenty or thirty a week. He put their death moments in a wooden box and asked me to take them home for him; I have to go back to the camp for the box. It's in my tent."

Isaac listened as Sam's mumbling faded away into snoring. He stood watching the man for several minutes before leaving the room and searching for Morgan. He found her in the ship's observation lounge.

"It will take a while," Isaac said in Sansheren. "But physically, I think he will be fine."

"I have to return to the planet, to coordinate the interim relief. Several Houses have offered generous relief packages. At least as generous as their support of the mercenaries was. I wish I had room for all the human survivors, but it will be crowded with the few people I am taking home with me." Morgan kept her back to him as she stared out the porthole at the planet below.

"But my Lady, by right this is your home, and your House now," Neavillii said with a smile as she entered the small room.

"The defections of an insane Sansadee's people say little of the permanence of my alleged promotion," Morgan replied, and did not turn to face either Neavillii or Isaac. "Tadesde has made me Ouosin, and I have no liking for the title."

"May I ask after the meaning of the title Ouosin's? I have heard it used but never learned the context." Isaac glanced from Morgan's back to Neavillii.

"It denotes one who holds a title without right or rank. One who has been promoted through a rank without merit," Neavillii said as she continued to watch Morgan.

"Tadesde's a valuable example of the danger found in this indulgence." Morgan turned from the porthole, and Isaac wondered at the sad smile she shared with them.

"The shuttle is ready, my love," Neavillii delivered her original message, and Isaac turned to leave the room.

"Contact me whenever necessary." Morgan's hand on his shoulder kept Isaac from leaving until after he'd acknowledged her request.

Chapter Eight - Bystocc - 2012

"Hey, careful now," Neavillii said in Sansheren as she grabbed Enrico's filthy coat by the collar, preventing him from falling down the stairwell she had just exited. He tried to balance on his one foot, and Neavillii noticed that his other leg's stump was bleeding red through its bandages. He twisted to give her a look of undeniable terror as he struggled in her grip.

"Hold her!" an old Sansheren called out from down the dim hall. She panted to a stop in front of them, and Neavillii saw that the other woman's hair was streaked with pale hints of green that almost matched the color of her single, faded banner. She was still pushing the wheelchair Neavillii realized Enrico had escaped from.

Neavillii watched with interest as the human child quit fighting her and held still. Frozen and trembling.

"This alien spawn has no sense of dignity or respect, your Ladyship. She should be beaten soundly and sent for apprenticeship early in my humble opinion." The old nursery worker moved to take the child back from Neavillii's control, but Enrico snarled, and she jerked away in fear.

"I have always found a strong will attractive in a child. I would think that it gave strength," Neavillii said as she used her body to block the woman and offer Enrico the chair.

"Then I must assume you have not fathered many children. If I might have her chair back, please," the old woman said as she moved to reclaim her quarry once more.

This time it was Neavillii's expression that caused the old woman to pause.

"My dear wife, Morganea, had a very deep sense of will as a child," Neavillii said. "I find myself thinking that her strength cannot be doubted." Neavillii smiled as she pushed the chair past the stunned woman. Enrico, Neavillii noted with a pause, was arching his back to stare up at her.

"My Lady. You must forgive my impudence. I had no idea that human children were so different from our own beloved. I should have deferred to your better judgment instantly," the nursery worker said, and was forced to run toward the retreating Neavillii, only to stop when she saw the expression still directed at her.

"Must I forgive you?" Neavillii asked, but did not wait for response. "Yes, I suppose. Why was this child not kept with the other humans?" Neavillii continued moving.

"The five children from the death camp were separated out from the other humans. How else could we screen them for regressions, my Lady?" and again the old nursery worker ran to catch up.

"I recall neither an alliance nor a marriage proposal," Neavillii started, and stopped to study the other woman. "I wonder that any would be so well trained as to be able to declare without pause the state of an alien child's evolution," Neavillii finished, and did not turn her gaze away when the frightened woman indicated a side hallway.

"My arrogance astounds even myself, oh most benevolent and understanding of patrons," the other stuttered, "but this child even now gives credence to my argument. See how she bares her teeth at me?"

Neavillii glanced down at Enrico in time to see him stifle a human grin, and again wondered how much of the conversation he could follow. "It is a smile, nearly a laugh. At your expense I admit," Neavillii said and stuck her tongue out at Enrico.

He stared at her for a moment before returning the gesture with far more moisture.

"I fail to see why so noble a Lady as you would indulge in such insolence. The children's room is through these doors."

Neavillii stuck her tongue out at the old woman's back as she led the way through the doors; what she saw inside sobered her.

Three children lay strapped to wooden boards scattered about the floor of the filthy room, a fourth board had cut straps, and Neavillii glanced at Enrico in respect before her gaze found an empty board propped up against a far wall. The smell of waste and infection nearly overpowered her. "What is this outrage?"

She demanded. Neavillii left Enrico's chair beside the door and moved to release the first child from the bonds that bit deep into her arms.

"But, surely a patron as intelligent and understanding as yourself will understand," the old woman said. "They are all near infancy. The doctors refused to see them. I did the best I could." The old woman found her retreat toward the doorway blocked by a teeth-baring Enrico.

"I am not your patron," Neavillii snapped without looking up from the rope that held the small child. "Nor do I think my most benevolent wife will be. Her benevolence might extend to allowing you this day to leave the planet. I doubt it will go much further," Neavillii said, and paused her attempts to untie the child as she made eye contact with the woman. Now she turned her full attention back to the thin ropes. Flexing her finger, she slid a nail between the two cords and worked at cutting outward.

"But, my Lady, I requested an audience." The old woman stared from Enrico to Neavillii and back again.

"You have not left yet? Child, move," Neavillii snapped, and Enrico's instant compliance confirmed her suspicions of his language skills. "Wait! What happened to the other child?" Neavillii did not look up as she continued to speak.

"Oh!" the old woman turned and ran to the door.

"That is what I was afraid of," was Neavillii's response as she brought her gaze up to meet Enrico's.

#

Neavillii spent the morning alternating between pacing the makeshift nursery's corridor and glaring at the medical staff that refused to treat the children while she waited for Morgan to arrive from the other side of the planet.

Morgan's arrival also brought Fanlelo, one of the few Sansheren doctors with any experience in treating humans, leaving both Morgan and Neavillii pacing in the corridor. Neavillii watched with a smile as Morgan vented her frustration by dismissing the other medics and then rescinding the order, but telling them they must become proficient in the treatment of at least one other species.

58

"How are they?" Morgan asked when Fanlelo open the door. Neavillii and Morgan moved to stand at the foot of the sleeping Enrico's bed.

"She has a strong will. She will be fine," Fanlelo said waving them back into the hallway.

"And the carrion responsible?" this time Morgan directed her question to Banessa, the Gulardee soldier who had appointed herself Morgan's personal bodyguard.

"I gave her this day to find transportation off planet," Neavillii interjected.

"She did not succeed," was Banessa's grim response, and Neavillii was not the only one to ignore the sharp teeth she exposed.

"What of the others?" Morgan turned back to Fanlelo without a pause.

"There is only one I fear for," Fanlelo said, and held the room's door for all to leave. "I do not have the knowledge to judge how fast your most beautiful species recovers from brain injuries," she continued as Morgan led the way down the hospital corridor. "The other two will recover fully, and should be ready for their apprenticeship test within the year," Fanlelo finished as the group approached the entry to the hospital.

"You must contact the human doctor, Isaacke," Morgan said as Banessa ran down the steps of the building and opened the door on the waiting aircar. "He will be able to answer your questions. Keep me informed," Morgan said to Neavillii with a tender smile.

"I will," Neavillii said with her own smile. She watched Morgan walk down the steps and climb into an aircar before turning back to the Doctor. "I am planning to schedule audiences through the dinner hour," Neavillii said in an offhand manner. "It will be late when I return."

"I will attend the children as if they were born of my favorite wife, my Lady." Fanlelo placed her hand on Neavillii's shoulder in a reassuring manner as she spoke.

"Indeed. A better incentive would be to treat them as if they were born of our most wonderful Morganea's favored wife," Neavillii said with an intimate inflection and a smile.

"I will. May I be so presumptuous as to plan a late meal for your wonderful person?" The other asked.

"I think I might enjoy that. Please do," Neavillii replied, and found her smile deepening as she turned to walk down the steps.

#

"Hello.   I have a meeting scheduled with Tadesde's administrator," Neavillii addressed a young clerk as she looked about the barren office. It was stripped of wall hangings and furniture, leaving a plain desk positioned in front of a closed door on the far wall.

"I am very embarrassed to be forced to admit that the Administrator Raceri has left the planet with my most former employer." The young administrator used an intimate inflection to distance herself from Tadesde. "If you would like to schedule an appointment with me, I will attempt to place your request before my next and most wonderful employer," the young clerk finished, and she never broke eye contact.

"Indeed.   Tell me, who did your administrator, Raceri, designate to smooth the transition to your next and truly most beautiful employer?" Neavillii smiled as she moved around the clerk's desk toward the doorway to her own new office.

"I am sorry to inform you that only my own humble self and a few of my friends chose to remain in Administration when the lady Tadesde declared her withdrawal. If you will kindly leave your name and business, I will pledge my honor that I will attempt to present your case, personally if necessary, to our future government," the clerk said as she stood and moved to prevent Neavillii from reaching the door.

"Oh, have you made this pledge to many?" Neavillii demanded, her smile fading. And then she remembered Banessa's argument for anonymity among Morgan's higher ranks. With a glance down at her own bannerless chest, Neavillii felt her smile return.

"In truth, no. It is just that you have the look of my father's second wife about you.   I felt you deserved respect for your obviously noble archetype," the clerk said and held Neavillii's gaze once more.

"Indeed," Neavillii whispered, more affected by the compliment than she wished to reveal. Instead, she reached forward, and stroked the young woman's cheek fur where a hint of green could still be seen mingling with her adult reddish orange.

"My Lady, I look forward to dining together soon. But now we're in a very public place, and I am awaiting my future employer." The clerk blushed as her eyes darted from Neavillii to the office doorway and back again.

"I will hold you to your invitation. Perhaps we should introduce ourselves?" Neavillii asked, and waited for the clerk to speak.

"I, my name is Thanera. I hold the Fifth rank of the Tamsatel," the clerk answered.

"It is my honor and pleasure to meet you, Thanera. As for my own humble self, I am Neavillii. I hold the Twelfth rank of Tamsatel, the Ninth rank of Gulardee, and the Fifth rank of Sansadee. And I have the extreme honor to name Morganea my wife," Neavillii said slowly in a vain attempt to soften the impact of her words.

"Oh," the sound was more a breath than a word, and Neavillii laughed as she helped the stunned Thanera to her chair.

"From my perspective, can you think of a better job interview?" Neavillii asked the recovering clerk.

"I would never presume to judge your motives, my Lady. I only feel foolish to have offered an evening with someone so obviously above my rank," Thanera said, and kept her head down, refusing to meet Neavillii's eyes.

"To have made the fifth rank of Tamsatel before fertility, anyone would be forced to admit the potential of rank. Besides, it is I who wear no banners, and none would fault your ambition," Neavillii said, and she knelt until her face was level with Thanera's.

When Thanera's head came up in protest, Neavillii stared deep into her startled eyes. "It was not ambition that spurred my offer," she whispered.

"Indeed, I thought not." Neavillii once again reached out to stroke the younger woman's cheek.

"Excuse me, but I think a touch of modesty is in order. Which of you belongs behind that desk?" Short by even Sansheren standards, the woman standing in the office doorway was bloated and nearly furless. Neavillii saw that she wore stained felt pants and a torn Gulardee banner that placed her within the ranks of the Houseless spacers.

"What may I do for you today?" Thanera asked, and nudged Neavillii before giving a quick glance to the office's picture window.

Neavillii took the hint and moved to stare out at the devastated city as she listened to the conversation.

"I demand an interview with the Arbitrator Morganea's representative." The obese Sansheren entered the room and headed toward the closed door with an assurance Neavillii felt misrepresented her rank.

"If you would so kindly give me your name and business, I will see that my most benevolent employer receives you in all due haste." Thanera stepped around her desk, and the other woman was forced to halt.

"I will not be put off so that you can return to your afternoon tryst. I insist that you contact your employer and tell her of my presence," she demanded with foul breath.

Neavillii watched the spacer's reflection in the glass and noticed that several of her dulled teeth were missing.

"If you would tell me your business, I would be pleased to schedule you an appointment with my honorable employer." Thanera kept her back to Neavillii as she spoke.

"I cannot afford to be put off by a front office clerk and her lover. I have a hold full of starches that will go stale long before you remember to tell your employer of my visit. I insist you inform your Lady now," the spacer demanded.

Neavillii saw Thanera's shoulders tense as the spacer's breath fouled the air in the large office.

"Why should this matter involve my employer?" Thanera asked with equal rudeness. "I feel confident that she will simply remind you that your ship's cargo became the Lady Morganea's property when Tadesde signed over this planet. And the benevolent Morganea has instructed all supplies be delivered up for general distribution," Thanera said as she moved past the spacer and opened the entry doorway.

"But I have not been paid for my cargo! Surely the Arbitrator Morganea could not expect me to surrender all hope of profit? Where is the justice in that?" the woman did not follow Thanera to the entry but instead hurried across the room toward the inner doorway.

"There is no one inside!" Thanera called out before the other could open the door. "If you will sit at my desk, I will see what can be done for you and your cargo of much needed starches." Thanera shrugged to Neavillii as she sat at her desk and activated her communication unit.

"Finally," the spacer said, and moved to sit where Thanera was pointing. "If you assist me in getting my payment, I promise I will not report you to your employer."

Neavillii felt herself having difficulty controlling the urge to laugh as the pompous spacer gestured in her direction.

"Indeed," Thanera said in a near perfect imitation of Neavillii. "Trizonu, I need a record checked. What was the name of your vessel?" she lowered the communication unit as she addressed the ship captain.

"The Slender Beauty, we made planet fall three days before the Arbitration," the obese woman said with an effort to sit straighter, and brushed at a stain on her single banner.

"The Slender Beauty. It did? It was? Thank you. Yes, I did meet her. I think it'll work. At dinner? Great," and in the window's reflection Neavillii made eye contact with Thanera as the young administrator spoke.

"Well? When will I receive my payment and lift authorization?"

Thanera brought her gaze from Neavillii back to the spacer in front of her. "Our records show that you made planet fall nearly two weeks before Arbitration and that Tadesde's people refused to pay more than half your asking price because the cargo was nearly rancid then. You will be placed on the lift queue immediately. You will be required to show that you are lifting empty. Good day." Thanera turned her body away from the spacer but continued to watch what she did.

"I will report you. I will file a complaint. I will have your job within the week." The fat woman continued to issue threats as the office door swung closed behind her.

"Well handled." Neavillii moved away from the window to join Thanera at her desk.

"Thank you; you truly are a most rewarding employer." Thanera lowered her head and blushed as she spoke.

"I am also an employer who favors openness and honesty over courtly behavior. Shall we tour my new domain?" Neavillii stood and moved toward the inner door.

Thanera lunged to grab Neavillii's arm and prevent her from opening the door. "Wait! It is not... It is not safe," she whispered. "I took the liberty of making arrangements for you to hold interviews in the cafeteria area. We are still fixing the computer linkups, but it should be ready for your presence," Thanera finished as Neavillii stepped back from the door.

"I have confidence your arrangements will be most suitable. Am I correct to assume that my predecessor did not, in fact, leave the planet?" Neavillii gave a tight nod to the closed door.

"Raceri, my lovely former employer, committed suicide within. I have been able to find no one to clear the room properly." Thanera leaned her back against the forbidding door.

"Indeed, to die alone is not a fate I desire," Neavillii said with a shudder, and then stepped forward to place her hands upon Thanera's shoulders.

"Nor I. But she was not alone. Tadesde herself was within the room when I heard the shot. Her staff has not yet acknowledged the paternity notice. My Lady... My employer had given me the name of the Fifth rank of Tamsatel that day. She told me I should stay on the planet, join Morganea in the reconstruction. It has been nearly one week, and now you are here." Thanera moved into Neavillii's arms to cry against her chest.

"You honor me with your presence. I can only hope your bravery is contagious," Neavillii began, and felt Thanera try to pull away, the young administrator's tear-streaked face betraying confusion as Neavillii finished the ceremonial words. "In the face of such devotion I can do no less than bring you closer to myself," and with that, Neavillii leaned to the young woman's ear and whispered a single word. The promotion ceremony was ancient and made simple through time, and Neavillii paused to savor the opportunity to elevate a new leader.

"But, my Lady, I..."

Neavillii laughed as the previously eloquent Thanera struggled for words. "Say nothing. You have given me the opportunity to actually feel and understand the words of the ceremony," Neavillii said and held one hand on Thanera's shoulder.

"I, oh. The cafeteria should be ready, would you follow me?" Thanera blushed as she moved across the room and held the door open.

"Indeed. Tell me just how many waited to follow my banner?" Neavillii exited the room and walked beside her clerk.

64

"Of the one hundred and fifty eight who worked for Administrator Raceri, seventy-three have struggled with me this week." Thanera's voice betrayed no pride.

"And how many bow their heads to you?" Neavillii continued to probe as they moved further into the maze of bureaucratic offices.

"Someone was needed to coordinate things, and as Raceri's aide, I fell into that position." Thanera kept her gaze straightforward as they walked.

"Was there a vote?" Neavillii stopped in the doorway of an office and addressed a Sixth rank Tamsatel. The woman also wore the banner of a First rank Sansadee. "Excuse me, would you have an additional banner of Sansadee, one that I might procure from you?"

The old administrator looked from the blushing Thanera to Neavillii and back before standing to remove a worn banner of order from a place of honor on a shelf. "It was given to me by my father. I am pleased to gift this to you, my friend." The old woman crossed the room and offered the banner to Thanera with outstretched hands and a head bowed.

"Thank you, Thatina. I will honor this," Thanera said, and Neavillii placed her hand on the older woman's shoulder. They both smiled with pride as Thanera tied on the banner.

Neavillii waved Thanera to resume walking down the hallway, gave the old clerk a slight bow of appreciation, and moved to catch up.

Thanera was silent the rest of the way to the cafeteria, and they entered the large crowded room without a word.

#

"We are still not clear on the exactness of your request. That Tadesde practiced genocide against your people, I will not deny, but surely you require more than just this acknowledgment from our House." Neavillii was seated on a raised platform next to Thanera in the far corner of a very large open room. A single door was open and guarded behind her, and the line of petitioners which claimed the center corridor of the room could be seen to block the room's other entrance.

"You are most wise and kind, general sir. I only wish to speak to your person of the numbers involved," a native said. "I wish the history to be recorded, and I feel certain that if any action is required, your most astute self will see this long before me." Twice the height of the tallest Sansheren in the room, the native speaking was taller than even Bystocc averages.

Neavillii had not yet ascertained its gender, and so had been using neutral terms. She hid a smile of amusement when it chose a gender role for her.

"If you have the numbers you mentioned in recorded form, I would be willing to review them this night and grant you the first audience in the morning," Neavillii said before turning to speak with Thanera.

The native spoke before she could. "Sir. I would not be so rude were it not for the fact of my own miserable failings, I have only learned to speak your beautiful words. My records are in my own primitive language."

Neavillii again suppressed a smile as the native petitioner ended his hurried plea by kneeling and pressing his face against the floor.

"Do we have a translator?" Neavillii addressed Thanera, who assured her of the availability of one. "Leave your records, my friend. We invite you to return in three days' time. Please schedule a time with my assistant." Neavillii held out her hand to the native before turning to the next petitioner.

"I am Kadage of the Ninth rank of Gulardee and the Seventh rank of the Tamsatel. I have come today to offer myself and my family line – some five hundred strong – to the rebuilding of the Western Continent's spaceport. I am willing to accrue all expenses myself."

Neavillii found herself paying more attention to the woman than her appearance or statement would have merited, as Thanera and many of the petitioners reacted to the name so proudly stated. Open hatred could be seen in the eyes of many.

"Indeed, that would be most generous of you. Why?" Barely within her sight, Neavillii watched Thanera clench her fists.

"Why? For the profit of course." The woman paid no attention to the others in the room as she barked out what Neavillii assumed must be a laugh.

"It will be a long time before this planet realizes any profit. Are you willing to wait those many years?" Neavillii forced a smile as she spoke.

"I assure you, most generous representative of the beautiful Morganea, if you give me the space port to rebuild and run, I will force a profit within one year." The woman's smile agonized Neavillii.

"The House Sheresuan will in no way profit from the exploitation of a desperate people," Neavillii said as she rose from her chair to emphasize her rank. The platform she was on added to her stature, and she towered over the other woman. "My love, Morganea, will personally kill you for such a hint. I, myself, will call a debt of honor against your face if I find you have not left the planet before the morning," Neavillii said, and finished her threat by turning her back to the confused petitioner.

"See that security escorts her from the building," Thanera addressed her assistant.

The stunned profiteer turned to walk down the central aisle, which opened before her and allowed a quick and silent passage.

#

"Yes?" Neavillii watched as the three natives moved forward and shuffled their papers yet one more time.

"It is our humble opinion, ma'am," one said, and Neavillii ignored the maternal pronoun as she noted the three Bystocc natives were old and ill-clothed, "that the survivors here would find their spirits greatly lifted by the production of a story. A story we, my friends and I, have written."

"Tell me a bit of the story, friend." She sat back and took a drink of water, and she watched as three sets of eyes followed the glass, and three tongues attempted to wet dry lips as she swallowed.

"It is about war-" "Actually, it is against war –" "Well, mostly it is about love." The three cut each other off as each attempted to explain his contribution to the play.

"Indeed? With the war so recently ended, I would think few here would want to relive the pain." The three in front of her slumped, as if every hope that had been keeping them alive had been removed.

"But, if this play were about Bystocc and the ravishes it endured, I think it would play well before the great Houses of the

Sansheren. And I would be honored to personally commission and sponsor such a play for touring, if not three plays. Of course, you will need a secure place to live while you polish your work, and a meager income with which to feed yourselves. My assistant will assign someone to make the necessary arrangements if you will speak with her," Neavillii said, and smiled at the transformation her words evoked.

The three before her now stood tall as they moved to Thanera.

"And you are?" the two bare-chested Sansheren Neavillii found herself addressing were well groomed.

"Yolunu, of the Fifth rank of Gulardee, I am trained in the sciences of communication." Yolunu did not move to sit as the other petitioners had.

"And?" Neavillii prompted.

"I would present my gentle spouse, Aldera, she who is of the Tenth rank of Tamsatel," Yolunu said. "We have come to request family status within the House Sheresuan and to the beautiful Morganea herself."

"Indeed, and who would you name as your reference?" Neavillii gestured to the chairs in front of her as she spoke.

"I have not had contact with the most noble House Sheresuan since the day I was sent for apprenticeship. Both my father and his wife were killed during the time of my apprenticing. Tadesde's predecessor, the most courageous Dejymo, offered me a position. In truth, I can think of no name with which to petition," Yolunu said.

She would not beg, Neavillii thought.

"Well, my friend. You leave me in a difficult position. Perhaps if you could present me with the names of your departed parents, I will contact the House registrar. It will take time, but it is possible that someone might remember the child you were and give you a reference. In the meantime, I would suggest finding quarters and private employment while awaiting notice." Neavillii regretted the decision custom forced upon her, but to grant family status to an unknown was not something she would do.

"We thank you for your time. Your honor is impeccable." Yolunu stepped forward to hand Thanera a card with the information Neavillii had requested already printed on it.

"Do you think the lovely Isaac will be able to help us to find a place to dwell?" Aldera asked of her wife.

"It is a hope." Yolunu placed her hand around her older wife's waist as she turned to walk away from the platform.

A group of petitioners took their place before the platform.

"The MaEryas Zoo is in desperate need of –"

"Isaac, that is not a Sansheren name," Neavillii interrupted the new petitioners to call to Yolunu as she and Aldera walked away.

"No. I mean, yes, it is not a Sansheren name," Aldera said, a little too loud, and Neavillii saw Yolunu squeeze her waist in response. "Isaac is a human. That is of the same species as the beautiful Morganea. We have spent a pleasant evening together; I was only wondering if he would have a place we could stay," her voice trailed off.

"Until your truly kind self has called us back," Yolunu finished.

"Indeed. Perhaps I could save you time and ask him for you?" Neavillii smiled even as Thanera motioned for the petitioners in front of her to resume their places in the line.

"We would not trouble you on so insignificant a point, most caring of patrons." Yolunu made no move to return to Neavillii, and held Aldera close to her as she spoke.

"It is no trouble," Neavillii replied. "I planned to call him later. If you will be seated, I will try to keep the conversation short." Neavillii removed her personal communication unit from her pocket and placed the call. "Isaac?"

Yolunu had no chance to protest before Tansea's voice reached her.

"I will wake him," was Tansea's response.

"What do you want, woman? Surely there are others you could be torturing right now?" Isaac demanded in English, and his voice echoed through the speakers long before his face appeared on the small screen. "Neavillii, truly a beautiful sight," Isaac said in Sansheren. "To what do I owe the honor?" he asked as he continued to rub the sleep from his eyes.

"I have just made the acquaintance of two friends of yours, and they were wondering if you might be able to provide them with lodging and employment until the question of their status might be addressed." Neavillii smiled at Isaac's further attempts to clear his eyes and head of sleep.

"The only Sansheren on the planet I would call friends would have to be the lovely Yolunu and her most delicious wife, Aldera.

Sure, go ahead and tell them they can stay with me. And ask after the infants for me." Isaac was struck in the head by a cushion as he spoke, and Neavillii laughed at the sight of Tansea in the background picking up another cushion.

"I will convey your congratulations to the parents," Neavillii signed off as Isaac turned towards Tansea and received the second cushion in his face.

"He speaks of our beloved Numane's death children," Aldera answered Neavillii's silent question.

"Why did you not mention this?" Neavillii asked.

"Our beloved was of the generation of the House founded by the courageous Dejymo. I did not want to burden you with this knowledge," Yolunu said, her head held high, and Neavillii felt her admiration for the other grow.

"Indeed. Your honor is impeccable. I have reviewed your request for family status. You have been given an acceptable if somewhat intimate reference. I will personally set your request before my generous mate Morganea. Until that time, you may consider yourselves on probation. My assistant will see to your housing needs. Have you made arrangements for the children?" Neavillii asked with a smile.

"If it pleases your kindness, our wife's children are currently in the public nursery that has been established only a few blocks from here. Would it be considered improper for me to call to your attention the pure squalor of that establishment?" Aldera rushed the words out.

"It would not be improper at all. Have you any experience in nursery care by which to pass this judgment?" Neavillii asked with a new smile.

"I was the assistant to the nursery head under Dejymo's House. I retired my position and consigned myself to running my wives' household after Tadesde assumed the Twelve," Aldera finished speaking with a blush.

"It would please me if you would trouble yourself to assume control of the nursery. Thanera will give you my authorization." Neavillii again smiled as she gestured to her assistant.

"I find myself humbled by your generosity and foresight. I would ask if any steps have been made to prepare the planet for when our Lady Morganea returns to House Sheresuan." Yolunu's thaw was slight but noticeable.

"Many preparations are underway. May I assume your inquiry is in concern to communications?" Neavillii asked.

"You are observant. The last I heard, all communications were being routed through the House Sheresuan flagship. When it leaves, we will be forced to relay messages without even the most basic of satellites in orbit," Yolunu said, and Neavillii wondered if the other woman was simply warming up to a subject that she knew well.

"I was not made aware of this problem. And what would be your solution?" Neavillii leaned forward to encourage Yolunu.

"I would never presume," Yolunu said and took a physical step back.

"Presume!" Neavillii demanded. "It is your problem, find me a solution. The flagship departs within the week, I want planetary communications reestablished, you have my banner to back you," Neavillii finished with a smile and waved Yolunu to Thanera.

"You were speaking of a zoo?" Neavillii turned to address the petitioners who had been forced back into line.

"Oh, yes, my Lady. The MaEryas' Interplanetary and Alien Species Zoo. We have been without support or supplies for quite some time. I fear the animals will all perish without support from your most kind government." A frail creature of a species unknown to Neavillii moved to reclaim its seat and was now perched on the back of the chair.

"These animals are very rare on their home worlds?" Neavillii asked.

"Oh, no, but they will die without food or water." The second in the group of four was an elderly Bystocc dressed in clothing that Thanera explained was maternal, and Neavillii winced as the other declined to attempt the chair wearing copper pants.

"Then, off their home planets, they can only be found here?" Neavillii forced her voice to remain encouraging.

"Not really, well, except the Perrisanns, a beautiful flier, I might add." The first speaker leaned forward.

"I do not understand, perhaps you could explain to me how it could fly in a zoo?" Neavillii also leaned forward.

"Oh, a joke, I would think. The Perrisanns is caged, as are all the fliers. But if you would tour the zoo, a lady as wise and generous as you would be forced to see the desperate plight of the animals." This time it was the third in the group who spoke, an average Sansheren with no banners of House or rank to give her right to the condescending tone she used.

"Indeed, then I think I shall not visit your zoo. I hate being forced into anything." Neavillii leaned away from the stunned foursome.

"But. At least tell me why," the fourth petitioner, also a native of Bystocc, said over the protests of his companions.

"I have heard that there was once a small flier on the Western Continent, whose song was a joy to hear. And that before the war, holidays were held in its honor." Neavillii looked at each of the four petitioners.

Only the fourth would meet her eye. "You have humbled me, kind Lady. I withdraw my name from this petition and will instead submit another in favor of the native animals and their habitats."

"Arrange for the Perrisanns to be gifted to another House's zoo and let me know when this new petition is ready to be considered," Neavillii smiled at the native as she waved her toward Thanera; the other three picked up their papers and left.

"Please step forward." Neavillii sighed as she addressed an elderly Bystocc wearing an elaborate bronze costume.

Chapter Nine - Sheresuan - 2012

"And may we be so forward as to ask toward the health of your newly found maternal family?" Neadesto asked Morgan who knelt with her own retainers on a mat in front of the ancient Sansheren leader.

Morgan considered the question. "I am sorry that my explanation was so inadequate. Sam is of the family I adopted on my first planet. He is not of my genetic heritage," Morgan replied to Neadesto who reclined amid the casual splendor of the room.

"Indeed. That would explain the visual differences, would it not, lovely Neadesto?" Iedonea said from her seat beside Neadesto.

Twice the age of any Sansheren in the room, Neadesto was the oldest Sansheren currently alive. At four hundred and seventy three years since birth, Neadesto had used her longevity to build the largest power base found within the Sansheren Houses.

"Yes it would," Neadesto agreed with Iedonea, the only child she loved enough to marry. "Tell me, how many defections did you receive? And what is your intention toward the planet Bystocc?" Neadesto's voice was soft, yet her tone was sharp.

"Two hundred and seventy-eight individuals requested asylum and another thirty-four asked kinship benefits. I humbly agreed to ferry their requests to your most loving and generous self," Morgan said with her head bowed in respect and told herself there was no reason for the edge of panic that made her heart jump.

"I asked how many you received," Neadesto said sharply. "Your honor to me is touching, but it does get in the way. Dispense with the court accent and sit by me," and Morgan watched as Neadesto shifted to make room between herself and Iedonea on the sprawling couch. Over three hundred retainers and court aides packed the room, and Morgan was aware of the public honor being offered.

"I will always honor you, my father," Morgan said as she stood. "As to defections, eight hundred and ninety-three professionals of various rank and title now claim to swear allegiance to my name. It feels strange, and I am certain that once reliable transportation routes are established most will return to their original House," Morgan finished and sat on the edge of the couch. She knew her heart was pounding loud enough for her own retainers sitting in the first row at Neadesto's feet to hear it and she worked at calming herself with a few focused breaths. The memory of sitting beside her grandmother before a smiling brass Buddha in a cool temple gave her focus and relief.

"But my most extremely humble wife, it is you whom they follow, not the convenience of your banner," Neavillii said from her assigned seat at the front of Morgan's retainers.

"It is true, child," Neadesto said. "I have heard of no one who stayed on Bystocc requesting a House audience. Of the thirty-four whose requests you brought me, all but nine asked me to release them from family obligations so that they might proudly wear your own banner. Even my own beautiful daughter Iedonea's descendant is proud to sit beside your wife, we see," Neadesto added with a new smile.

Morgan's heart started pounding anew, and she closed her eyes, if only for a moment. "I am truly upset if I have acted in any way improperly toward you, my most loved and respected aunt," she said as the room's attention shifted from her to her retainers.

"You are as a daughter to me, you know this," Iedonea said. "It is with pleasure that I see my blood sit with you. And it is with joy that I find this line of my honor still preserved. Come child, I would see you better," and Iedonea made eye contact with the frightened Nealoie.

"Surely you are joking at my willing expense," Nealoie said, and her voice could barely be heard as she moved forward and knelt before the couch. "I cannot be of so noble a blood as you, my Lady."

"Indeed," Iedonea said. "It is like looking in the mirror and seeing how I feel. I have never liked this old face that stares at me. Perhaps your most kind and wonderful new father would allow you to spend a few days with us. Would you like that?" Iedonea asked, and Nealoie bowed her head. Soft sobs could be heard by all.

"Now we have upset you. We are sorry, child. Perhaps you would do us the pleasure at some future time when the shock of the war is behind you?" Neadesto said with genuine concern.

"I would do you the honor now. If my most wonderful and new father would permit me the days?" Nealoie asked while looking at Morgan.

"Of course I would allow you the time to rediscover your heritage," Morgan said, and a sudden calm enveloped her. "In fact, I would ask that you become my ambassador to the House Sheresuan since everyone present thinks I will be dealing with the planet Bystocc for some time to come." Morgan resisted a smile as she announced the forming of her own small House. Those in her party laughed and clapped.

Iedonea was forced to hold up her hands for silence so that Neadesto could speak.

"It has been barely a blink since I found you dying," Neadesto said. "You not only lived, but have blossomed beyond my wildest dreams. Even your most ardent detractors have been forced to reassess their opinions of you. I am informed that many Houses have retainers who have expressed an interest in rebuilding Bystocc. When you return to your new home, you will discover that the thousand loyalists you left have grown to over ten thousand. Be assured that they will bring their own supplies."

"I have also been in contact with the Royal House of the planet Dreco. She sends her thanks to your honored family for recording the death moments of her people, as well as gifts of gold and jewels. She is a very powerful leader, and you would be wise to encourage further contact with her."

Neadesto reached to pull out a banner of ranked order from behind Iedonea. "I had this banner stitched when you left on this assignment. Never did my faith in your honor and integrity waiver. I am pleased to request that you be entered into the annals of the House Sheresuan as the first to reach the rank of Tenth in the order of the Sansadee before the age of fifty. Or forty. Or perhaps even thirty. We are proud of you," Neadesto said and handed Morgan the banner without any more ceremony. "Have you decided on the name of your new House?"

"The name I would choose would be asking bad luck upon us both," Morgan said. "But I do not know of another that I would feel so close to."

"I am honored again," Neadesto said with a soft chuckle. "It is a pity I am not dead yet, for I would enjoy the thought of the House with my unworthy name."

The room was quiet as everyone set themselves to the question of a name.

"Please excuse my presumptuousness, most charming and lovely fathers. I have thought of a name that might be found acceptable for this new House that rises from the ashes of Tadesde's greed," Neavillii said with a smile, and Morgan tensed in anticipation of an insult to Tadesde.

"Indeed. We would hear such a name that would imply so much at Tadesde's expense," Iedonea said and smiled.

"I would humbly submit the name, House Timone."

The room was silent before laughter erupted, and all semblance of order was lost.

"To honor the dead mercenary who so humiliated Tadesde, that is a tempting name, I admit, and it would have personal value as well," Morgan said over the residual laughter.

"But still bad luck, I fear," Neadesto said through her own laughter. "I have reliable sources who assure me that the good Captain Timone, and a few of his men, escaped capture and is now on the planet Wergol awaiting the pirate ships to replenish his forces."

"Indeed?" Morgan managed to ask in a mock serious voice before the laughter erupted anew.

"For the exuberance of youth, eh, father?" Iedonea asked Neadesto as the two of them stood and walked from the room.

Morgan watched with a sad smile as Nealoie ran after her newfound family.

Chapter Ten - Earth - 1997

"He followed me home, can I keep him?" Greg asked in a crude imitation of Morgan's accented English as he removed his glasses and rubbed his eyes. "Most kids just bring home stray puppies; I have to have the only roommate who adopts the homeless."

"Were you waiting up for me?" Morgan returned as she tried to help the injured and drugged Sam walk to the couch.

"No. I always stay up until three when I have to be at work by six. What gives, little sister?" Greg asked as he followed her into the living room and spread a blanket over the already unconscious Sam.

"I got jumped. He saved me. I couldn't just leave him." Morgan glared through the exhaustion that blurred her eyes.

"Tim's still out looking for you. Hell, where you been hiding?" Greg asked as he moved toward the kitchen.

"I took him to Riverside County Hospital." Morgan followed Greg. "We waited for the police. They never came," Morgan said.

Tim stood in the kitchen doorway. She felt tears fill her eyes as the shock of the day caught up with her.

"You ever find a cop when you need one?" Tim demanded. "Shit, why didn't you call home?" Tim's green eyes burned out of his dark face.

"The phone was busy." Morgan returned his glare without flinching until a yawn overwhelmed her.

"That would be Denise, I told you we need another line," Greg said with a bitter grin.

"Shut up, Greg, don't you need to go to work?" Tim turned his back on both and started rummaging in the fridge.

"Oh, I have plenty of time." Greg smiled at Tim's back before heading for the hallway.

"Who ate all the ham? Jesus, there's nothing in here." Tim

closed the door hard before turning away empty handed.

"I could make you some soup." Morgan stood and walked toward the stove. Kicking her stool, she climbed up and reached for a can.

"Or," Greg paused in the doorway and frowned, "he could make his own."

"Go to work, Greg." Tim's expression was far more serious than his voice.

"I won't say a thing." Greg's voice sounded far more serious than his expression, and a puzzled Morgan glanced up from her cooking.

#

Morgan forced herself to eat the soup Tim insisted on sharing. It made her nervous and self-conscious to have him watch her. A faint buzz offered her an escape.

"That's Greg's alarm clock, I'll get it." Morgan moved away from the table and went to turn off the alarm.

"You finished with this?" Tim held up her almost full bowl, and Morgan paused in the doorway, but she couldn't look back.

"Yeah," she whispered before leaving the room.

Tim followed her into Greg's room and sat on the bed as she picked up the alarm.

"Are you going to tell me what happened?" Tim held a serious look, until he noticed the difficulty she was having finding an off button on the alarm.

Morgan told herself he wasn't laughing at her. "I got jumped on the way home from school." Morgan didn't make eye contact as she hit a random button on the alarm and set it down.

"Hey, this is me," Tim said and cupped her small face in his hand.

Morgan felt her resolve drown in the depths of his green eyes. "They were going to touch me," she said, and finally cried. She felt Tim hold her to his chest as she cried.

"But they didn't. It's going to be okay. I'm here." Tim's voice was barely audible as he stroked Morgan's long hair.

"They held me down, and they kept trying to touch me. He saved me. I couldn't just leave him." Morgan continued crying.

"You're okay, you're okay," he repeated. Tim held her close with one arm and used the other hand to continue stroking her hair and shoulders. "It's over now. You're safe."

"I feel safe, now," Morgan whispered, and dared to think what she was saying.

"I'm here," Tim repeated while his hand moved from the top of her head down her shoulders and to her back.

"With you," Morgan, no longer crying, leaned into Tim's embrace and turned her head up to see his face. Morgan saw the surprise in his eyes and bit her lip as she waited for his rejection.

His free hand moved from her shoulders along her neck until it again cupped her face. "It's time for you to get some sleep," was not what she thought he meant to say, but, after it came out, she knew it was the best thing he could have said.

"Would you stay with me?" Morgan hoped her expression didn't betray the emotions she did not understand.

"Damn," Tim ran his thumb over her mouth before pulling away and standing up.

"I'm sorry," was her comment as she held her arms around herself tightly, and hoped Tim couldn't see her shaking. She kept her eyes closed as she waited for the tears that refused to fall.

"It's against the law, kid. Besides, you're only eleven years old; there's nothing you could get from it. Please, believe me, it would hurt you. I never want to hurt you," Tim whispered as he knelt on the floor and put his forehead on Morgan's knees.

"I'm sorry," Morgan whispered again, and the shaking continued as she stared down at Tim's head.

"I won't hurt you. When you're older. Will you wait for me?" Tim moved forward on his knees so that their faces were level and inches apart.

"Yes," Morgan moved toward Tim until their lips met.

Tim did not move a muscle as Morgan began exploring his mouth with her lips. She felt him shudder when her tongue began to lick his lips.

She wondered if she should stop when he finally relaxed his lips and allowed her tongue to slide inside. Morgan thought he might have been holding his breath when, with a sigh, he shifted forward, slid his hand into her hair until it pulled, and supported her neck against the pressure of his kiss. He pushed her back against the bed. His other hand supported his own weight as he kissed her, again. Her small body shivering, she reached up and under his tee shirt, sliding both of her hands around the small of his back. She tried to pull his warmth toward her like a blanket, her body arching up to meet him.

His body remained tense as his kiss stole her breath. The alarm clock rang again. And Tim was standing and moving towards the door even as Morgan identified the sound.

"I'm sorry," Morgan whispered to the closing door, and felt the empty darkness of Greg's room invade her.

Chapter Eleven - Sheresuan - 2012

"Would you like me to rub your shoulders?" Morgan heard Neavillii say from behind her in the dark.

"No, go back to sleep, I'm fine," Morgan said as she sat at the edge of her bed and tried not to think about the memory.

"You dreamed of her again," Neavillii said without accusation, and Morgan felt her move. "A wife could find herself jealous of a ghost." Neavillii began to rub Morgan's shoulders.

"I love you," was all Morgan could bring herself to say as Neavillii's massage worked through the tension in her body.

"So, it was the ghost. I would listen if you wished." Neavillii continued to rub.

"It was after I found Sam. He found me? It was when we came back from the hospital. I lived in a home with others who were older. I was a child, eleven. Tim lived there too, I loved him, you know this," Morgan said with a sigh, and moved to lie upon her stomach.

"This was not your genetic family, it was the family you loved and still cry about?" and the concern in Neavillii's soft voice disturbed Morgan.

"It has been years since last I cried," Morgan said.

"Years since anyone caught you, my love." Neavillii paused in her rub.

"It has been years since I dreamed of them, or him. Why now?" Morgan asked, and turned to lay on her side facing Neavillii.

"You have found one, is it wrong to want to find the rest of your first home?" Neavillii's hand began to massage Morgan's thigh.

"Sam's mind is trapped in the hell of the prison camp. Isaac says he may never recover," Morgan said. "And the others? We were separated. It is a fool's hope to chase ghosts." Morgan placed her hand on top of Neavillii's to stop the distraction.

"Sam was high in Timone's organization," Neavillii said.

And Morgan was at first thankful that Neavillii did not voice the speculation that was circulating throughout Morgan's retainers. When the silence grew between them, Morgan sighed, and decided to give voice to the thought herself. "And Timone is human, I know the rumors, and there are six billion humans on Earth, and who knows how many more in the galaxy. The chance of him being my Tim is too small to base a hope on." Morgan was impatient as she shifted to begin massaging Neavillii's closer leg roughly.

"But any hope of finding lost family," Neavillii protested. "Must you not pursue this? For your honor, if nothing else?" Neavillii asked as she allowed Morgan to massage her legs.

"I have a House to attend to, children to father." Morgan moved her massage to Neavillii's midriff. "I have a life now," she finished with a sigh.

"Honor is seldom convenient. And your House will be stronger for the knowledge of your effort. Besides, it is I who would bear your first children, my love," Neavillii said, and smiled as she turned to reach into a drawer for a small communication unit.

"Now?" Morgan asked, and her surprised response evoked a laugh from Neavillii.

"If you wish, yes. This way I will be healed and ready to serve in your stead on Bystocc when you leave for Wergol next week. I have already negotiated a loan of one of Neadesto's nurseries for us and any of your retainers who wish to transfer their young until we can get a nursery properly established on your planet." Neavillii still held the com unit out to Morgan.

"The children I father would have to be transferred to my planet immediately," Morgan said in a whisper.

"Of course," Neavillii said, and thumbed the com unit's standby button.

"I am beginning to suspect that you have outmaneuvered me, my most lovely wife." Morgan laughed as she took the communication unit from Neavillii, and pushed the call button.

"I look forward to waking to your beauty in the morning," Neavillii said as Morgan's massage became even more aggressive.

#

An eternity later, Morgan sat on the edge of the bed as the resuscitation team finished preparing the revived Neavillii for transport. Her thoughts kept circling around the fact that it was far different to understand intellectually how children were produced than to be involved in the actual process. Morgan watched the movement under Neavillii's skin and was awestruck at the speed of new life.

Following behind the jogging doctors, Morgan thumbed her communication unit and asked the nurse to locate Isaac at the main hospital and send him to the nursery hospital.

#

"The miracle of pregnancy. I would enjoy the opportunity to observe some time," Isaac said when he entered Neavillii's room later that day. Neavillii lay flat on a bed; a large bandage could be seen on her stomach.

Morgan watched Isaac look around the room in puzzlement as the Sansheren present began laughing.

"We all enjoy the opportunity to watch when it presents itself, do we not?" Morgan's doctor, Fanlelo, nudged Isaac as she moved towards the room's exit.

"Would you accompany me to the nursery, my wonderful physician?" Morgan said and moved past the still-confused Isaac. "I will be back soon, my love," Morgan added to Neavillii before she left the room.

"And I thought French was impossible," Isaac said as he bowed his head to Neavillii's, and followed Morgan out the door.

Fanlelo caught up with them when Morgan stopped to speak with the ever vigilant Banessa. "Assign someone to watch the dear and wonderful mother of my children," Morgan said, and placed her hand upon Banessa's arm before moving down the hall, not waiting for a response.

"Power becomes you, my Lady," Fanlelo said, and Morgan glanced at the old medic. Her age showed as confidence, and Morgan realized Fanlelo was now at the pinnacle of her career and might be ready to retire. Might be looking for a dominant wife.

Morgan smiled as she decided that she would have to watch her natural generosity or she would find herself with more spouses than bedrooms, and fathering children more often than sleeping.

"Um, I missed something," Isaac said as they walked through a set of swinging doors labeled Sheresuan nursery.

"Oh, what was that?" Morgan asked with a chuckle.

"A few birds and a few bees. Maybe the flowers and trees. You tell me?" and this time it was the Sansheren doctor's turn to be confused as Morgan laughed along with Isaac.

"I wonder if we're speaking in the same House?" Fanlelo questioned politely.

"This is my observation room. I think we will spend some time within," Morgan said as she dismissed the medic. Taking Isaac by the arm, she led him into a dim room.

The room was small, with comfortable lounging chairs facing a wall of solid glass that looked into another, bigger room.

"May I present my children?" Morgan waved her hand at the glass partition and then moved to sit on one of the lounges.

"But, we can't.., I mean we could, but it can't do any good," Isaac finished in English as he moved to the glass wall. A fine mist covered the glass, blurring the jungle-like setting behind the glass. The nursery room was filled with plants of all shades of green; a thick grass carpeted the floor.

"We can, and it does. I think. They don't seem to need much help," Morgan finished with a shrug, and reached toward the table beside her lounge, and helped herself to a bowl of fruit.

"You mean they can all have babies? That there's only one sex to the species?" Isaac asked. He still had his back to her as he peered into the nursery, trying to see a child among the plants.

"All are mothers, only the best are fathers. An old saying. You are looking in the wrong area." Morgan leaned forward and pointed to a small lump of dark green under a fern-like plant.

"I've heard multiple births are the norm?" Isaac asked as he stared at the mossy looking ball and found three shapes blended together.

"Most have two, a few one. We were honored with three. They say the more siblings you have, the smarter you become." Morgan beamed with pride as she gestured for Isaac to sit beside her.

"How long will they sleep?" Isaac asked with a continued curiosity about the newborns.

"I will ask," Morgan said before she moved to an intercom by the door and spoke with an attendant, who assured her they would be fed soon. "How strong is your stomach?" Morgan smiled without showing her teeth.

"Carnivorous? Seeing the adult's teeth. Live food? That would explain the relative independence of the room." Isaac never took his eyes off the green bundle Morgan pointed out.

"They are completely independent at birth. And very dangerous. The panel, see?" Morgan gestured to the opposite wall where a small panel could be seen opening. A cage was held to the opening and a small animal the size of a young pig was pushed forward into the room, then panel dropped closed.

"Where did they go?" Isaac pointed to the spot where the green balls had been sleeping.

"They hunt."

The prey was glimpsed as it ran from one plant to the next, trying to find something to hide under. One of the taller plants came crashing down as the frightened creature dug at its base. Movement pulled Isaac's eyes toward the corner of the glass wall. One of Morgan's three children was moving toward its dinner. The prey looked straight at its tormentor before bolting away: right into the range of the other two. Once caught, dinner was eaten in a blur of splattered blood. Isaac sat back in shock as the three infants began to lick at the pool of blood left behind.

"Bones and all, how efficient." His shocked voice was low.

"I did warn you. They're not human," Morgan said before she picked up another piece of fruit and began eating. Her small children finished licking up the blood and again curled themselves at the base of a plant to sleep, their bellies distended.

"I forget sometimes. I have to remind myself that Tansea isn't a small woman in a costume, you know?" Isaac was sitting as far back in the chair as he could. He did not take his eyes from the green balls of fur.

"I look into the mirror, sometimes, to remember that I am not in costume, myself." Morgan looked at Isaac, and he tore his eyes away to meet her gaze.

"How old were you?" and his question hung in the air for several minutes before Morgan looked at him again.

"Almost thirteen. And yourself?" was the polite response.

"Thirty-two. I was in a Central American country, Panama. Pirates grabbed the Shithook helicopter I was in before it crashed. They saved our lives." Isaac looked back into the nursery room.

"We were in L.A.; they grabbed us in an alley." Morgan knew she sounded far more bitter than she felt.

"I... I know you're their father. But?" Isaac said, and then hesitated. "I mean," and his question fell, unasked.

"I was a girl," Morgan said, filling the silence that threatened to overwhelm her. She could almost feel Isaac resist the urge to look at her muscular, androgynous body, and she realized curiosity must have filled him from the first time he saw her, only growing after Neavillii asked him to help the surviving humans.

"I was bought by a Santrey cargo ship; they needed someone small enough to crawl under the deck plating. When I started- I skipped a few months, and when I started my period, they thought I was dying. They left me on the next planet they docked at, Faldebbia. The doctors there had never worked on a human female before; they had only seen male mercenaries. They thought it was cancer, I guess. Neadesto was there negotiating a contract in person, and the Faldebbians asked her to transport me to Wergol; they had no use for me. I guess they thought I could link up with the other humans on Wergol. Neadesto brought me home instead." Morgan leaned her head back against the couch, and wished Isaac would gather her into his arms.

"They must've removed your ovaries and uterus. Hormone replacement would help." Isaac held his hand out toward her.

Morgan smiled before she reached out. His grasp was firm and warm, she was surprised to notice. "Help what?" Morgan asked as she watched Isaac blush.

"Help you to develop," Isaac said and Morgan did not look away. "Physically. Visually." Isaac used his free hand to cup his own breast.

"Must I?" Morgan whispered when she realized what Isaac was offering. "Talk to the good Doctor Fanlelo, she will know where you can find what you need." Morgan sat forward and pulled her hand free with a gesture toward the door.

"You don't have to, you know. I'll speak with her though. We've synthesized some medication I think will help Sam. You might want to stop by his room later." Isaac stood and moved to the door.

"Thank you. For listening." Morgan did not turn to the door; even as Isaac left, she sat staring at her sleeping children.

#

Sam woke. He did not have the hangover he was expecting. He smiled to himself as he remembered the doctor's attempts to fake drinking from the bottle.

"I should cry now," he said aloud.

"If it would help release what is inside you, please do so," a soft voice said in accented English, and Sam turned to see the doctor's assistant, Tansea. The small alien moved from a chair by the window and climbed up onto the edge of the bed.

"English? Are you my keeper?" Sam asked as he pulled his hand back and then moved away from Tansea. His body moved with a stiff, shaky ache that left him weak and wondering how long he had slept.

"No," Tansea said. Her long, reddish hair tangled about her, and she spent several moments straightening it out. He noticed that there was more hair than body, though she did not look fragile, and he watched her twist her fingers through her hair, pulling out knots.

The small alien reached her hand out to brush a lock of hair from Sam's eyes. The tiny hand was red brown and scaled with two blunt fingers and a nub of a thumb.

"Everything is in such commotion, with the new House. How would you say that in English? Country, I believe? Yes, everything is in such commotion with the forming of Morgan's new government and the preparations to return to Bystocc. I came in here to read." Tansea held up two small rods of black wood with a strip of blue cloth connecting them.

"Morgan?" Sam stared at the ceiling in shock.

"Your child, yes," Tansea answered, and Sam glanced at her. "You must forgive my English, as a child she was your friend, you lived in the same home once." Tansea leaned against the head of the bed as she placed the scroll into a slim pocket in the leg of her outfit.

"Morgan," Sam whispered. "I dreamed about her, except she

was a man and I wanted to kiss her. I thought I'd gone insane. I kept dreaming I was a homosexual with a man who was a little girl, things kept changing and I couldn't find my way out of the dream," Sam said and turned to the person beside him. "Have you ever heard anything so crazy?"

"The Asterex have no word for dreaming. The Drecos, no word for insane. And the Sansheren? They have no word for homosexual, or heterosexual, that I've heard. I find it interesting, you can tell a lot about a people by what words they do not have." Tansea moved until she was lying next to Sam and then turned slightly towards him.

"When can I see her?" Sam asked.

"When you wake up, child," Tansea said, and curled against Sam's side and closed her eyes. Sam lay very still, staring at the ceiling for several hours before drifting off.

Chapter Twelve - Bystocc - 2012

"Your beautiful wife has not come home yet," Yolunu heard Thanera say, and looked to see the young administrator standing in her own doorway across the short hallway.

"In truth? She seems to come home later each day. I worry about her," Yolunu said, and forced a smile as she leaned against her unopened door. The hallway was dimly lit in an attempt to save energy, and Yolunu hoped Thanera could not see the depth of her concern.

"She does you honor in her work. I saw her this afternoon," Thanera said as she moved across the hallway and smiled in return.

"She does herself honor. I only wish that my work was half as successful." Yolunu brought her hand to her face, and rubbed her eyes as she spoke, but she still felt exhausted when she stopped.

"But your work is by its nature less rewarding. Even the slightest progress must be considered a triumph. I do not hold you responsible for setbacks that were engineered long before Tadesde left this rock. No one can consider you at fault for the mag-mines." Thanera stepped closer to Yolunu and placed a hand on her shoulder.

"I can," Yolunu said as she turned away and unlocked the door. The door refused to open, and Yolunu sighed; Isaac's tent was better maintained than the building that had been converted into a temporary housing for those who pledged directly to Morgan.

"I could assign you more assistants if you would like," Thanera offered, and Yolunu was pleased that Thanera did not move back despite the obvious rebuff.

"You are very generous, my Lady," Yolunu said as she opened the door with a violent yank and cold air enveloped them. "I do not need more assistants. I need a flight crew willing to take a few more risks. We will never clear the mag-mines Tadesde scattered in orbit if my crew continues to panic with each new mine. Do you realize that we clear only one mine a day?" Yolunu asked as she leaned against the open door.

"If you are willing to deal with mercenaries, I am sure I can find a braver crew for you. My own wish is to find a thermostat specialist," Thanera smiled and placed her hand on Yolunu's arm.

This time Yolunu offered no rejection. "I do not see how we can pay for mercenaries, with the number of ships hitting dirt increasing every day? It seems a miracle we can feed ourselves." Yolunu placed her own hand over Thanera's and smiled.

"We would welcome you within our humble home."

Both turned to Aldera's voice, and Yolunu smiled when Thanera stepped away from her. Aldera's approach was half hidden by the open door, and she now stood beside them, her clothing filthy and still damp in places. Her look of exhaustion far surpassed Yolunu's.

"My wife, come; I will fix you dinner." Yolunu moved into the apartment to be followed by Aldera and a blushing Thanera.

"Please do not trouble yourself for me, love. A shipment of supplies arrived today for the nursery. House Decado had the honor to send us everything necessary to start a field nursery. I ate with my few staff members. I suspect I will have new employees tomorrow when word circulates that there is uncontaminated food for those who would work a shift." Aldera moved through the room, pausing in the doorway to the next room as she finished speaking.

"Please tell the representative of the House Decado to visit me tomorrow so that I can be certain that their generosity is recorded." Thanera spoke to the empty doorway.

"Will you dine with me then?" Yolunu asked after the silence built.

"It would please me greatly. I have a package of sweet-meats I was going to dine upon. Let me contribute these," Thanera said as she reached into the side pocket of her pants.

Yolunu followed Aldera into the sleeping room.

"I wish you luck with the young administrator. I am just tired. We find a new regressive every day. Right now, I want to sleep, maybe I will dream of you and your date. That would be pleasant, my dear." Aldera smiled up at her wife as she drifted off to sleep.

Yolunu smoothed the blankets and turned to leave, in time to see Thanera backing out of the doorway.

"If I offended you, I will leave." Thanera waved her hand in the direction of the door.

"Of course not. Let us go into the kitchen."

"Your beautiful wife spoke of regressions. I confess to having a rather morbid curiosity toward the subject." Thanera accepted an instrument from her host and began to open the small tin she had contributed.

"I think everyone has a fascination with the subject. That an arbitrary decision by a nursery worker could lead you to an 'accident.' It frightens me, the power they wield." Yolunu said. She worked at filling a small cloth spread on the floor as they talked, and soon she and Thanera were sitting down sampling various near-empty plates.

"Are they having such a problem with regressions? And why has no report been filed? I warned you I was curious."

They both laughed as Yolunu offered her guest a bit of meat from a plate close to her.

"Yesterday she said she and her staff had decided to take no action until after each of the suspected infants had been given adequate food for at least a week. I suppose this new shipment will give them their week. And yes, there are far more who are regressed than there should be, by anyone's estimate." Yolunu accepted a portion of the meats Thanera offered.

"Do you think she will file a report? What a topic to discuss over dinner," Thanera said with a laugh.

"Not a topic for polite discussion, I agree. And no, I do not think you'll be forced to finalize a report." Yolunu placed her hand upon Thanera's as she, too, laughed.

#

Enrico was tired and his missing foot hurt, but Tracy looked so alone when he wheeled past her bed. He couldn't resist offering to play a game. Hide and seek had been her idea, one that Gerry quickly agreed to. And now, as he tried to move quietly without the aid of his chair, he knew he had made the right decision. He could see the younger boy smiling in the reflection of the room's single window as he hopped past the hidden children, and searched in the farthest corner.

"Freedom!" Tracy shouted in English, and grinned as she supported most of her small compatriot's weight.

"Three times, little seniorita!" Enrico said in English with his own laugh as he moved toward the center of the room. "It is your turn to search for me, amigos."

"Sure," Tracy said, and Enrico watched as she and the small boy, Gerry, hid their heads in their arms and began counting aloud. Tracy's voice was the only one he could hear, piping clear and loud. She was seven she told him, with a confidence he doubted but wished he could imitate. The other boy looked around four, but without a common language, Enrico could not be certain.

Tracy's counting sped up, and he realized she was about to finish. With a painful hop, he managed to hide behind the bed of the fourth child in the room before Tracy shouted twenty and went silent.

Gerry was the first to make a sound, a soft giggle that hinted at his discovery. But the younger children moved in the other direction, and Enrico relaxed for a moment.

The breathing sounds of the fourth child soon masked the noises of pursuit.

Enrico risked a peek over the top of the bed and was rewarded with a glimpse of Tracy boosting Gerry up to check the corner countertops. Kneeling down once more, Enrico brushed against the hand of the child whose bed he was hiding behind.

The hand had fallen out of the secured blankets when he bumped the bed.

A girl's hand, he thought as he tucked it back into the blankets. A girl my age, and he moved to look over the top once more, to see where his pursuers had chosen to look next and to see the face of the girl the doctors said would never wake up.

The two children were busy digging through the closet he had hidden in the last time.

The teenage girl was still, pale and bruised, and looking very much like what he kept telling himself death should look like. Not the swollen, black, cracked look he knew too well.

The human doctor had come and looked at her while he was still confined to his bed. The doctor told the human woman the girl was dead, her body just didn't know better. Enrico remembered seeing the woman nod her head and leave. The girl was still there with them, and he wondered when her body would discover its fate.

"Tag! We got you! We got you!" Tracy shouted from one side of the bed. Enrico looked to see a smiling Gerry blocking the other side of the bed.

"Oh yeah. Roar! Roar!" he laughed and shouted as he lunged forward at the girl. Grabbing her, he started to tickle her, Gerry moved to them and started pounding feebly on his shoulders and adding his own laughter to the mix. Enrico was the only one to notice the attention their play was drawing.

"Has anyone called a team?" Enrico heard a nurse ask in the alien's language from the room's open doorway.

"I, my Lady. I thought they were playing." The younger medic still clutched the lunch tray she was bringing to the children to her chest, food and liquid staining her banners.

"At hunting each other?" The older nurse demanded.

"They are alien, my Lady. They bare their teeth for pleasure. Our Lady Morganea said so. I thought they were playing until she shouted and grabbed the little one. I called for help," the medic said, and her grasp on the tray tightened, and several more liquids ran free and down her front.

"Well, child. I hope they get here soon," was the other's response as four Sansheren dressed in green appeared. The two in the doorway moved out of the way.

"Where?" was the comment from the new team's leader as Enrico watched her fit a small dart into a hand weapon.

"Within, it is killing one of the others, you can see. Strange, I thought it would have been the small one to lose its bearing, she does not even have a language yet," the older nurse said and moved from the doorway.

Enrico wondered if those outside the nursery room could see him watching them as he played; Tracy and Gerry were on the floor rolling and fighting him and each other. The new Sansheren listened to the younger children's squeals and screams.

\#

"One should leave decisions of regression to the nursery staff, thank you." With that comment, Aldera shook her head at her assistant and holstered her still loaded weapon.

Aldera clapped her hands together twice as she entered the room of the three children, who rewarded her with silent, frightened looks.

"You have caused enough trouble for today, now get in your beds and be good." She used her father's voice, soft and reassuring. Hoping it was something their two species had in common. Loving parents.

Making eye contact with each child, she pointed to a bed at random, and was rewarded with small giggles as the youngest two climbed into opposite beds. She saw terror in the eyes of the youngest one as she helped her pull her blanket up. The middle child was afraid, but had control of herself, Aldera was pleased to note. She stroked the child's long hair, once.

"And why do I get the feeling you know better?" Aldera asked as she moved to help Enrico climb into his bed.

"I know lots," Enrico said in barely understandable Sansheren. "Better what?" he grinned, showing most of his discolored teeth.

Aldera stepped away from his grin before the meaning of his words registered.

"Better than to pretend to hunt, better than to scare your elders." Aldera moved back to his side as she chastised him.

"I do not understand, eat what? I do not understand, know older?" the child asked. He quit smiling, and she realized he was trying to understand her. He spoke with an accent she was unfamiliar with, and she realized he must be having far more difficulty with her own accent.

"You hunt to eat. Elder – older? An elder is older than you and takes care of you." Aldera found herself speaking slower and watching Enrico's face for small signs of comprehension.

"Hunt eat, same word, not..." Enrico paused, and she could see him unfocus his small eyes as he tried to express what he understood. "Not same word time! Older, old. Elder, older family!" he declared and glared at her. "I no family."

"Word time is tense," Aldera said, and wondered at the

94

moisture that filled his eyes, threatening to overflow. "An elder does not have to be family, an elder is one who takes care of you, helps you, heals you." She wanted to touch her finger to his chin as he clenched his jaw tight and glared at her.

"I no family, no mother, no father!"

He continued to glare as she compromised and moved her hand to touch his arm where the blanket and his shirt did not meet.

He did not move away.

"As you wish," she said, not breaking eye contact.

"Hunt to eat?" he asked, and she thought he might be focusing on the words he wanted and not the feelings he didn't. "Tracy, Gerry friends, amigos. Why hunt? Why eat?"

"They were afraid you had regressed, had become an infant." Aldera gestured for the small crowd still gathered at the door.

"I do not understand? Infant – not older? Know mother, father, family. Know infant not older understand waa. Waa!" Enrico demonstrated rocking something in his arms while crying.

"We are not the same, you and I," Aldera said, and tried to understand just how different he was. "Human infants may go waa," and she, too, pantomimed rocking something. "But Sansheren infants go ROAR!" she lunged forward and made him cower. She was sorry even before she finished.

"Roar?" Enrico swallowed and Aldera and found herself skeptical of the tone of disbelief he tried to speak in.

"ROAR. I will show you," she offered by way of an apology for frightening him.

"Roar. Safe? No eat, no hunt?" Enrico said, and she knew he was trying to bare his teeth in a human smile.

"Yes, it is safe. Here, let me," Aldera said and reached for his blanket. She gave way when Enrico shrugged off her hand, and she let him struggle alone as he swung his legs free of the bed.

"I better," he gave a sharp gesture toward his dangling leg. "No elder, no family."

"No help then." Aldera moved away while keeping her hip and leg behind the wheelchair to keep it from rolling. The young human she realized she was beginning to find attractive struggled, and she wondered when humans looked for mates.

"Are you ready to go?" she waved toward the door and they both smiled to see the small group of onlookers flinch and back away.

"Go? Yes," he said with a grin that cleared the doorway and the hall of those who hesitated.

She looked down in time to see his lips come together.

"You should not bare your teeth to anyone you do not intend to hunt." Aldera ended her sentence by baring her sharp teeth to Enrico.

"No teeth? No hunt? I understand teeth eat, hunt. Yes." He moved his chair through the door she held open, pausing to aim a ferocious grin at the older nurse who had stood her ground.

Aldera resisted her own smile when the woman brought her hand to her chest and ran down the corridor.

#

"Where'd ya go?"

Enrico had started to fall asleep even before Aldera left the room. Tracy's question roused him.

"The zoo," he said, too loudly, before turning away from his young friend, and tried to recapture the exhaustion that had threatened to overwhelmed him before.

Wide awake, staring at the ceiling, he listened to the sounds of the hospital. Two people hurried down the corridor, speaking in Sansheren too soft for him to catch any words. His grasp of the language was limited but he found its small vocabulary easier to recall than English. He knew he often missed the inflections that turned a no into a yes, but even the enemy Sansheren he had encountered were willing to repeat themselves as long as he made the effort. A guard at the camp had spent hours explaining the variations of the single word thirst one day, and Enrico winced as the memory echoed.

Thirst, with a smile, is for the dryness of your mouth with a new lover. Thirst, with a laugh, is for desire of another. Thirst, when the eyes laugh but the mouth is sad, is for the memory of friendship and wine.

What about water? How say I thirst water?

Thirst. It is always there with the word.

He forced himself focusing on the murmur of machinery, noticeable in the quiet night. Thrum, thrum, he tried to put his mind into the sound, tried to hear only that while he saw only the ceiling. It isn't working, he decided. And slowly opened his mind to the memory of the day.

The Sansheren had taken him to visit the children of its wife.

"Roar," Enrico whispered with a smile that faded.

He thought back to the camp, to the night Sam burned the guard. He understood, finally, and wondered if he would ever see his friend again. To apologize for what he had thought.

"Hey, you awake?" Tracy barely mouthed the words.

"Yeah," he whispered back.

"Why'd he take you to the zoo?" she asked, and he heard her rise.

"To show me his kids," he answered as he continued to stare at the ceiling. "It wasn't a zoo, just a nursery."

"Oh," she sounded almost disappointed, Enrico thought as she lay back down.

"They're green, with lots of teeth," he offered, more to tell her he hadn't been mad earlier when he turned away, only tired and a little afraid.

"Really? Neat."

He smiled at the enthusiasm in her voice. "Not really, they hunt. Like wild dogs. Lots of blood." He didn't want her to go through the shock he had experienced.

"Cool," her voice was muted, and he thought she might be drifting to sleep.

"That's why everyone's afraid of us; they think we're still wild." Enrico lowered his voice as he spoke and was rewarded by a soft murmur from Tracy in response.

"Don't bare teeth at anyone you don't intend to eat," he whispered to himself. The Sansheren wanted to teach him that today, and he had learned.

\#

"What um, what you? Enrico. Enrico," Enrico ended, pointing to his chest in what Yolunu thought to be frustration.

"Name. You are Enrico, I am Aldera. Name." Aldera took Enrico's hand and placed it on her chest when she pronounced her own name before moving their hands to his own chest.

"Name, understand. What you name?" Enrico pulled his hand

from her as he turned toward Yolunu. He and Aldera were sharing an evening meal in the nursery when Yolunu arrived.

"Yolunu," and anything she might have added was cut off by the shrill whine of Aldera's communication unit.

"Where? It will take us a while to get there, go ahead and call Nogina. Right. As soon as I can," Aldera finished as she stood to leave. She paused to kiss Yolunu's cheek, saw Enrico, and stopped.

"I can take her back to the hospital," Yolunu offered in answer to the panicked expression that flooded her wife's face.

"Thank you," Aldera smiled, patted Enrico's hand, and left.

Yolunu listened to her running down the corridor.

"Aldera go, why?" Enrico asked, and once more Yolunu thought he was frustrated by his limited vocabulary.

"Someone must've found an infant," Yolunu said, and didn't try to keep the worry out of her voice.

"Hungry infant hunt, Aldera safe?" Enrico held her eye and Yolunu realized that he was also worried.

"They will feed the infant before they try to get close. She will be fine." Yolunu did not meet his eyes as she told them both the same lie she told herself every day.

"Feed – eat? No hungry is safe?" he brought his hand to hers as he spoke.

"Yes," Yolunu tried to reassure him by smiling; only to realize the young human would not recognize the expression. "Your lesson for today is in expressions," she intoned with mock seriousness.

"I do not understand," he left the sentence hanging in the air.

"I know," Yolunu said with a smile and a sigh. "See – I do not understand – is confusion. Like this." First she pointed to her eyes and then his before trying to school her eyes into a confused or blank expression.

"I do not understand – confusion?" Enrico tried to mimic the expression.

He succeeded in looking dazed or drugged, Yolunu thought. "Right, now try this one, happy," again Yolunu gave an exaggerated expression.

"What happy?" he asked.

98

#

"Enrico," Tracy paused until he looked her way. "Can we go with you tomorrow?"

"I don't know, senorita. I'll ask, if you want me to?" he felt the silence build.

"It's been days, and you don't play anymore. It's really boring when you're gone. And you're learning to talk like them," she finished in a rush, and he tried to hear if she was crying.

"Hey, little princess." He hopped across the room. "We'll play tomorrow, and maybe I can teach you how to speak like them. Would you like that?" he stood beside her bed and pretended not to notice the tears she wiped away.

"Promise you'll play tomorrow?" she sniffled while she waited for his nod. "Then I'll let you teach me and Gerry how to talk like them."

He smiled at her logic before patting her arm and moving back to his bed.

#

"Enrico, wake up," someone said in Sansheren.

A dark shape was standing over him in the night; Enrico screamed in terror as he pulled away, only to become tangled in his blankets. He felt strong hands catch him when he started to fall.

"Enrico, it is Aldera. Wake up." Aldera's voice was louder but still soft as she held his struggling, crying form. "Turn the lights on, Nogina, the others must be awake by now. It is Aldera, your friend. Wake up. I need your help." The voice continued to shout in Sansheren as Enrico twisted in his blankets.

The bright light only served to further panic him and make his struggles more violent.

"Leave him alone!" He heard Tracy shout, and then a Sansheren cursed. "Help, Enrico, help!"

"Aldera?" Enrico whispered. Tracy's voice brought him out of the nightmare and into the room instantly. He now stared, confused, first at Aldera, and then at his young friend.

"Let her go, Nogina," Aldera said even as Gerry joined them by grabbing Tracy's captor around the leg and trying to bite through the baggy pants.

"Confusion. I do not understand," Enrico said to his Sansheren friend even as they both started laughing at the others.

"I need your help. Nogina needs your help." Aldera found it difficult to speak through the laughter that continued to swell up.

The other Sansheren adult released Tracy only to have the girl turn and attack her other leg. With a child on each leg, the woman had fallen backwards and was leaning against one of the bed supports. Each of her hands was firmly against the chest of a child; the children looked as if they had been caught in mid lunge.

"Tracy, Gerry, it's okay. Let him up," Enrico called out in English, and schooled his expression before the two younger children looked his way. "Let him up," he said again, this time more forcefully.

"Thank you," Nogina said in Sansheren before she turned and fled the room.

"Thank you for trying to help me, it was just a nightmare," Enrico said in English but did not elaborate, and the other children knew enough about their own nightmares not to press.

"I need your help," Aldera said once more in Sansheren.

"I understand help. Why?" he sat up straighter and reached for the handle of his chair.

"A human is about to burst, she cries in pain from the infant. You must explain to the other humans that we would help." Aldera braced the chair as she spoke.

"Human create infant, you help?" he asked, and Aldera's nod confirmed his grasp of the situation. He dropped into his chair and started toward the door.

Aldera move to the doorway and turned off the lights.

"Enrico, you promised to play tomorrow. You promised," Tracy whispered from her bed.

"A human woman needs my help Tracy. I have to go. When I get back, okay?" he moved his chair parallel to her bed.

"Okay," she said, and he knew she remained unconvinced as she turned away from him in the now dark room.

#

Tracy was asleep when Enrico returned to their room, he noted gratefully. He had been awake for the entire night and well into the next day.

The human woman had indeed been in labor, luckily there were no complications to the birth. The little girl screamed almost before she was clear of her mother.

He was hard pressed to explain to the Sansheren medics that the human woman didn't need any help.

He was stumped for Sansheren words he did not know, and it had been very frustrating to make eye contact with Alistair, the old man who had taught him most of the little Sansheren he did know. Alistair had at first pretended not to know him until Enrico told the room of humans he was not going to betray any information they held. Alistair then muttered that knowledge is power before coaching him by spelling out, in English, the phonetics of some Sansheren words.

He thought Aldera noticed the hints, but she never said anything. Her attention was on trying to help the mother. Enrico watched how hostile the adult humans were towards the Sansheren, and told the room that they were there to help, and that his sister died in childbirth and they should be thankful for the help. Things had gone a bit smoother after that, and only one man called him a toad, to be silenced by looks from Alistair.

Aldera accompanied him back to his room the following night. After he had repeatedly explained to her and the other Sansheren medics that they would not succeed in separating the mother from her newborn. He had tried to pay attention to the route they took while explaining to Aldera that human mothers stayed very close to their babies for years, that the baby might die if they took it away. That human children needed parents. He still didn't know if he made himself clear when they reached his room, and he said good night.

#

"Where is Stripes?" Enrico had planned to visit Aldera at the preschool room, when he noticed another absence. He found himself visiting daily since little Teresa's birth two weeks prior.

He and the other three children had been moved in with the adult humans as soon as he woke the day after the birth. Tracy and Gerry flourished; Gerry had someone who spoke his language. And Enrico succeeded in convincing some of the humans to sit in on the quick language classes Yolunu offered when she had time. Now, almost half of the humans joined the classes, and most of the rest listened.

"Stee-ripe-ees," Nogina said phonetically, "choked on her dinner." Aldera's aide, Nogina placed her hand on his shoulder, trying to soften the blow of the lie.

"Choked? You mean dead?" Enrico shrugged the weight off his shoulder as he raised his voice.

"Yes, I know you liked her, but these things happen," again she tried to place her hand on his arm in comfort, to be stopped by his expression.

"You know nothing. Where is Aldera?" he left the room and started toward her office.

"I will tell her you want to see her; you might wait in her nursery." Nogina moved to intercept him and steered him into a different room.

\#

"He is waiting with your wife's children. I didn't think you would want to explain to him as head of the nursery. My Lady, I hope I have not overstepped my position to assume that you would want to speak to him as a friend." The aide kept her head bowed as she blurted out the situation and glanced up at the end of her rehearsed explanation.

"You did well to anticipate, my friend." Aldera placed her hand on the woman's shoulder in passing and missed the look of adoration cast her way.

\#

"You wish to speak with me?" she stood in the doorway, her eyes on the darkened window across the room.

"Why you kill older infants?" Enrico tried to tell himself that it didn't matter if the alien children were dying, but it did matter to him if his alien friend was responsible.

"Because they're still infants. They still hunt." Aldera sat down on the lounge opposite his and sighed.

"Infants hunt, stripes hunt, older no hunt." He tried hard to organize his thoughts into Sansheren words.

"Steripes was not an infant anymore. She still tried to hunt others, to eat others. She was a regressive. Like we'd thought you were," Aldera said.

Enrico noticed for the first time how old his friend was. "Stripes older? Know better no hunt?" he sat staring at his friend.

"Yes, Steripes should have known better. A regressive does not grow up, does not become an elder, family. It is better they die, they are too dangerous." Aldera leaned her head back and closed her eyes as she spoke.

"Regressive, kill, regressive are not old? Not Patches?" her silence answered his question.

"Furball?"

No answer.

"Annunu and Innura?" he tried again.

"Annunu and Innura will be fine, they have each other." Aldera sat forward and smiled toward the dark glass.

"Tadesde infants die." A hard edge entered his voice when he realized that orphans were the only ones dying.

"Not all, only those who were born alone. Those who were hungry too long. Some of ours will die too, infants always die. It keeps us strong," Aldera said, but to Enrico it sounded as if she was talking to reassure herself.

"Infants born hungry, alone die? Tadesde infants born hungry, alone. Lots?" he thought about the conditions toward the end of the war that might have caused Tadesde's people to give birth alone. He understood far more than he wanted to.

"Yes," Aldera said, and Enrico allowed her to put a hand on his shoulder, this time.

Chapter Thirteen - Sheresuan - 2012

"We are pleased to hear that you have finally chosen to search for your first family. It has been an honor and pleasure to father you, my dearest child. And now, we are in agreement that your House demands the resolution of your history. It is my sincere wish that you find success in searching for those who meant so much to you," Neadesto said from where she stood leaning against Nealoie.

Morgan paused in the doorway of the private audience chamber and considered her response. A large room, outfitted with many cushions for petitioners, the chamber would have fit unnoticed into a corner of the formal audience room in which Morgan had declared the forming of her own House.

"I will always honor you first, my dearest father. I would beg loan of a ship from you with which to accomplish my travels," Morgan said as she knelt in front of Neadesto.

"Stand. Child. You rule a House now, to bow is mockery." Neadesto frowned as she reached forward and held her hand out to Morgan.

Morgan took a breath to push down the fear.

"To bow shows all where my own allegiance falls." Morgan stood, and took care not to put weight on Neadesto's frail arm.

"Your allegiance must now fall to your own family and House, my dear. Neadesto moved toward the only lounge in the room.

"Do you then divorce me, my father?" Morgan asked, and her voice echoed Neadesto's chastising tone. She sat beside the older, more powerful leader, and forced herself to relax.

"Never. But I will not loan you a ship. It is not seemly for so neutral a House as mine to grant loans. I will give you, my adopted child and apprentice, the good ship Yonxine. She has

104

been in service almost as long as I have been Twelve. She is not fast, but she will serve you well." Neadesto smiled as Morgan felt her fear and disappointment shift to excitement and pleasure.

"The Yonxine was Neavillii's first command, you know. She speaks of it frequently. I am afraid she will not want to attend to Bystocc when she finds that I will be traveling in her first love," Morgan said with a smile and Neadesto echoed her with a soft laugh.

"Your bold and daring wife is recovering nicely, I am told. You have done well; triplets have not been born in this House for over a century. Tell her I would be honored if she would present them to me herself," Neadesto said.

"I will convey your message, my Lady," Morgan said with a brief but sincere bow of her head.

"Have you thought toward a crew for your new possession?" Neadesto asked, and then turned to whisper something to the kneeling Nealoie.

"I did not know I had this new treasure before you told me; it will take some time to find a crew worthy of such a wonderful craft." Amused suspicion crept into her voice as Morgan watched Nealoie cross the room and speak with someone in the doorway.

"The current crew is very fond of her, you might try asking them," and Neadesto chuckled as Nealoie, followed by four others, walked across the room.

"If it pleases your most wonderful ladies, I would present, Vilhade, the one who fathered my most loved aunt, Neavillii." Nealoie bowed before turning to indicate the eldest woman behind her.

"Indeed," Morgan said, to Neadesto's soft laughter.

"I am honored by this audience, my great and loving aunt. And I am doubly honored to meet again the young apprentice who so recently wed my lovely daughter." Vilhade, like Neavillii, was tall by Sansheren standards, four feet, eight inches. Her bones were thinner than most and Morgan always suspected her of spacing before she was matured.

"Vilhade, the honor is mine as well." Morgan leaned back into her chair.

#

"You're awake, shh," Isaac said with a smile to the still groggy Sam. "I thought the two of you would sleep all day."

"What day?" Sam asked as he shifted his weight. "I feel like I've been out for weeks." He was careful not to disturb Tansea who nestled against his side.

"It's been nearly a month since we rescued you." Isaac moved to the side of the bed, and tried to be quiet as he removed the various tubes that were connected to Sam's body.

"I don't remember much, just a dream that wouldn't go away. Your friend said Morgan was.., real?" Sam grimaced as the tape came free from his hand.

"Shock. You shut down until you could deal with everything. Morgan will be by later, to visit her wife. She doesn't know you're awake yet. I thought we might surprise her." Isaac smiled as he removed the last of the tubes.

"I'm game. Think I could get a shower first, though?" Sam ran his hand over his face, feeling his scant but long facial hair.

"Shit, shower and shave coming right up." Isaac laughed as he moved toward the door.

"I don't need the first now, but I appreciate the others." Sam also smiled.

"Wait until you eat the food here. You'll need it." Isaac shared a laugh with Sam before leaving, and Sam hoped it was to make arrangements for the promised shower.

#

Isaac stood in the doorway to Iedonea's office and watched the Sansheren work. Iedonea's coloring was unusual, he noted, streaked with red and faint hints of green.

"Morganea asked me to notify her when Sam regained consciousness," Isaac told Neadesto.

"And has she?" the older Sansheren looked up from her work with an impatient frown.

Isaac met her frown with an annoyed looking human smile. "My grasp of your wonderful language must not be as strong as I thought. Sam is awake, Morganea requested I inform her immediately," Isaac said while staring the other in the eyes.

"You may petition her any time you wish, but I am sorry to

note that my niece is taking her obligations of House far more seriously than her obligations of family. She has not even visited her spouse, the lovely Neavillii, yet today." Iedonea set aside her work with the new frown.

"A new House is an intimidating obligation. It is possible she wants to have things under control before she relaxes and indulges her personal obligations," Isaac offered, thinking in human terms.

"The obligations of the Sansadee are the obligations of the House. She shames herself," Iedonea said and picked up a model flier from her desk.

"You're a pilot?" Isaac asked in surprise.

"I have little time to indulge such passions now. I second Neadesto, it is better that I do the desk work." Iedonea set the model aside.

"Most pilots I have known consider flying a desk worse than death," Isaac said.

"I would agree, but the work must be done." Iedonea stroked a claw-tip down the wing of the model before returning her gaze back to Isaac. "Is there anything else you would ask?"

"No. But thinking of Morgan, what if we were to shame her?" Isaac asked with a polite smile and watched as Iedonea returned it with far more enthusiasm. It took several minutes to finalize their plans.

#

Sam stared at the door, waiting, until an overwhelming itch began in his left stump. Moving slowly, he attempted to shift his leg enough to rub the stump against the bedding. This caused the itch to intensify and to be joined by one on his other stump. He shifted again and succeeded in knocking the blanket that was spread over his lower body onto the floor.

"Damn. Well, I see I'm a bit shorter now," Sam said as he stared at the bandages that now ended above his knees.

"It was needed, believe me, please." Tansea opened her eyes and smiled up at Sam before stretching and sitting up.

"Yeah, no doubt. The doc was here, I think he'll be right back." Sam was not embarrassed to be in bed with a person he did not know, but the intimacy combined with the realization that the other person wasn't human left him uncomfortable.

"Doc? Doctor? Isaac?" Tansea made no move to leave Sam's side.

"Yeah. Um, what species are you? If you don't mind my asking ma'am. Uh, I mean, um." Sam felt his face flush as he tried to twist to face Tansea.

"Ma'am is fine. I am from Greos." Tansea made no attempt to face Sam, but instead leaned toward him until they were in contact again.

"Um, I- That is-" Sam continued to stare at her small head as she snuggled into his side.

"Are you uncomfortable with her presence?" Isaac said from the doorway. "Tansea, move your cold-blooded little butt."

Tansea stuck her long tongue out at the returning Isaac before moving to make eye contact with the confused Sam; she then resumed her previous position.

"It's okay, doc." Sam smiled down at Tansea's head before noticing the wheelchair in the doorway behind Isaac.

"Morgan is so busy she hasn't even stopped by to see her spouse yet. So I thought we'd surprise her a bit." Isaac moved the chair to the bed while smiling at Sam's puzzled expression.

"What have you planned, you devious child?" Tansea climbed out of the bed and took Sam's blanket with her.

"Yeah, doc. What gives? Shower?" Sam tried to lift his weight and transfer himself to the chair, but the months of near starvation followed by weeks of confinement had weakened him far more than he realized.

"Hey, wait until I get someone to help us." Isaacs's voice showed his strain as he shifted Sam back onto the bed and then went to the door and flagged down a passerby.

"Gently. You still haven't explained your plan," Tansea said, first in English and then again in Sansheren in politeness to their assistant.

"I'll tell you on the way." Isaac then thanked the Sansheren and pushed Sam out of the room.

Tansea was forced to jog to keep up.

#

"It is my opinion that a father who does not attend her ailing child is not worthy of the title," Iedonea said in a disapproving voice from behind Morgan and Neadesto.

"I was just at the nursery less than an hour past. Tell me you're mistaken, my most loving and caring aunt." Morgan stood and turned to face Iedonea even as all conversation in the room came to a halt.

"I have just left the most beautiful and distraught Neavillii, who is even now being forced to discuss, alone, the distasteful concept of disposal with the nursery staff." Iedonea continued to frown, and Morgan heard Nealoie's gasp as Neadesto struggled to her feet.

"It is not our place to interfere, most loving father to us all. This is a matter between spouses," Iedonea said to Neadesto, and Morgan cringed at the cold tone in her voice. "I do trust you will go and take the burden from the brave Neavillii's shoulders, my niece?" Iedonea left no doubt that she expected instant obedience from Morgan, who was already halfway to the door when Iedonea finished speaking.

Bowing, out of habit, Morgan allowed the door to swing closed of its own accord and took off running down the hallway.

"Why was I not contacted?" Morgan shouted at the Sansheren medic who was just leaving the nursery corridor.

"My most kind and lovely Morganea, we know you're very busy, and your lovely wife insisted-"

Morgan pushed past the surprised older medic whose words trailed behind her. Racing down the corridor, she neared the crossroad that led to her spouse. Grabbing the side of the archway, she threw herself around the corner and then avoided colliding with a somber-faced Banessa.

"Why was I not contacted?" and again Morgan did not wait for a response but shoved herself past and into the observation room.

Someone sat huddled in the far left chair with the lights turned out and only the dim glow from the nursery for illumination.

Morgan moved to her wife, anger already giving way to tears. "No one told me," Morgan whispered as she placed her hand on the blanket covered shoulder.

"I know," Neavillii said from the doorway behind her.

And Morgan blinked. "Then, who?" Morgan asked, and realized it was a human beside her. "Sam!" Morgan cried, and Sam shrugged off the blanket when he heard his name. Morgan stared first to Neavillii and then Sam before smiling in relief.

"It was your good doctor's idea," Neavillii said with a laugh.

"I confess, I confess." A proud looking Isaac put his hand on the shorter Neavillii's elbow and walked her into the room, freeing up the doorway so that Iedonea could enter with Neadesto.

"He is admitting he is childish," Tansea said in English and Morgan looked over to see her climb onto Sam's lap.

#

Tansea continued to translate the conversations that swirled about the room, but Sam lost track of who was who as he stared at Morgan.

He kept thinking about her as a child and watching her move as an adult and his mind could not reconcile the two images. This was someone else wearing Morgan's body he kept thinking, and then dismissing each time she used a gesture or expression he remembered.

#

"Why do you do that?" Sam asked.

Morgan was smiling to the departing Iedonea, and Sam's English did not register until after he finished speaking and the silence built.

"Do what?" She asked, speaking softly, to him only. Then she waved to Neadesto, who was awaiting eye contact before leaving.

"There, the way you scrunch your mouth and raise your eyebrows?" Sam asked as he leaned toward where Morgan sat.

Morgan smiled when Tansea's sleeping form halted him, and he smiled down at her.

"It's a smile, a Sansheren smile. I see you made a friend." Morgan forced herself to use a human smile as she pointed to the frail looking creature who was under most of Sam's lap blanket.

"Yeah, her name's Tansea. I think her and the doc have something going on. Anyway, she's cold-blooded, and it's way too cool in here for her. Weird, huh?" Sam returned Morgan's smile, but with less success at faking it, she noted.

110

"Don't believe her, she's an incorrigible nymphomaniac," Isaac said from the doorway.

Tansea moved, and gave a soft sound of protest when Isaac's loud voice filled the room.

Morgan began laughing, and Sam just stared between the three and looked confused.

"You see in others what you fear the most, young man." Tansea sat up, kissed Sam's cheek, slipped to the floor, and glared at Isaac, before wrapping Sam's blanket about her shoulders and walking to the door. "I will see you children after we leave for Wergol, if not sooner. Come infant, we'll see how much warmth you can exude."

Isaac gave an exaggerated look of fright before laughing out loud and following Tansea out of the room.

Sam stared at the room's exit for several long seconds before Morgan felt him turn toward her. She continued to look at the door despite the pressure of his gaze.

"We're going to Wergol?" Sam asked, and Morgan could not miss the hope that tinged his voice.

"Neadesto has word that Tim is there. It is Tim, isn't it?" Morgan did not allow herself to feel any emotion and was afraid Sam would hear everything in her voice.

"It is," Sam said.

And Morgan used the silence to absorb the news.

"We've always spent a lot of time there," Sam continued. "Most humans do. The government is human, and they have a register you can sign onto if you want someone to find you. That's how I found Denise, and we found Tim," Sam said, and again Morgan felt the pressure of his gaze as she tried not to cry.

"I didn't know. I never thought to look. I wanted to, believe me I did. But somehow I never thought about how to look," Morgan said, and Sam leaned forward to offer his hand to her.

It was a long time before Morgan accepted his touch.

"You did good for yourself, I hear you own your own planet and everything. No one will think badly of you just because you haven't had the time to search us out," Sam said as Morgan stared at the glass, and her sleeping children. "Hell, it hasn't been that long. We wouldn't hold a grudge for at least another five years," Sam said with a bitter laugh, and Morgan thought he knew his attempt at humor was unsuccessful even before she started crying.

She didn't know how long it had been since the last comment, and Morgan felt a pressure to talk as she dried her eyes.

"Bystocc."

"A nightmare best forgotten, why?" Sam asked, and Morgan noticed that he still held her hand.

"My planet, it's Bystocc. Tadesde abandoned the prize. I pledged my House to restoring it." Morgan gave one last moist sniffle before straightening up and smiling to Sam.

"That planet is dying. The only reason Tim agreed to a cease-fire with that bastard is because he was afraid Tadesde would blow the sun, the suicidal asshole!" Sam let go of Morgan's hand to clench the arms of his chair.

"Who broke the cease-fire?" She needed to know.

"I don't know. I think they both did. Tim planned to double-cross her and I think she double-crossed him as well," Sam said, and Morgan felt a cold spot begin to grow inside of her.

"Is that when you were captured?" Morgan refused to look at his legs, so Sam did.

"Yeah, I held the rear. God, I hope they made it out okay." Sam gave up his self-control, and it was Morgan's turn to put her hand on top of his and wait for the storm of emotions to pass.

The entire time Sam was crying, Morgan kept thinking to herself, with an absolute certainty she didn't understand, "He's dead."

And then she had to wonder if it was a premonition or a wish.

"We'll find out, we leave for Wergol the day after tomorrow. In the meantime, you need to rest, and I have business. We'll speak again on the trip. Promise?" Morgan tried to keep her voice neutral and reassuring even as she moved across the room to the intercom panel and signaled for an attendant to take Sam back to his room.

"Sure," Sam answered as he was wheeled out of the room.

Morgan had already left.

Chapter Fourteen - Bystocc - 2012

"What you have accomplished is amazing," Neavillii said from where she stood in the doorway of the preschool room and watched the small children working at their toys.

"In truth, my Lady, the Great Houses have been most generous. I would have little to show you were it not for their donations," Aldera said with her head bowed low.

"Indeed?" Neavillii asked, and heard Thanera laugh behind her. "I am certain the progress I see is more an indication of your skill and leadership. Another would surely have wasted the resources and squandered her time." Neavillii turned to share a smile with Thanera over Aldera's blushing head.

"Would you view the room I have set aside for your clever and intelligent children, most beautiful of patrons?" Aldera asked. She kept her eyes low as she brushed past Neavillii and hurried from the room.

"Of course," Neavillii answered to Aldera's retreating back as the other woman hurried down the corridor. "But I warn you, if you continue to flirt with me, I will hold you to the offer." Neavillii laughed aloud when Aldera stopped her hurried pace and spun around to stare at her.

"I would never presume a place in your lovely bed, my Lady. I only meant to honor you." Aldera stumbled over a formal inflection as Neavillii reached her side.

"Then you do not find our Lady beautiful?" Thanera asked with an formal inflection and a smile.

"Our Lady, you are indeed most beautiful," Aldera said. "I meant that sincerely, I just did not think one so esteemed would take seriously the devotions of someone as low as myself." Aldera continued to switch her gaze from Neavillii to Thanera.

"Indeed?" Thanera imitated Neavillii's inflection. "Then

perhaps something should be done about the low image you hold of yourself."

"Indeed," Neavillii said with an exaggerated copy of Thanera as imitation. "Would you have the honor? Or, perhaps as the subject of her devotion, and it should, by rights, be myself."

"Indeed!" Thanera said with a laugh. "It should be you, my Lady." Thanera moved to stand behind Aldera and placed her hands on her confused friend's shoulders.

"Indeed," Neavillii said with her own soft laugh. "Well, I shall try to give you a memory suitable to this moment," and she took a deep breath before beginning. "You honor me with your presence, and I can only hope your bravery is contagious, for in the face of such devotion, I can do no less than bring you closer to myself," and with a stifled laugh, Neavillii leaned forward to whisper Aldera's promotion to the Eleventh rank of Tamsatel in her ear.

Thanera paused and whispered the promotion of the First rank of Sansadee in her other ear.

"Look what we have done with our lover's giggles, she is crying. Please don't cry, please." Neavillii put her arm around Aldera and exchanged a concerned glance with Thanera.

"If we ruined the moment for you, I will never forgive myself. Yolunu will never forgive me." Thanera placed her hand on Aldera's shoulder, who was attempting to pull gently away from Neavillii.

"You did not ruin it for me," Aldera said and took a deep breath. "It was the best moment I've experienced since I was released from apprenticeship and the wonderful Dejymo accepted my pledge personally." Aldera tried to laugh, but her voice was still shaky from the emotions that overwhelmed her.

"Why don't we take this into the nursery? I see we have attracted an audience." Neavillii gestured toward the older children who stood watching and waiting for them to stop blocking the corridor.

"Indeed," Aldera manage to choke out before all three gave way to laughter.

#

Enrico stood for several minutes in the darkened observation room, watching the three Sansheren infants' violent game of hunting each other, before he realized he was not alone. "Forgive me, noble patron. I thought the room was empty," Enrico said as he turned away from the form in the darkness and moved toward the room's door.

"I would welcome you," Neavillii said. "Sit. You are the human Enrico?"

"Yes," Enrico said, and continued facing the closed door. "Have you met many of my species?" he asked the expected question before leaning his cane against the wall, and turning back to the room. He shifted his stump in his new prosthetic.

"I am honored to call the human, Morgan, my mate. Sit with me a moment so that I can see how you have fared since last we met." Neavillii slid the dimmer control up until Enrico could see her clearly.

"You are Neavillii, then?" Enrico asked as he limped across the small room. "I am in your debt, how may I serve you?" Enrico limped forward to kneel between Neavillii and the glass partition.

"Sit by me, please. You speak the court tongue, I am pleased to note," she said with a wave toward the empty lounge. "Tell me, are you so eager for parenthood that you view other's children?" And again she indicated the other lounge.

Enrico kept his head bowed as he remained kneeling on the floor. "The patient and wise Yolunu has been generous enough to spend her evening hours coaching the surviving humans on your beautiful language," Enrico said as his stump began to throb. "Learning seemed necessary to our survival." He had yet to shift his position.

"Yolunu, wife to Aldera? I must see that she understands my appreciation of her foresight. But you have not answered my question." Neavillii leaned forward, and Enrico hoped she would not notice the beads of sweat forming on his forehead. "Nor have you sat with me."

"Custom states that one must not sit at a height equal or above one whom you are either decidedly beneath or that you owe an honor debt to," Enrico said through clenched teeth, and he never wavered in his stance as the throb intensified.

"Except for the purpose of dining. Have you not covered that lesson yet? Sit and share some fruit with me." She waved to a bowl of shriveled, pale produce sitting on a small table out of reach of both of the lounges.

"I have been taught that one may accept an equal seating while dining, if by invitation and if said invitation includes a night of pleasure as well. Are you asking me into your bed, my Lady?" Enrico asked with a sharp glance up, and felt himself sway. He used his left hand to brace against the empty lounge.

"I am asking you to sit with me!" She said, and he heard the frustration in her voice. "Here. Alone. In the dark. Court behavior belongs in the court. Leave it there."

"And what if someone enters, uninvited as I did?" Enrico asked, and felt the sweat begin to trickle down his face. "Will not your honor suffer from such a sight?" he shifted enough to allow his arm to take some of his weight.

"In two other situations may we sit as equals. Can you name them?" she tried a different tact.

"The personal guard sits always to the right of her chosen master. I know of no other reason to breach protocol." The sweat ran from his forehead to sting his eyes.

"An apprentice sits with her master when they eat alone; otherwise she stands to offer service." Neavillii held her hand out to him.

"And as no one would believe me to be your bodyguard, and I am not your apprentice, I will hold my position. My Lady." He raised his eyes, to watch the hand pull back.

It didn't.

"A personal guard chooses whom she will guard," Neavillii said, and Enrico thought she was chastising him. "There have been some unlikely guards within our history. You would be accepted, were that your choice. If not, I am offering an apprenticeship."

The hand remained, and Enrico clenched his teeth in pain. "I would not presume the skills necessary to protect your lovely self. Therefore, I am forced to accept your offer of apprenticeship," Enrico said and reached out with his right hand. The same as she offered him, but he used his left arm to push himself up from his knees. The blood returning to his stump was painful and forced him into the lounge.

"It was not my intention to force you into this agreement," Neavillii said, and Enrico felt her watch him sit. "I simply wanted to spend some time speaking with you. Something I could not in good conscience do with you kneeling in front of me. How is your wound?" She asked, pointing to the wrong leg.

"Then I release you from your offer. One as low as I should have realized it was in jest." He bowed his head and moved forward, intending to kneel once more.

"Stop! It is not the place of the apprenticed to release the master. Sit."

He heard her voice soften toward the end.

"As you wish." He sat back. The sweat stung his eyes.

"I wish. How is your leg?"

Enrico met her eyes. "It heals," and looked away. "The talented doctors gifted me with a wonderful prosthetic and cane." He nodded toward the door and the cane he had left there. He did not look down at the fake orange fur that bristled at the end of his pant leg.

"Court language is unnecessary between us; you're a part of my family now," Neavillii said, and offered a polite smile. "Dispense with any compliments you do not feel."

"Dispense?" he asked, and tried to force his face into a Sansheren smile long enough for her to notice.

"Dispense – drop – do not use. Like your smile. A human smile is pleasant enough once one becomes accustomed to it." Her own Sansheren smile grew at the forced expression on his face.

"A human smile is not appropriate. I live in your world now. I must practice your expressions, lest I forget one day and bare my teeth at someone I do not intend to eat. " He held the smile an extra moment before relaxing and rubbing his face.

"Indeed. Remind me some time to tell you about when my wonderful mate Morgan announced the arbitration to Tadesde's retainers. Regardless, you never answered my question, why do you view other people's children?" Neavillii shifted in her chair until she was again facing the viewing window.

"Any answer I offered would either be a lie or an insult, most generous of patrons." He, too, shifted until he could see into the nursery, and Neavillii dimmed the lights as he spoke.

"I think perhaps we have not known each other long enough to grasp what will offend the other," she whispered.

"I concede," Enrico responded and glanced toward her. The

room was dark with only the diffused light from the nursery to cast dim shadows about them.

"Would the truth be that you knew I was within and hoped for this audience?" Again, the whisper. The children continued to stalk each other in turn, oblivious to the glass wall.

"No," he said, and debated the truth before continuing; "I just like visiting the zoo."

"Indeed?" she asked with a chuckle, and the loudness of her voice startled Enrico after the whispers.

"They're so wild, so cruel. I like that. I really do," he gave up trying to explain to her what he couldn't explain to himself. He just felt an attraction to the alien children who needed no adults, no help.

"Human children are very different, I realize. When the most beautiful Neadesto brought my mate Morgan onboard her flagship, I remember she was very quiet. Very frightened. You had the same eyes as her, when we first met in the corridor. I wanted to help you the same way Neadesto helped Morgan," the whisper was back as neither looked away from the window.

"You were honor bound to leave with Morgan and I fared well." This time it was his voice that was loud in the room.

"Indeed. Tell me..," Neavillii said and paused with a sigh. "Tell me what you would have me know about yourself?"

Enrico saw her glance from the window in time to see his expression, and he hoped she didn't recognize it as having to do with nightmares and unshed tears. "I do not know what of my life would interest you," he said in an empty voice.

"I will not pry, child," Neavillii said, and it felt like a mild rebuke. "I only wish to know you better so that I might help you."

"I do not remember requesting help, my patron." He sat stiff, staring at the glass and not the room.

"I am not your patron any longer. It would please me if you would consider us family, you and I." Neavillii leaned across the space separating them to touch his knee.

"I have no family. Does apprenticeship require that I become physically intimate with you?" and knew he startled her when he turned his gaze to her in challenge.

"No. No, it does not," Neavillii said, and pulled her hand from his knee. "It does not require that you even like me. How must your family have treated you, to react so?" Neavillii moved back until her head rested against the cushioned riser and closed her eyes.

"You saved Sam's life, and for that I honor you. For that, I'm grateful. I can give little else." He bowed his head and closed his eyes.

"Then it is I who must do the giving. Come, it is late, we should leave now." She opened her eyes, moved forward and stood, offering her hand.

"They will feed soon, I wanted to watch." Enrico remained seated, ignoring her hand.

"Another time." Neavillii moved across the room and retrieved his cane from where it leaned against the door frame.

"As you wish, my patron," Enrico said, and wondered if his inflection was insulting. With a sigh, he stood and turned toward the door, to find Neavillii beside him holding out the cane.

"I have accepted an invitation to dine with the lovely ladies Aldera, Yolunu, and Thanera," Neavillii said, and he knew she chose to ignore the inflection. "You will share my quarters, but tonight, I think, you will sleep alone." Neavillii smiled as she held the door open for Enrico.

"I have to stop by and tell Tracy I will not be there for dinner." Enrico paused on the ramp leading out of the subterranean nursery.

"I should visit the other human survivors as well. Tracy is your mate?" Neavillii put her hand on the small of his back and nudged him into moving.

"She is just a little girl who has a - is devoted to me." He searched for the Sansheren word before shrugging and continuing up the long slope.

"The English word is crush, I believe," Neavillii said in English, and Enrico stumbled.

He threw a quick glance in her direction and saw that she was smiling. "I was not aware of your talent for language," Enrico said in Sansheren, and struggled to continue walking up the ramp as his knuckles turned white on his cane. "You humble me."

"I thought we agreed not to use the court speech between us?" Neavillii asked, again in English, and moved to take his free elbow. To help him, he thought.

"You told me not to use court language, my patron," Enrico said in Sansheren. "You also told me to voice only those compliments I felt. I apologize if I've misunderstood your instructions," and he stepped forward quickly, to lose her hand at his side, but only succeeded in getting even more off balance.

"Indeed, I did," she said, and hesitated before letting go of his elbow.

He fell, catching himself with one knee and the railing. He quietly righted himself and continued up the ramp.

"There is a lift," Neavillii said from behind him.

"I need the exercise," he said, not raising his gaze from the path before him.

"I agree," Neavillii said without continuing, and Enrico felt forced to turn around and join her at the entrance to a level corridor. "But I desire speed. Come."

"As you wish, my patron," Enrico said, and followed Neavillii into an elevator. He leaned against the wall until they reached the ground level where she led him outside to a parked ground car.

The sun's light was blocked by clouds and too feeble to penetrate the vehicle's darkened windows on the short ride to the converted warehouse that the human survivors used as a barracks.

"It is not the word one should listen to, but the inflection. Try it once more: beautiful," Yolunu said in Sansheren, and Enrico looked across the large room to the corner where eighteen humans formed a semicircle around his Sansheren friend. The rest of the humans sat about the room in small clumps or lay on their cots pretending not to listen to the language lessons.

"Beautiful." The word echoed through the room from more than just those sitting in on the class, and Enrico could hear Tracy's voice through the rest.

"When the brave Enrico told me you were giving language lessons I did not imagine it included the art of insults, most lovely and talented Yolunu," Neavillii called from the doorway of the cavernous room.

And Enrico turned to watch Neavillii.

"My Lady," Yolunu said with a startled gasp as she moved to a kneeling position before standing, and Enrico wondered at

Neavillii's position among the Sansheren. "It is but an incentive I've offered the intelligent humans whom it is my pleasure to teach."

"Indeed. Tell me, have they all learned to speak with the same stubborn eloquence of my new apprentice here?" Neavillii asked as she nodded her head toward Enrico.

Enrico froze as Neavillii placed a hand on his shoulder before she continued her slow move into the room. All activity in the room stopped as the humans sat, staring at Neavillii with open distrust, and Enrico tried to ignore Tracy's shock.

"Only a few. I am ashamed to admit that my skill in teaching is not nearly up to their need to be taught," Yolunu said with her head bowed, but Enrico saw that she continued to study Neavillii's approach.

"I remember well the difficulty of teaching my beautiful wife the many facets of our language. Do not feel discouraged," Neavillii said as she joined Yolunu in the corner of the room.

Enrico still stood in the doorway watching and trying to follow their conversation. None of the humans would meet his eye.

"Is he our new owner boy?" Alistair asked in a whisper from where he lay on a bunk to Enrico's left.

"No," Enrico answered, and resisted the urge to turn. "She's married to a human named Morgan, he's our new owner." His eyes never left Neavillii.

"So Morgan is human. He, you said?" the old man continued to stare at the two aliens talking in the corner of the room.

"Yeah, I guess. Tell me something. You ever heard that their bodyguards are self-appointed?" he darted a glance at his friend.

"Yeah, something like that. Why?" and their eyes met, if only for a moment.

"Just thinking. Here they come," he turned his body away from the old man.

"Enrico, would you be so kind as to ask everyone to sit in the chairs so that I might speak with them?" Neavillii waved her hand toward the corner that still contained the language class students.

"I am sorry to inform you, my patron, that it is impossible for me to comply with your request." Enrico stood stiff, not leaning on his cane.

"May I ask why not?" Neavillii placed a hand on Yolunu's shoulder when the other started to speak and asked the question herself.

"You are my patron; you may ask anything of me. I cannot comply with your request because not everyone present can sit in those chairs," he nodded toward the few high-backed chairs that were empty in the corner.

"Indeed. Would you be so kind as to make arrangements for everyone to gather in the corner in whatever manner is most comfortable and convenient?" Neavillii smiled as she turned her back on him and walked to the corner.

Enrico felt Yolunu's questioning gaze and looked up to meet her eye before she walked away.

"What were you trying to prove?" Alistair asked in a low voice as Enrico moved to his side and helped him strap on a prosthetic leg.

"I don't know. Come help me with Josef," and he limped away.

#

Neavillii waited as Enrico moved from group to group

The room was a large converted warehouse, she surmised. Big and drafty, it now contained almost two hundred humans of various races, sex, and age. At some point during her absence the injured humans had been moved from the hospital rooms and in with the mercenaries Tadesde had captured.

Her thoughts were interrupted when she noticed Enrico crossing the room toward her. Less than half of the remaining humans joined those in the corner.

"Is there a medical reason they do not follow you?" She leaned against the wall and called to him.

A shrug was his response.

"Then I must conclude I did not make my request clear enough. Tell them this: anyone who comes and sits with me will be free to leave this planet when I have finished speaking. Tell them that only." She glanced from him back to Yolunu who looked confused.

"My most generous mate has seen fit to declare family all human who choose to make this planet home. Or, if they choose, to provide them with transportation to the planet Wergol."

122

Neavillii shifted so that she could watch Enrico's progress.

"Then they are truly honored, to be listed in the scrolls as founders of a new House," Yolunu said.

"An honor you share, I am pleased to state." She laughed as Yolunu reached blindly for a chair to support herself, only to find the shoulder of a sitting human.

#

"Is he trying to say this Morgan has adopted us?" the question echoed through the room as Alistair translated the French into English for Enrico.

Enrico did not translate into Sansheren before answering. "I think so, yes. We all have five years in which to learn the language and customs." He kept his gaze to the room; not wanting to see Neavillii's expression.

Alistair spoke for some time as he translated. Another man translated into Arabic, and the Arabic became Chinese.

"After five years, those who can, must work," Neavillii said when the room became quiet again.

"It's not a free ride; we will be expected to work."

Alistair had already translated Neavillii's statement, he added Enrico's on.

"Doing what? All I know is fighting." The speaker was an old woman, the language was English, and again he did not translate. But only stood waiting for Neavillii's response.

"What would you have me tell them, my patron?" he bowed his head to her, for a moment.

"If you would be so kind as to tell me the question, I would gladly give you a response." The bite in Neavillii's voice was distinct, and Enrico tightened his grip on his cane.

"She is old, and she said she knows no skills but fighting. The question, my most intelligent of patrons, is what job is there for her?" Enrico kept his face to the crowd of humans, making eye contact with Alistair, and that but briefly.

"All have five years to choose a job. She may choose any career that appeals to her, surgeon if that would be her choice. She will be apprenticed to the best in her field that is available. We're a small House on a desperate planet; I would hope that most choose a job they are already proficient at. To the soldiers, we are in desperate need of defense personnel to assist the Gulardee soldiers," Neavillii said, watching the crowd.

"You can pick any job you want, brain surgeon for all they care. You apprentice to someone until you'll learn the job. She reminds us of the shape this planet is in and asks that we choose jobs we are already trained for. As for the mercenaries, they need them."

As Enrico spoke, Neavillii drifted away from him to stand beside Yolunu.

"It speaks English, don't it?" Alistair asked in a low voice before beginning his translation.

"And you, my friend, speak Sansheren. Perhaps we could both cast the ruse aside." The room went silent as Neavillii spoke in English.

"As you wish, most wise and intelligent Lady." Alistair offered a mock bow from his seated position.

"I wish," again in English. "Please, your translations," she said with a wave to the silent room.

#

"I fear my new apprentice has an agenda quite her own." Neavillii sat on the floor of Aldera and Yolunu's apartment.

"He forced your hand about knowing their language, it would seem," Yolunu said with more than a touch of pride and then held out a plate of food.

"So it seemed to me," Neavillii accepted the plate, took some of the meats from it and offered it to Aldera.

"How?" Thanera asked as she accepted the nearly empty plate from Aldera.

"By not translating everything I said, by asking my opinion without having first translated what the humans said. The thing that confuses me is she betrayed the human's knowledge of Sansheren to trap me." Neavillii leaned back as she spoke.

"She betrayed no one; I knew a few humans spoke Sansheren better than they admitted to. Think, who taught Enrico to speak our language to begin with?" Yolunu reached for a stack of flat bread.

"It is something we have discussed: he is smart. He would

have known you would inform our lovely patron of their held knowledge." Aldera accepted half of the bread from her wife.

"Indeed. Then it would seem that the only thing she sacrificed was a day of knowledge and one person. How many others do you think speak our tongue well?" Neavillii reached to retrieve an uneaten piece of bread from Yolunu's plate only to have her hand slapped at.

"I would be honored to serve your most beautiful person. More than five but less than ten. It is hard to tell." Yolunu held the bread out to Neavillii, but Aldera had already placed a piece on her plate.

"I am overwhelmed," Neavillii laughed as she accepted Yolunu's offering and gave it to Thanera with a smile.

"But why betray you, her patron?" Thanera accepted the bread with her own shy smile as she spoke.

"I must have forced her to choose between myself and the humans. In the future, I will have to be careful of the position I place her in." Neavillii shrugged as she spoke.

"But one's loyalty must always be the one's patron, why was she in conflict?" Thanera asked, and Yolunu thought she was puzzled.

"Our customs are not theirs. But tell me, as a new apprentice, would you not feel conflict if your master's House declared war upon your father's House?" Yolunu held a small cup of fermented juice to Thanera as a way to soften her words.

"Oh," was the response as Thanera sipped from the cup.

"Indeed. My friend and mate Morgan was a child when she came into the lovely Neadesto's home. Enrico is older, and I fear she has been ill-treated by those who should have protected her." Neavillii also sipped from a small cup given to her by Yolunu.

"Did he tell you, then?" Aldera asked as she offered a cup to Yolunu.

"She told me little. The pain was there to read." Neavillii did not ask the questions that Yolunu could see burned her tongue like the wine they were sharing.

"Then I will not betray his confidence, only, it was his family who sold him into slavery." Aldera met and held Neavillii's eye for a long time as the others in the room sat and waited.

"I cannot fathom her pain. My resolved to help her is strengthened by this knowledge. Thank you." Neavillii held her hand out to Aldera.

"Another point, my Lady. Humans are sexually limited, Enrico is a masculine person. He can be nothing else," Aldera stated after she released Neavillii's hand.

"Indeed. I knew that of humans, I just never thought to ask his limit. I will be more careful when I assign gender with the humans." Neavillii placed her hand over her plate as Thanera moved to put a bit of meat on it.

"I too am full, my Lady." Aldera bowed her head and blushed when Neavillii's smile answered her compliment.

"Go, both of you. We will clean up," Yolunu said, and her laughter was joined by Thanera's as Aldera's blush deepened.

Neavillii stood and offered her hand to her new lover.

\#

"I may have found a crew, finally," Yolunu said, and Thanera rolled away, trying to untangle the blanket that wrapped itself about their legs.

"An orbital crew, to hunt mines with? I thought you were halfway done?" Thanera asked as she shifted her position to grab the second blanket which had fallen from them unnoticed.

"Barely half finished. I do not see any reason to continue at this slow pace when five of the human mercenaries have offered to fly a ship which belonged to them originally," Yolunu said. The first blanket twisted beneath her, and she was forced to raise herself onto one elbow to free it.

"They are competent?" A casual question in a sleepy voice.

"So they say. One speaks a minimum of Sansheren. In the accent of the House Medori of all things. I have a meeting with them tomorrow; we will see." Yolunu finished speaking in time to hear Thanera's faint snore.

Chapter Fifteen - Wergol - 2012

Morgan stared out of the cramped ground car as Sam struggled to climb into the seat beside her. She knew Isaac was watching her as she again adjusted the banners of order and House that crossed her chest.

"So, the black banner is for being the Sansadee?" Isaac asked a question he already knew the answer to, she thought.

"The color black says that I am Sansadee. The banner says I'm of the Tenth rank," Morgan answered in a distracted manner, never bringing her gaze into the vehicle as they started moving away from her shuttle. She focused on a large mural on a far building that showed a human woman with black skin and metallic green eyes and bone white teeth offering a plate of steaming food to a group of small children.

Sam sat with the now ever-present Tansea sleeping at his side.

"And the red, white, and blue is for America," Isaac said.

"No. The multicolor banner always denotes one's House. I choose red to compliment my father, Neadesto. I then added the white and blue to personalize it. I named my House America." Morgan continued watching outside the ground car as they passed several grounded shuttle craft. Each craft had a human woman painted on its side and Morgan startled when she realized that she had never seen a picture or painting while living as a Sansheren and that she had never questioned the absence.

"I don't understand why you made the colors so bright." Sam pointed with a smile, and Morgan glanced down at her newly developed breasts before again readjusting the way the banners covered herself. No mirrors, she thought with a new start. Glass and metal surfaces everywhere but no deliberate mirrors.

The hormone therapy that Isaac synthesized before leaving the House Sheresuan was effective in starting the maturation of

Morgan's body. It had not helped her adjust to this new body she could not visualize.

"The House Gashere already wears red, white, and blue. Theirs are paler colors though, and in a different order." Morgan looked back out the window. They were finally leaving the spaceport tarmac and moving much faster as they headed for the city whose light could be seen against the sky ahead.

"I thought you're just being patriotic?" Isaac tried once more to distract Morgan from her nervousness.

"I guess. I'm not an American, you know. I just wanted to name my House so that other humans would know they could approach it." Morgan met Isaac's eyes, and he was the one that looked away first.

Sam leaned over Tansea to place his hand on Morgan's bare shoulder. "They'll know, believe me, they'll know." Sam let go of Morgan's shoulder and turned his gaze out the window as she adjusted the banner, again.

They rode in silence for several minutes as their car, and the other cars with them, moved in between the first buildings of the city. Posters and billboards were a riot of color, and humans could be seen on the streets and in doorways. A few other species were also represented, but Morgan was astounded by the sheer number of humans. They came in all shapes and sizes, all colors and costumes, and she had difficulty distinguishing people from print as the vehicle moved deeper into the city.

"How many are there?" Morgan asked.

"Don't know. Doubt if anyone does. The slavers work out of the port, people just seem to come back here, if they can." Sam hadn't turned from the window.

"Wergol is the planet for pirates bringing in humans, that's certain. I hear there's a planet in the Mydex system for Greos." Isaac gave Tansea's sleeping form a tender look.

"Slavers. They're called slavers. Pirates is too romantic." Sam sat forward, and his eyes widened as his look challenged Isaac to deny his comment.

Morgan noticed that Isaac never realized the danger as he turned his gaze outside the car.

"Slavers, pirates, I don't see much of a difference. They pull people off backwards, destructive planets and give them a chance to experience the entirety of the universe. Surely you don't begrudge a few years of indentured service as compensation for the ride?" Isaac turned back to the car's interior just as Morgan shifted her weight and intercepted the awkward blow Sam aimed at the other man's head.

"Hey! What was that for?" Isaac asked, and Morgan was annoyed to hear his indignation.

"A few years of indentured service? You toad." Sam spit out. "The average contract for a mercenary is seven years. The average life span is three! Don't talk to me about the wonders of the universe and all that crap, I've seen too many kids die out here." Sam threw himself back into his seat and clenched and unclenched his hands.

"But surely... I mean, the benefits, to be... Most people benefit from... The pirates help... I mean..." Isaac stared at Sam and then Morgan as his voice sputtered out under their harsh frowns.

"They're called Slavers," Tansea said as she sat forward, and placed her hand upon the now silent Isaac's.

They remained tense and quiet until they entered a rundown neighborhood and Sam sat forward to stare out the window instead of at the glass.

"How much further?" Morgan asked into the silence.

"The address your most loved family member supplied us with is just around this corner."

When Banessa answered, Morgan realized she spoke in Sansheren.

Turning back to the window, Morgan's gaze fell on a human man walking in the opposite direction. He was tall and black, with short cropped hair and a proud walk that was enhanced by a slight limp. Morgan turned her head to watch and, just as the car passed him, he paused at the door of a tavern. Standing for a moment, he cast a quick glance at the ground car, and Morgan knew she recognized him.

"Stop!" she gasped, and flung the door open as the car slowed to a stop. She ran toward the building Greg had just entered.

Banessa's loud curse followed her into the bar, and she stepped to the side of the doorway as her eyes tried to adjust to the darkened room.

It was Greg, she was sure. She stood and watched him sit

down at the counter. A short, large, pale skinned human woman walked up to Greg, and Morgan saw how familiar they were with each other. She had long, brown hair and Morgan did not recognize her until she laughed. It was a high pitched, forced laugh that reminded her of the Earth. Denise. Her face bore wrinkles that Morgan did not think came from laughter, and after she finished laughing she looked sadder than before.

Banessa opened the door and walked in. Looking the room over for possible threats, Morgan thought to herself with a smile. Morgan looked around herself and noted that the room was large and split into two sections by a half wall; there was a group of Sansheren casting stones in the far corner. The dim light prevented her from seeing either their House or order, but most of the other assorted patrons of the establishment wore the uniforms of spacers, and she dismissed their group from her mind. Serving the room were females of several different species, although she did not see any patrons of similar species. Morgan watched as one Dreco server led a laughing human toward a flight of stairs. There were no fewer than thirty people in the bar.

Tansea opened the door next, and then stood holding it as Isaac maneuvered Sam's chair over the threshold. Denise again glanced up, to see who was coming in. It was an almost robotic upward nod of her head, and she was already looking at Greg again when Morgan saw recognition flood her face.

"Sam! Sam, damn you!" Denise said, slamming her hand down on the bar, and Sam grinned as she ran to him and stooped to throw her arms around his neck.

Banessa moved to stand between Morgan and the room, almost blocking her view.

"Move," Morgan hissed, and her bodyguard shifted, if slightly.

"Tim, old boy. Have I got a surprise for you." Greg was standing behind the bar grinning into a communication camera. "No. Just come. Yes, now." Greg disconnected the line even though sound could still be heard from the wall unit. He moved out from behind the counter and walked to Sam.

Morgan saw the smile on Greg's face slacken when he saw the amputations Sam had suffered. Then, without losing his stride, he bent forward and began to cry into Sam's shoulder.

Sam looked over Greg's shoulder and made eye contact with

Morgan. Denise followed his gaze and gasped as she realized who stood before her. Morgan shook her head at Sam and then gave a shy smile to Denise.

The door was thrown open again by an impatient and unwashed looking Tim. His greasy, black hair was pulled tight at his neck and allowed to hang down his back. His brown skin was pale and Morgan stared at his gaunt cheekbones, so prominent in his chiseled face.

"This had better... Be... Good..." Tim didn't move as he stared at Sam.

Greg wiped his eyes and stood up. "Hey man, I always deliver," Greg said in a forced exaggeration of masculine bravado.

"You said you were dying," Tim said as he moved out of the doorway and pulled a chair over to sit beside Sam. He sat with his back to Morgan, who saw Denise smile as the old friends became reacquainted.

"Man, I never should've left you behind. How could you let me leave you, man?" Tim's pain was visible to anyone watching.

"It's okay. Hey, it all worked out fine." Sam was trying to laugh and joke, but he, too, felt Tim's pain and Morgan knew that the only way to abort the pain would be to step forward.

"Okay? Those fucking Sansheren whores blew your legs off, man! How could that be okay? I never should've backed down from that bastard Tadesde. That illegitimate spawn of a dead animal needs to be taught a lesson."

When Banessa laughed, Morgan realized with a start that Tim used a single Sansheren word, most politely defined as retrogressive or unevolved, for his insult.

The Sansheren in the far corner, upon hearing Tadesde's name and the insult from the same direction, stood, and Morgan could see that they wore Tadesde's purple House banner.

"Hey, it's OK. Believe me. It was worth it, you got everyone out, besides I found someone." Sam waved his hand to Morgan just as one of Tadesde's people drew a gun. A very small, very shiny, very lethal gun.

Morgan watched in silence as Tim stood and placed his hand on top of his own side-holstered weapon.

"You will deny this insult to our most lovely and intelligent Lady," the armed Sansheren said in her own language.

Morgan was still and watched as first Tim drew his own pistol and Banessa moved to stand beside Sam.

"I don't know what you said, but those pretty banners give me a good idea," Tim spoke, in English, before he spat on the floor between himself and the five armed Sansheren.

"You are insulting my family," Morgan said in Sansheren. She made eye contact with each of Tadesde's retainers with a deliberate teeth-barring grin for the entire room to see. "You childishly allow yourself to be insulted by someone who has just discovered her lover to be crippled. Do you deny that you would also curse, were it your favorite wife?"

Tim did not turn his head to see who was speaking.

Greg, stared open-mouthed at Morgan from within Tim's line of sight, his own hand under the bar countertop.

"I am most embarrassed at my behavior. Of course, you are correct. The human is insane with grief, and we will forgive the insult." The first Sansheren to draw a weapon was also the first to holster and Morgan relaxed her grin as she watched the first three frightened Sansheren move to the door. The remaining two Sansheren bowed to Morgan before nodding their heads to Sam and Tim as they left.

"What the hell did you say to them?" Tim asked with a feral grin as he turned to Morgan.

She watched him freeze as he assimilated her appearance. And for the first time she wondered what she looked like to other humans. Orange make-up, no shirt, silk pants, sandals, and Sansheren banners crossing her chest.

"Morgan!" it was Greg who first made the leap. He moved to her and engulfed her in a giant hug the likes of which she was certain she had not experienced since Earth.

Denise moved forward and was included in Greg's overflowing joy.

Morgan tried to center herself on the room and made eye contact with Tim.

His expression was unreadable. "Well kid, it looks like you landed on your feet," and he turned and walked away.

Morgan watched him move to the bar as no one said a thing.

"I told them Sam was your family, and you had reason to be bitter toward Tadesde." Morgan walked to the bar and watched Tim in the mirror that faced them both. She tried to stare at Tim as her reflection watched her.

"What do they care what you say?   You go native or something?" Tim met her eyes in the mirror. He made a point of staring at first her banners and then her makeup.

Morgan had worn a pale orange blush the entire time she lived with Neadesto; she had almost forgotten this was not her normal skin color.

"I apprenticed in the House of Neadesto. She saved my life." Morgan refused to look away from Tim's hard gaze.

"You went native." Tim dropped his eyes and reached for a bottle that sat on the counter a few feet to his left, away from Morgan, and poured himself a drink.

"Chill, man. Morgan saved my life, and freed Bystocc," Sam said as Denise wheeled his chair to the counter.

Tim looked up from his drink and turned to make eye contact with Morgan. "Glad to hear it," he said as he reached out and took her hand. "Let's do lunch," he said with a brief handshake.

The room was silent as Tim stood and walked from the bar to the stairway. He paused long enough to nod his head to one of the alien servers before starting up the stairs. His steps were heavy, and the silence lingered until both he and the alien were out of sight.

Morgan felt numb as she picked up Tim's drink and downed it in one gulp before walking over to a table with the bottle. Sam and Greg moved to join her, but nothing was said between them as they each got drunk for different reasons.

Chapter Sixteen - Earth: Taiwan - 1995

Lui Moih-Gan sat on her mother's knee, and felt her unborn brother kick her from behind. She could hear her grandmother in the kitchen cooking, and her grandfather humming on the balcony as he painted. She watched her father come in the room from the kitchen, a steamed dumpling in his hand. He handed her half of it as he sat on the chair opposite of her and her mother. She knew something was going to happen, she felt it during breakfast, and again throughout the day as her normally happy grandmother cried. Even her grandfather called her out to his balcony: to show her how to paint, he said. But Lui Moih-Gan felt the tension in his hands as he showed her how to hold the brush.

She twisted her body around to see her mother, only to have her mother turn her to face her father. Lui Moih-Gan watched her father's solemn face as she picked at the sweetmeats within her half of the dumpling.

"My son lives in America. Your teachers tell me you have learned English well, my daughter. It is time for you to join my son." Her father took a bite of his dumpling.

"I am happy we're going," Lui Moih-Gan said with a smile.

"There will be a new baby soon; it is time for you to grow up, dear. We're not going. You leave tomorrow. The schools in America are easier and you can go to college there," her mother said gently into her ear, and Lui Moih-Gan was puzzled at the tears she could hear.

"But I'm not ready for college yet. My tenth birthday is months away, and grandfather promised to teach me how to paint. Must I go now?"

Her father set his unfinished dumpling on the table in front of them and frowned at her.

She was afraid; she had never questioned him before.

"You leave tomorrow. It is best for your future to go to school in America." Her father stood and left the room and then the apartment.

Lui Moih-Gan did not move from her mother's lap, and her mother continued crying long into the night.

#

"Isn't she just a little doll baby?" the old woman asked in English in a loud whisper and Lui Moih-Gan refuse to look at her.

"She's much too young to be traveling by herself. What kind of mother would leave her child alone on an international flight? Why, what if there were hijackers?" the old woman continued to whisper in a loud hiss as she stared around the first class cabin trying to decide who to suspect.

"You don't have to whisper, Ethel. These people can't speak English." The husband of the woman was large enough that they had been forced to purchase first class tickets.

They were the only Americans on the Taiwan to Tokyo leg of the Asiana Airways flight to Los Angeles, and Lui Moih-Gan watched them curiously in the embarking lounge before boarding. Their appeal to her had worn off quickly, and Lui Moih-Gan remembered her fear and unease.

"I'll bet she's one of them parachute kids, you know, like the ones we saw in that special report last year." The woman was still leaning forward in her seat so she could watch Lui Moih-Gan.

"The special about Asian street kids. I don't see as she can afford a first class ticket, then. The damn things cost a fortune. Just another way to soak a hard-working man, I say." The husband glanced at Lui Moih-Gan one time before returning his to attention to his in-flight magazine.

"No, of course not. The one about Taiwanese children being sent to live in America alone. You remember. They said that because the schools in Taiwan are so hard, less than half of the students finish high school and only five percent go on to college. We watched it last February, remember? It had all the kids with blacked out faces." The wife turned her attention from Lui Moih-Gan to glare at her husband.

He didn't notice.

"The only thing I remember from February were the college playoffs. Who would have thought the Cats could drop it after being ahead by three. I had fifty bucks riding on them. I tell you, it's just another way to soak the hard-working man." He never looked up from his magazine.

"It was Monday night, before Rush, you remember." The wife was insistent.

"Now Rush, he understands the hard-working man. No twinkies or slants for him, just a hard-working American man." The page of the magazine turned slowly.

"They spent the entire half hour on it. They send the kids here to America to live, alone. It's a shame. There should be a law against doing that to such a pretty little girl." The old woman threw herself back in her seat as the seat belt sign winked out and the captain started speaking.

"Well, at least they have a real American flying this death trap," the husband said as the pilot worked through the flight explanation in both Chinese and then English with a drawling West Virginia accent.

Three hours later, Lui Moih-Gan listened as the pilot announced their landing at Narida International in Tokyo. When the other passengers stood and moved around, she sat still in her seat, long after landing.

Her bladder was full, but her father's harsh admonition not to bother the attendants kept coming into her mind. She resisted the urge to squirm around for a more comfortable position. The layover was over two hours long with the disembarkation of most of the Asian passengers and the boarding of the mostly white, American tourists and business travelers.

The woman who took the center seat beside Lui Moih-Gan did not look happy at sitting next to a child, even when Lui Moih-Gan smiled shyly at her. The woman was middle-aged and very thin, wearing a severely cut suit dress; she made a point of pulling all available material away from Lui Moih-Gan.

The man who sat in the aisle seat was old, with white hair cut short and wrinkles on his hands. Lui Moih-Gan watched him from the corner of her eye as she pretended to stare out the window. He opened his briefcase on his knees and began reading.

Nothing was said between the three as the seat belt sign

136

flashed back on and the attendant began speaking at the front of the plane.

When she woke up it was to bright sunlight streaming through her window as the plane banked into its approach pattern. The Captain was apologizing for the delay and said it was three o'clock local time. "Thank you for flying Asiana Airways flight three five four originating in Taipei and terminating in Los Angeles."

Lui Moih-Gan sat very still as the other passenger's stood and tried to shove their way into the aisle politely. The husband of the old woman stood and pushed the business man into the sharply dressed woman standing beside Lui Moih-Gan. The American made his way down the aisle sideways with no regard for anyone else. The other passengers mumbled their apologies and bowed, but she could see their disgust and loathing for the fat man.

Lui Moih-Gan stood as the last passenger was bowed out the door by the lead flight attendant. She began to climb on the chair arm to reach her bag over her head, but one of the other attendants chastised her in her own language. Lui Moih-Gan stood still in the aisle as the woman reached for her bag. Her bladder had begun to ache, but she followed the woman out of the plane and to the ticket counter. The attendant dropped her bag at her feet and then flagged a skycap.

"Give him your baggage ticket," the attendant said in an urban Taiwanese dialect.

Lui Moih-Gan handed her ticket envelope and passport to the attendant who ripped out the stubs.

"When he comes back, give him five dollars. You do have American dollars, don't you?"

Lui Moih-Gan reached into her little purse and pulled out several hundred dollars in U.S. currency.

"Don't wave that around! America is full of thieves." The attendant shoved Moih-Gan's hand back into her purse, before separating out a five dollar bill and placing it in Lui Moih-Gan's other hand.

"Are you expecting someone, or do you need a car?" the attendant asked with an impatient glance at her watch.

"I don't know," she whispered, looking around for the brother she had never met.

"Well, I have to go now. I'll ask the counter man to keep an eye out for you. Listen to me; do not leave this area alone. It's dangerous for little girls in this country. Do not accept any offers for a ride, and if you take a cab, make sure it's an expensive one. Do you understand me?"

The attendant was leaning over Lui Moih-Gan, and her fierce expression was far more frightening to the girl than the surrounding chaos that was the visible portion of the airport.

"Yes." She did not think she spoke loud enough to be heard and was preparing to speak again when the attendant straightened her shoulders and moved to speak with the man behind the information counter.

"She's a dump, make certain no pervert picks her up before she gets tired and then get her a cab. Okay?" the attendant prompted in accented English.

Lui Moih-Gan followed the conversation above her without looking away from the sprawling mass of humanity that surged past on the concourse.

"How do I guarantee that the cabbie isn't the pervert you're worried about?" the young man asked with a smile.

Lui Moih-Gan stared up at him as he spoke. His voice was deep, and his tanned face was accented by his bleached hair. She decided he had not been an adult for very long and returned to staring at the people around her.

"I wish I knew. Look, I have to run for my login. Just try and take care of her, okay?" the attendant flipped her wrist up and looked at her watch again as she finished speaking.

"If no one shows in an hour, I'll call the cops. They can sort it out. Deal?"

The attended nodded her head impatiently before turning and speaking in the same Taiwanese dialect.

"If no one comes for you, the police will take you to your home. Do you understand?"

This time Lui Moih-Gan was certain she did not wait for a response.

"Make certain they sent a female cop, you never know." The attendant left the counter area with that comment in English and walked into the crowd.

Lui Moih-Gan followed her with her eyes until the throng of people obliterated her. Looking back to make eye contact with the counterman she remembered she needed the use the restroom. She turned back to watch humanity flow past without saying a word to the already busy man.

#

Lui Moih-Gan was sitting on her luggage, leaning against the side of the counter, and watching the man across the way take something out of the pocket of an unsuspecting woman when a man in uniform spoke.

"This the kid?" he was tall, and she had to tip her head back to see his round, black face and his white teeth as he grinned down to her. The other officer was waiting for the counter man's answer; she was almost as tall but much thinner. Her black hair was pulled back in a severe bun, and Lui Moih-Gan decided she might be North American Spanish.

"Yeah, the flight came in over two hours ago, no one's showed up. Looks like she got dumped. We get them every now and then, you know."

Lui Moih-Gan was still watching the female officer as the woman wrote something in a small notebook she then placed into a pocket.

"She speak English?" the large black cop turned to the counter without looking at Lui Moih-Gan again.

"I don't think so. Here are her flight papers and passport; she gave them to a stew earlier." The man reached under the counter and handed the male officer the papers before turning to help another flyer.

"Student visa, it figures. Here's an address, grab some bags and let's go." The woman was reading the papers upside down. They stooped and picked up Lui Moih-Gan's stuff without saying anything to her. She was forced to walk very fast to keep up, and the whole time her abdomen was burning.

#

"You ever been in one of these houses?"

Lui Moih-Gan was not the only one in the car who stared at the widely spaced two and three story houses that sat like fortresses upon small hills on either side of the street.

"I responded to a homicide in this neighborhood once, a domestic mess that never made the papers," the female officer said without looking away from her driving.

"Yeah, I know what you mean. Turn left here. Man, this must be Gook Street." The black officer nodded his head as they drove past a small Asian woman pushing a stroller and trailed by three even smaller children.

"Hey!" the female nodded her head back to indicate Lui Moih-Gan as they pulled into the long driveway of a large formal looking house.

"Yeah, sure. If they're this rich, why didn't they send a car, shit," the male officer said but did not turn to look at her.

The car came to a stop under an overhanging that protected the front doorway. Before they could get all of the baggage out of the trunk, an elderly woman opened the front door.

"What is the problem officers?" the old woman wore a white starched dress.

"She's been sitting down at LAX for hours, thought we'd give her a lift, is all. Any family members home?" the female officer stepped forward and began speaking to the maid.

"Her worthless brother is out drinking. He told me she was to come this week but he did not say today. He is a member of a gang, a tong they are called." The maid crossed herself.

Lui Moih-Gan bit her lip to keep from crying or peeing her pants. Already she felt a dampness seeping through her underwear.

"Yeah well, give us a call if there's any problem. We have to run now. She's all yours," the female officer finished speaking and turned to the car.

The male officer smiled down to Lui Moih-Gan and then went to the trunk of the car. He came back from the car and handed her a small stuffed bear wearing a police uniform.

"Why'd you do that?" His partner asked, standing half in the passenger door.

"The poor kid looks like she's about to cry. Remind me to look up her brother and introduce myself sometime," the black cop said with a parting smile in Lui Moih-Gan's direction as he got into the car.

"Step in line," was the last Lui Moih-Gan heard as the cop

rolled up the window and drove down the driveway.

"Moegan? Follow, please." The old woman's English was strongly accented, and Lui Moih-Gan turned toward the door of the house.

When she reached for her smallest bag, the old woman gave an inpatient sigh and said "no" before walking away.

The entryway was all wood, and she ran her hand along the banister as they climbed the stairs that were the centerpiece of the large room. Each step dampened her panties a little more, and she felt a single tear begin to trace its way down her cheek as she entered the room the maid indicated. The large bed with white pillows and blanket dominated the room. There was an adult sized computer desk complete with printer and fax in one corner, and a matching black dresser in the other corner. Under the window was a bookcase full of reading material appropriate for someone much older than her nine years.

"Moegan," the maid said, bringing her attention to the bed and an envelope that was lost in the sea of white.

When Lui Moih-Gan walked to the bed, her abdomen burning, and her panties damp, the maid turned and closed the door behind her.

Dear sister,

Sink or swim. That's what this country is all about. You seem to be swimming fine, little girl. This is your ATM card, the code number is 7746. I told our dearest father to set you up with a separate account so you could learn to handle your own money, and so I wouldn't have to deal with your every need. $1000 a month, mail them your report card. Your grades go down, he sends less money. He sends a bonus for straight A's. I'll meet you after school Monday; enjoy your first weekend in the land of opportunity, little sister.

The letter was unsigned and written in very sloppy English. As Lui Moih-Gan finished reading it, she felt her bladder give way and the stinging hot fluid course down her leg. She stood holding the letter in her hand without crying, until hours later she noticed the room was dark.

She climbed up into the bed without undressing and stared at the ceiling.

Renewed pressure on her bladder roused her from the almost sleep. And Morgan became dizzy as she realized that she inhabited an adult body. Sitting back down on the dirty white sheets, she put her face into her hands and whispered to herself, "It's only a dream." She said this three times before the tears began.

Chapter Seventeen - Bystocc – 2012

"Come on, Amigo. It's right there." Enrico sat alone in the dark of a nursery viewing room.

The Sansheren child sat near the glass and stared back at him.

"It's right there, just get up and get it." Enrico pointed at the small food animal that cowered in the far corner of the nursery.

The child shifted its gaze to his fingertip.

"If you don't eat, they will kill you," his comments were interrupted by the opening of the viewing room door behind him.

The Sansheren child responded to the sudden light by darting into the already occupied corner, and the food animal fled with a loud squeal into the center of the room.

"Does she hunt?" Aldera asked, but Enrico could hear no hope in her voice as she closed the door behind her.

"No. Why can't you put dead food in the room? You did for Mistrata yesterday." He did not shift his gaze from the child who was moving back toward the glass.

"Mistrata is nearly five years since her first parent's travail, it was her time. This child is too young to be approaching the change. Soon its hunger will drive it to hunt." Aldera ended the sentence with a sigh.

"But then it will be too late. You've already decided, haven't you?" his accusation was greeted by a slow nod of acknowledgment. "Then what would it hurt to feed it?"

The child was back at the glass, looking from one to the other.

"What would it hurt? You ask me to defy common sense, to risk creating another Tadesde. If the child is not advanced enough it is best that–"

"Wait! If it is medically possible for your species to regress genetically, then what are the chances of a child being more advanced?" Enrico moved from his seat to kneel in front of Aldera.

"There have been a few, whose brilliance could not be denied. I will not bore you with history. But even those few did not leave the hunt behind until well within their fourth year. This child cannot be even three." Aldera turned her eyes away from Enrico's pained gaze and shot a questioning look at the child.

"How do you know?" he asked as he moved to regain his seat.

"Know?" Aldera asked as she stood and moved to the glass wall.

The child scooted back.

"Know how old it is? Why can it not be real small, like the old patron who works in the kitchen upstairs?" Enrico watched as Aldera held up a hand against the glass and the child responded in kind.

"It is possible. Still, the child is an orphan. What kind of life will she enjoy living on the charity of the House?" Aldera stifled a smile as the child bumped its head on the glass it could not quite focus on.

"By custom, anyone can adopt an orphan, true?" Enrico moved to the glass.

Staring at the child, he missed Aldera's frown.

"True, although it is generally accepted that an apprentice will not acquire any new responsibilities before being freed from her master." Aldera took her hand from the glass and placed it on Enrico shoulder.

"But it is a custom that can be ignored. Right? A child in need takes priority. That's how the custom is enforced, correct?" Enrico looked from the child to Aldera, and back.

"You are within the law if you choose this path," Aldera's voice dropped as she spoke. "My friend, please, do not do this."

In the end, she left Enrico standing at the glass.

His vigil ended an hour later when a small slot opened on the far wall of the room, and a dart struck the child from behind.

\#

"I would ask as to the health of your newly adopted child," Neavillii spoke from the doorway, and he heard her anger.

"She ate, and played with some toys, then fell asleep. Aldera said he thought it was a promising first day." Enrico refused to

144

turn from the computer screen he was studying.

"Indeed. It is customary that an apprentice not accept new responsibilities without the knowledge and consent of her master." Neavillii moved across the room and turned the computer off.

"So I was informed, my most generous and understanding of patrons." Enrico bowed his head and moved to kneel, only to be halted by Neavillii's quick grasp upon his arm.

"Then why did you not discuss this with me?" Neavillii sat beside him.

"I did, last night. And the night before. You did not show an interest in the subject, my patron." Still, he kept his head bowed.

"You spoke of a regressive during the dinner hour, and I told you the subject was distasteful. You never said anything about adopting this child." Neavillii tilted her head to the side in an attempt to see his face.

"I spoke of a child who needed help. You did not offer," and he looked up quickly, startling them both.

"Then I am to fault. You have my apology. What is to happen now?" she reached her hand forward to stroke his cheek, and he knew he flinched, if only slightly, when she pulled away.

"Aldera said that he would give me a week, no more. I would ask permission to spend my time at the nursery." He placed his hand on hers, as an apology for the flinch.

"Custom requires it. You are released from your studies for the week; do not expect more." She smiled before standing and offering her hand.

"Thanera asks that you join her for dinner. I have already eaten." He ignored her hand and turned on the computer.

"Indeed."

He stared unseeing at the computer as she walked from the room. It was several minutes before he could focus on the screen enough to read the study of Sansheren childhood he had called up. And several more minutes before he realized he would need to reread the page.

#

"Captura, captura." Enrico sat on the floor of the nursery and rolled the ball to his adopted child.

The child watched it roll by. Five days had passed, and the child's progress astounded him.

"Capt, capt," the child whispered and rolled the ball back to Enrico.

"You might want to focus on teaching her Sansheren words before your own." Aldera's voice echoed through the intercom.

"I concede the wisdom of your advice. Have you come to pass judgment?" Enrico asked without turning his gaze to Aldera, who was standing on the other side of the glass.

"I came to watch, that is all." Aldera sat down on a lounge.

"Oh. Here, say it this way Amigo: catch.., Catch," and this time he spoke to the child in Sansheren as he rolled the ball.

The child ignored him and moved to stare out the glass at Aldera.

Aldera smiled and waved.

The child raised its hand as if to wave, and then sat with a thud as it stared at its own hand.

"That is your hand. Hand." Enrico crawled over to where the child sat and held up his own hand.

The child touched his thumb before turning its gaze back to Aldera.

"Hand." It said in an exaggerated mimic of the Sansheren word, its hand held up and still for Aldera to see.

"Yes, that is your hand." Aldera moved to stand beside the glass once more.

"Hand," Enrico said holding his own hand back up with a tight smile.

The smile faded when the child hit Enrico's hand out of its way with a casual violence, then smiled shyly to Aldera, and held its hand out again.

"Hand," it said to Aldera.

"You should come out, it's not safe," Aldera said, her eyes focused on the child, but seeing the blood that dripped from between Enrico's fingers.

"No. She didn't realize she hurt me. Besides she just doesn't understand the differences between our species." Enrico took a cloth out of his pocket and began wrapping up the small cuts.

"! Ay!" the child said in Spanish.

"Yes, ouch. Amigo's hand ouched Enrico's hand," Enrico said in

Sansheren and reached out to use the child's hand to pantomime the swipe that drew blood.

"Ouch. Enrico," the child said in Sansheren and moved closer to him.

Enrico could see Aldera tense out of the corner of his eye.

"Yes, ouch. Enrico's hand hurts."

"Enrico hand ouch. Amigo hand ouch," the child said, and Enrico saw Aldera relax, a little, when the child cradled its own hand as if injured.

"Amigo's hand not hurt. No ouch. Enrico's hand hurts," Enrico said with a laugh at the serious expression on the child's face.

"Amigo hurt Enrico?" the child asked, and Aldera moved back to sit on the lounge once more.

"Yes, Amigo hurt Enrico." He relaxed as Aldera moved away. Relaxed, but he kept his finger on the trigger of the dart gun he wrapped into the palm of his injured hand with the cloth.

"Enrico hurt. Enrico blood. Taste? Taste?" the child begged and Enrico moved his hand out of reach with a frown directed at the child.

"No. No taste. You do not taste anyone you're not going to eat." He saw Aldera move forward in her chair. The child gave up its attempts to reach his hand after putting several new pinpricks into his arm.

"Pull your claws, Amigo. No taste Enrico. No taste Amigo. No taste Aldera. No taste people." Enrico worked hard to keep his voice calm.

"No taste. Aldera?" the child turned and stared out of the glass at her.

"Aldera," she echoed in agreement.

"Aldera hand. Aldera claws. Amigo hand claws. Enrico hand no claws." Amigo offered her hand to Aldera again.

"That is right. Aldera and Amigo have claws on their hands. Enrico does not have claws. Aldera and Amigo are Sansheren. Enrico is human," Aldera said and enunciated as she placed her hand against the glass.

"Hands," and with that Amigo moved across the room and curled up into a ball in the corner.

Enrico shrugged to Aldera before he turned to leave the room.

"I would speak with you, tonight."

Aldera's voice held him for a moment, and Enrico opened the

door and left.

#

"The risk was not necessary," Aldera said from where she sat on the floor of Neavillii's apartment.

"I had the gun ready; did you want me waving it in her face?" Enrico demanded from the kitchen as he finished piling one plate full of meats.

"It is customary that children be taught in a firm manner of the danger their reflexes pose to others. Yes, I would have you openly handle the dart gun." Aldera met Enrico's frown with an equally formidable expression.

"It does not offend the child if she does not know what it is for," Yolunu offered as an interruption.

"I will not lie and I will not shoot if my life is not clearly in danger." Enrico sat and placed his plate among the others on the floor.

"If your life is not clearly in danger? Do you think you would see the attack in time to respond? Your confidence is commendable, but foolhardy, my apprentice." Neavillii followed him into the room and added a plate of dry fruit to the spread.

"I have told him it is much too soon to go into the nursery," Aldera said as she passed a plate to the silent Thanera.

"And if I had not sped up the customary process of getting a child used to others? Would she still be alive?" Enrico challenged first Aldera and then the others present.

"I think not," was Aldera's reply.

"I would hope not," Neavillii vehemently added.

"I have not met the child and so my opinion is not worth expressing," Yolunu said while handing Neavillii a cup of wine.

"I have not met the child either, only… I myself left the nursery at just barely four years. I feel for this child. Enrico, my friend, I would be honored to be introduced to your child tomorrow during the lunch hour." Thanera's comments startled the room.

"My apprentice has piloting lessons scheduled for the entire day," Neavillii said firmly.

"We could plan for two runs, and be back for the lunch hour."

Yolunu offered through a bite of food.

"That is not necessary. I am certain that the talented nursery staff can handle one small child tomorrow," Neavillii said, and Enrico bristled at the warning look she gave Yolunu.

"As you wish, my patron," Enrico said through clenched teeth after the silent exchange passed.

"Amigo will be introduced to a crèche of other children tomorrow. It is best that she not be disturbed," Aldera offered.

#

"What happened?" Neavillii kept tight control of her voice as she stormed into the infirmary.

"The children refused to accept the child Amigo. Only the bravery and reflexes of the most beautiful Aldera saved its life." The nursery medic bowed to first Neavillii and then Thanera.

"Is she okay?" Neavillii asked as she moved further into the room in search of the correct bed.

"The brave child Amigo refused to defend herself and thus suffered severe injuries. But they are no longer life threatening." The nursery medic pointed at a bed on the far side of the room. A small, unidentified lump could be seen amid the tangle of tubes and wires.

"The child Amigo has been adopted by my apprentice and so I am honor bound to care for it. I am under no obligation to care about it. I was asking for the health of the valiant Aldera." Neavillii spotted her target and left the confused medic standing with Thanera.

"I will visit the child," Thanera said into the awkward silence before she moved away.

The medic paused in the doorway and then crossed to stand beside Aldera's bed. "She is sleeping now; she suffered only a few injuries. The most notable was here," she pointed out a long but shallow gash on the sleeping Aldera's arm. "She should be on her feet tomorrow," the medic finished.

"And the other children, how has this incident affected them?" Neavillii did not raise her eyes from Aldera's face.

"They show no signs of distress. I think we were lucky, although I will not allow Amigo back into any crèche. The others agree with my decision." The medic's voice did not sound as confident as her words.

"That is understandable. Your performance has been exemplary; no one will question your decision." Neavillii looked up and held the eye of the other.

"What of your apprentice? It is known that she has strong feelings of attachment to the child. Should we take care of the matter while she is not present?"

Neavillii glanced to the corner where Thanera was sitting.

"No. He has been hurt too much. I will tell you when, not before." She punctuated her sentence by holding the medics gaze once more before moving to stand beside Thanera.

"What does she say?" Neavillii felt her hostility toward the child soften as she stared down at the small face.

So obviously in pain, the child kept whispering words.

"A human word, I don't know it. She also asks for Aldera by name, and Enrico. When will he be here?" Thanera heard the faint accusation in her voice but could not call back her words.

"They landed even as I called you, he should be here soon. The word is for pain. Curious, she keeps saying it for Aldera, not herself." Neavillii brought her finger to the child's face and stroked a small bare spot.

"Her concern for Aldera was noted when we cleared the room. Though she would not defend herself, Nogina has stated that the child bared her teeth and used a fallen dart gun in defense of the beautiful Aldera." The medic shrugged, devaluing her own words.

"Indeed." Neavillii looked from the child to the doorway of the infirmary. Running feet accented by the occasional clash of Enrico's metal cane could be heard approaching.

"Where is he?" Enrico shoved the doors open.

"Your brave child is here, my friend." Neavillii moved to give him room.

"You said Aldera was hurt, where is he?" he glanced at the bed before walking down the aisle toward the one bed that held an adult form.

"The lovely Aldera is sleeping off the effect of her injuries. She will be fine." Neavillii walked in his direction, a frown growing on her face.

"It is my fault. I should've listened to him. I should've listened to you." Enrico sat on the edge of Aldera's bed and fought the tears that pressed against his eyelids. One tear escaped and trickled down his face.

"While it is always nice to hear an apprentice say such things, I would rather you believed to begin with. In this instance, it is I who should have listened." Neavillii placed her hand on his shoulder.

"He could have died," another tear escape when he turned to stare at Neavillii.

"She would have died were it not for your brave Amigo. The child would not defend herself but did defend Aldera." Neavillii reached her free hand to his face and caught the third tear in the recess of a claw.

"He would not have been in danger if I had listened-" his words were cut off by Neavillii's claws pressed against his mouth.

"Do not say in despair what you'll regret later. Aldera is fine. Your child needs you now. She worries after Aldera and needs to see your love." Neavillii held her fingers close for a moment longer and then stood and held her hand to him. Enrico moved slowly as he accepted it, not bothering to wipe clear the blood that dripped from his cut lip.

"Maybe later, I do not think I can right now." And he reached for his cane.

"Would you shame me so? Your child is injured, comfort it," and she walked away.

#

"I told you to comfort it, not bring it home," Neavillii said from the apartment doorway, and Enrico turned to see her staring warily at the small child that sat on the floor rolling the ball against a wall.

"I had no choice." Enrico sat on the couch. He was unwashed, and the faintest hint of black chin hairs could be seen on his face.

Three days had passed since the nursery incident and he had spent his entire time floating from Aldera's bed to Amigo's. Aldera was up and around the next day as predicted, and Amigo healed far more rapidly than Enrico ever believed possible, short of a miracle. The medic's lecture about clot factors and tissue death did nothing to dissuade him from what he knew was superstition.

"Indeed. I suppose the nursery would've been rather adamant about her removal. The empty room will serve. Place her within and go wash yourself, you stink." Neavillii wrinkled her entire face in objection to the body odor that permeated the room.

"Stink," Amigo added with an attempt to imitate Neavillii's expression.

"Thanks for the vote of confidence, Amigo." Enrico laughed as he pushed through his exhaustion to stand.

"Apestan," the child repeated in Spanish before sneezing violently and then shaking its head.

"C'mon kid," he said with a smile.

"No. Enrico stink." The child scooted across the floor without standing until it was sitting at a wary Neavillii's feet.

"You need to go into your room now." Enrico did not move toward the two as he spoke.

"No sleep. Catch." Amigo picked up her ball and gently threw it upwards so that it crested just above Neavillii's head.

"Catch, huh? Go ahead, we will be fine." Neavillii caught the ball as it started its descent and threw it across the room. Amigo moved in a blur that Enrico couldn't follow, and caught the ball before it hit the floor.

#

"I have found some sobering news; I would ask your opinion as to whether I should lose it again?" Thanera asked by way of opening as she walked into Neavillii's office.

"Indeed," Neavillii said as an encouragement.

"Perhaps I should take my question to another," Thanera reconsidered.   "I'm sorry to have bothered you, my Lady." Thanera turned and walked to the door.

"Hold. Come back and sit," Neavillii said loud enough to stop her.

"I should not have brought this to your attention, my Lady. He is your apprentice, you would be honor bound to include his feelings in your opinion." Thanera sat in the offered chair.

"If you will tell me the information, I promise to answer you first without considering my apprentice and second with emotion. You may choose which to accept." Neavillii smiled as she leaned forward to offer Thanera a small candy from her desk.

"It is Amigo; in attempting to determine her age, I have found evidence of her birth line. Her mother is still alive," Thanera said, and Neavillii frowned at the bad news.

"Indeed. And who is this parent that would leave her child behind during an evacuation? Was she so badly injured?" Neavillii took a piece of candy and collected her thoughts.

"No, she was not injured. It was Tadesde. Amigo is of Tadesde's blood. Do we have to notify her?" Thanera gave Neavillii a desperate look.

"So it would seem. Tell me, who is responsible for the child's creation?" Neavillii tried to find a solution to the dilemma she felt herself sliding into.

"The records show that Tadesde was hospitalized after she betrayed the peace talks with the mercenary Timone three years ago." Thanera kept glancing up from the printouts she held to Neavillii.

"Indeed. Immediately after?" Neavillii allowed a slight smile to escape.

"Yes, the resuscitation team filed a paternity complaint against the mercenary Timone, only to have it rescinded by Tadesde," Thanera said, and gave Neavillii a confused look with the hardcopy.

"Then, House politics aside, Timone could be considered the child's father, would you not agree?" Neavillii's smile grew at Thanera's confusion.

"I... Yes, it could be said." And she waited for Neavillii to reveal her thinking.

"Timone is the human Tim. Family to my most loved wife Morgan. Is it not totally unheard of for an apprentice to foster the child of a master's beloved's other wife?" Neavillii nodded her head to herself as she concluded her logic.

"Morganea is your wife and Timone is Morganea's wife? And Enrico is your apprentice so he is only fostering Amigo? It is just politics," Thanera stated with a frown.

"Was the child named?" Neavillii asked.

"Politics," Thanera repeated. "But it is preferable to contacting a mother who did not care enough to evacuate her own unnamed child. Especially if that mother is Tadesde." Thanera smiled sadly with a shrug as she finished piecing the entire idea together.

"I will correct the records. What will you tell Enrico?" Thanera asked.

"The truth." Neavillii sat back in her chair with a new frown.

Chapter Eighteen - Wergol - 2012

"I'll have whatever I had last night." Morgan was the only customer at the bar, and only a few patrons occupied the tables throughout the tavern.

"Hair o' the dog, coming right up." Denise moved from the center of the counter where she was drying glasses and poured Morgan a half shot of whiskey.

Morgan downed the liquor without thought and then spent several seconds coughing. "It didn't hurt last night. What do you have that's a bit friendlier?" Morgan wiped moisture from her eyes as she spoke.

Denise was laughing bitterly. "You hurt last night, the whisky just made it bearable. Here, this is Demmesole. It's made from flowers and is the choice of most of my Sansheren patrons." Denise poured a delicate, stemmed glass full of a lavender colored wine.

"It smells wonderful," Morgan sipped from the glass cautiously. "Lilacs!" Morgan made eye contact with Denise as the memories flooded back.

"I forgot," Denise said, and Morgan thought it was an apology.

"There's no reason for you to remember me." Morgan stared at the wine as she twirled the glass between her fingers.

"You might have remembered if you hadn't been in the sack with Timmy boy every time you came over," Greg said from behind Morgan.

She didn't look up as he sat beside her.

"The lilacs were in bloom, remember?" Morgan turned and held the wine glass to Greg.

"I would have been doing schoolwork if Tim hadn't swept me off my feet." Denise smiled, but they could see the edge of her self-control.

"I remember you looked beautiful with the lilacs in your hair," Greg said to Morgan after smiling sadly in agreement to Denise.

"She's beautiful now," Denise said in a wistful voice.

"Tim once said you would be the kind of woman wars are fought over: god, he was right." Greg reached out and ran a fingertip through an escaped strand of hair on the side of Morgan's neck.

Morgan continued to look down at a glass of wine without moving.

"You had a crush on Tim, didn't you?" Denise asked. She was pouring Greg a glass of beer and did not notice the blush that darkened Morgan's face.

"Yes," Morgan blurted out before gulping at the last of her wine.

"Shit. I'm sorry," Denise said as she and Greg realized the state of Morgan's current emotions.

"He got married. She worked here with Denise. Before we bought out Denise's contract," Greg said and took a long swallow from his own glass before continuing.

"That was ten years ago. Some Sansheren bought her for a party, to entertain Tadesde we heard." Denise poured Morgan a second glass of wine and then slammed the bottle down in awkward anger before walking away, to serve another client.

"The bastard raped her! He raped her and cut her up for sport. His whole court watched and laughed. Damn! That's why Tim took the Bystocc contract. We didn't think we had a chance. Tim just wanted a shot at that murdering bastard," Greg said passionately, and Morgan stared at his reflection in the mirror and remembered her fear of his anger.

"Sansheren can't physically rape anyone. They don't have the equipment. They're all female. As for killing for sport, I've heard other rumors no less vicious," Morgan said with a shrug that she hoped would show how little she valued her own statement.

"Why doesn't the Sansheren government stop him, her then?" Denise asked with a frown as she joined them once more.

"Sansheren government? There is no Sansheren government. Sansheren means 'children of the Shere', the home planet. Tadesde is her own government; she rules her own planet. She holds the Twelfth and highest rank of Sansadee, she's autonomous. There are no laws to bind her, only a council that discusses customs and traditions and issues declarations of disappointments to chastise and she's been held to task a dozen times. She doesn't care." Morgan looked from Denise to Greg, surprised at the puzzled looks on their faces.

"So who can stop her?" Greg asked, and Morgan frowned at his disbelief.

"One of her peers. It would take a declaration of war. There hasn't been an inter-House war in two centuries, I'm told. It would be simpler if someone assassinated her, or one of her own people staged a defection. That's possible; she lost a lot of stature when she abandoned Bystocc." Morgan did not explain that she was the one to gain the most from Tadesde's loss.

"Why doesn't another House call her to task then?" Greg asked, and Morgan knew he was still trying to understand.

"Before Bystocc, Tadesde was the second most powerful Sansadee. Now, no one knows her true strength or weakness. It will take a few years for things to even out and the House intelligence units to decide her standing," Morgan said as Denise poured Greg a second glass.

"If the bitch is number two, why doesn't the number one knock her down a notch are two?" Denise asked as she handed Greg his drink.

"The most loved Sansadee is my adoptive father, Neadesto. Her House has honored a pledge of neutrality for over eight hundred years. She will not fight Tadesde openly. And without her support, no other House will dare. The best you could expect from the various Sansheren Houses is clandestine support to any planet opposing Tadesde." Morgan set her glass down without drinking.

"Yeah, we got help from several different Houses during the war. Tim always hated them for using us to fight their battles." Greg sat his glass down.

"He hates the Sansheren, now," Denise said.

"Hey, kid. You have a good life, why don't you just forget us old losers." Greg moved to put his arm around Morgan's stooped shoulders.

"Go home," Denise said.

"I thought I did," she answered as she shrugged free of him and sat up straighter.

The door of the tavern burst open with a bright flash of light. Denise continued to watch after the door closed and Morgan turned when she heard Banessa challenge the newcomer.

"I must speak with the most lovely Morganea, I must," insisted a young Sansheren who wore the banner of Tadesde. She was out of breath and close to tears as she came to stand beside Banessa.

Morgan noted she was a crew member of a merchant class starship.

"Well," Morgan said from where she still sat as she waited for the young spacer to collect herself.

"Oh most lovely and kind father. Please forgive my worthless self the sins of my family, I beg you," the spacer shouted past Banessa, and then grasped the multi-colored purple banner that crossed her chest - ripping it free from her body. She bared her teeth and spat in the general direction it fell.

"It depends upon the sins your family has committed against mine," Morgan said with a serious expression.

"Please understand that my wife and I had nothing to do with the dishonorable plotting of my shipmates. My wife even now runs to the one you defended yesterday to warn her of her danger. But I am sorry to admit, neither of us speaks the language of your most wonderful family." The spacer was close to tears and kept shifting toward the door even as she spoke.

Greg shook his head in answer to Denise's questioning look as the flow of the alien language surpassed his ability to follow.

"What danger?" Morgan asked as she made eye contact with Banessa, who was already speaking on her radio.

"They planned an ambush of the one I assume is your family. Come, I will take you to the place," the spacer said, and again moved as if to flee.

Banessa held out her hand to prevent the other from leaving.

"It could be a trap, let me handle it," Banessa said to Morgan, and let go of the spacer with a tight nod to the door.

Morgan watched the two Sansheren leave without looking at the curious Greg or Denise as she waited for Banessa to clear the doorway. She was in motion the moment her personal guard was out of sight. "Ambush," was all she said as she ran out the door.

Years of experience had shown Morgan that she could not keep

158

up with an athletic Sansheren; it was her hope to just keep them in sight as they raced down the street. She paid no attention to Greg or Denise as they struggled to keep her in sight.

Morgan stopped just inside the alley entrance; she had been running into the sunlight and her eyes balked, adjusting to the dim lighting.

The Sansheren who warned her was kneeling over an unmoving form that Morgan assumed was her wife. No injuries could be seen. But blood was pooling around the body. The young spacer looked up and met Morgan's eyes with a sad pleading look that forced Morgan to break contact first.

"Just get here!" Banessa's cry for help drew Morgan farther into the alley.

Morgan moved around some refuse boxes to find her guard and friend holding one unarmed ambusher against the wall while clutching her own bleeding side. The Tadesde banner could be seen on the captive's chest. Morgan moved forward to aid Banessa.

"Farther back, go!" Banessa tightened her one hand grip and drew her weapon with the bloody hand. The desperate woman stopped her struggling when she noticed the muzzle of the weapon against her abdomen.

Morgan moved into the darkness of the alley. She paused as she was forced to step over the body of a Sansheren spacer. Bending quietly, she picked up the spacer's discarded weapon, and then continued into the depths of the alley.

"Death!"

A form detached itself from the wall and lunged toward Morgan, who fired her weapon more in reflex than thought. A Sansheren collapsed at her feet, and Morgan could see several wounds even though she only remembered firing once. A loud shot echoed from behind a stack of crates, and she turned to run, without regard for her safety.

Tim crouched in the far corner, his back against a half wall that ended the alleyway, a locked gate beside him.

Morgan could see one body prone at his feet. Another Tadesde retainer leaned against the wall to his left and Morgan could see a pool of blood at her feet. There was a movement to the right, and Morgan shifted in time to see a third attacker finish loading a weapon. Morgan took careful aim this time, and smiled at the other's look of surprise when the impact of the bullet beat the sound of the shot.

"What took you so long?" Tim's voice was as strained as his smile, and Morgan moved toward him without relaxing her defenses. Before she could cross the space between them, Tim closed his eyes and slid down the wall.

Morgan stopped moving and stared at his immobile form for several seconds before screaming to Banessa.

Chapter Nineteen - Bystocc - 2012

"Would you tell him there is no way I'm going to allow that to fly my ship?" the human pilot gestured to Enrico as he finished his impassioned sentence.

"Handsome Jeffrey, be assured that I have voiced my own concerns, but I'm afraid that my apprentice is very determined," Neavillii said to the pilot and exchanged bemused glances with Yolunu.

"Well, he can be very determined in someone else's shuttle. That bird is all I own, and I'm not turning it over to his pet." The pilot finished speaking and stormed over to Enrico, who was walking Amigo through the preflight checklist procedure.

"May I assume that our talented pilot is less thrilled about this than we?" Yolunu asked in Sansheren. She leaned against the small shuttle craft as she spoke.

"One might even assume that the intelligent Jeffrey is less patient with the idea than we," Neavillii agreed with a laugh.

"Then I hope he has more success in his objections." Yolunu added her own nervous sounding laugh.

"It ain't gonna happen, boy," the pilot said, and Enrico glanced up to find the man blocking the hatch.

"That's what you said about teaching me, Jeff. Amigo says she can handle it." Enrico made a move to step forward; the pilot held his ground.

"You still couldn't handle her in bad weather - that takes hundreds of hours of flight time, boy. And your friend has only been on board a few times. I ain't letting it near my controls," Jeff said.

The pilot failed to notice Amigo sneaking on board, and Enrico hoped he would not realize the cause of Neavillii and Yolunu's smiles as they watched the standoff.

"It is my Foster child, and her name is Amigo," Enrico said through clenched teeth and moved away from the hatch.

"I don't care if its name is God, it ain't flying my ship," Jeff finished speaking just as the engines of the craft fired. Cursing loudly, he turned to grab the hatch handle only to be knocked to the ground by the lifting ship.

The ship rose a few feet up and spun to the left several rotations, stopped, and swung back to the right until Amigo could be seen in the pilot's window, a very human grin on her face showing a mouth full of tiny pointed teeth.

"Damn," Jeff muttered from the ground.

The ship hovered a moment longer and then zoomed straight up until it was a speck against the high clouds. It held, and then began soaring downward, making wide circles and lazy eights.

The pilot was pacing when Amigo finally landed. "If you're done hot-shotting around, maybe we can get going," Jeff addressed Amigo angrily as she opened the hatchway.

"Hot shotting? You fly," Amigo said, before she moved out of the doorway, and sat in the passenger seat.

"Hot-shotting! Showing off!" Jeff shouted over his shoulder as he settled himself behind the controls.

"Sure thing, boss." Amigo grinned once more as she offered the pilot a thumbs up gesture using both hands to imitate the human thumb.

Jeff snorted in response.

#

"We are still not certain of your request. Would you be so kind as to repeat it once more?" Neavillii asked from where she sat on a raised dais.

It was late in the day, and Enrico and Amigo had long since grown tired of the endless stream of Bystocc natives Neavillii was giving audience to.

"It is simply that we most humbly petition your most gracious body. It is our faithful desire only to be loyal to you, our love. And in showing our love to your most delectable self we bow low and request the most undeserved privilege to be allowed to toil upon your exquisite behalf." The tall thin native kept its face pressed against the floor as it spoke, thus obscuring the inflections and further garbling its message.

"Either they want jobs or they're proposing a group marriage?" Neavillii leaned back in her chair and muttered in English to Enrico who was sitting beside her on the floor.

"Definitely marriage," Enrico whispered back as he tossed the ball to Amigo.

"Though we are truly flattered by your sincere compliments, we find it difficult to think with our head swooning. Please state your request in one sentence. No compliments and no detractions. And look at me, please," Neavillii ended with a smile.

"We-" Whatever the native may have been proposing became of no importance when Neavillii and Enrico's communication units both screamed at once.

The high pitched, ear-splitting sound was replaced by Yolunu's voice.

"Attack! Planetary attack! Tadesde forces-" her broadcast was cut by static.

Neavillii stood in the now silent room and turned her gaze to Enrico who still sat, ball in hand.

"We have to get out of the city," Enrico said as he tried to jump to his feet. He forgot about his amputated foot with its mismatched prosthetic, and only Amigo's quick reflexes buffered his fall.

"Agreed," Neavillii said as she bent and picked him up. Amigo grabbed his cane and trailed the running Neavillii.

"Move!" Neavillii shouted to the crowd of petitioners, both Sansheren and Bystocc.

But the entire room had heard the emergency broadcast and everyone now milled about in various degrees of panic and confusion. Amigo stepped in front of Neavillii and growled at the people blocking their path to the entrance. The Sansheren closest cowered backward in fear, bumping into others and causing an even worse traffic snarl.

"But, my Lady, what should we do?"

The native petitioner from before fell at Neavillii's feet.

"Survive, my friend, survive." Neavillii tried to step around him to find her path blocked by others.

"This way, I have an escape." The voice came from the right; it belonged to a different native. Four natives encircled them and began shoving a path to the left.

Neavillii allowed herself to be escorted through the crowd, still carrying Enrico.

#

"Are we sealed in?" Aldera directed her question to her assistant Nogina.

"Yes, my Lady. There is still time. Perhaps we should use the escape exit and flee the city," Nogina said, and Aldera saw several others nod their heads in agreement.

"There is no time. The Administration building is but a few blocks down. It will be the first place targeted." Even as she spoke, the room shook slightly.

"Then we're doomed," said a voice from the back of the room.

"So be it. Our duty is to the children, we can last at least fifty days, and we will do our best. Who would accept the honor of keeping a journal?" Aldera looked about the room; thirty Sansheren sat in their cafeteria. None would meet her eye.

"Then I would ask that each would keep her own journal, and I will keep the formal accounting." The room shook once more as if to punctuate her sentence.

#

"There is no hope for survival and no honor in cowering. I will meet Tadesde on the front steps of the building." Thanera opened the door of the shelter.

They were deep within the building, but not safe from the violent shaking that accompanied each explosion.

"No! My Lady, we should wait here for our forces to drive back the carrion eaters above." The young aide Thanera had never met grabbed her arm and held her within the room.

"We have no forces, my love," Thanera said while attempting to remove the other's hands from her own arm. "I was speaking to the brave Yolunu in orbit when Tadesde struck. What few ships we had were destroyed immediately. Our patron Morganea will return too late. But she will avenge us," Thanera finished. She quit trying to free herself from the panicked aide and turned

164

to step into the hallway. The young aide followed her mutely. A few of the others in the room walked out to join them as they proceeded up the stairs.

Opening the main door to the Administration building, Thanera and her group avoided the fall of debris from above. The aircar responsible for the strafing saw them and circled to land.

"It is a privilege to surrender to one as beautiful as you," Thanera said without kneeling or bowing.

Tadesde piloted the aircar and now stood grinning at them.

"My Lady, she might have a weapon." One of Tadesde's s aides rushed forward from the aircar and attempted to prevent Tadesde from moving forward.

Tadesde paused to rake her claws across the retainer's face before continuing on. "Will there be futile resistance?" Tadesde asked after climbing the stairs.

"I can speak for no one but myself." Thanera continued to meet her conqueror's eye.

"Very well. I am hungry. See that my meal is cooked." Tadesde waved her hand in Thanera's general direction before continuing into the building.

The aides that followed her stopped in their tracks as they assimilated her order.

Thanera turned to watch Tadesde's departing back as she drew a small gun and placed the muzzle beneath her own chin. It was the same weapon that killed her first lover, the administrator Raceri. Neither Tadesde's aides nor Thanera's moved as Thanera pulled the trigger.

Tadesde's laugh came out of the building to chase the crack of the weapon through the street.

#

"Red dog leader to anybody out there. Red dog leader to anybody out there. The baby's in the wash. Repeat, the baby's in the wash. We're planning a revival on Bootleg Hill. Copy."

The shuttle pilot Jeffrey started when Enrico's voice came over the ship's radio. He was in the communication room of the mercenary ship Yolunu had hired to sweep for mines.

.

"That was Enrico," Jeff said as a short human woman joined

him in the room; several others floated in the corridor.

The minor damage the ship suffered from Tadesde's strike was offset by Yolunu lying unconscious on a table in a central compartment. Yolunu was not the only one injured when the captain shut off all power and assumed a lifeless attitude: a spiraling drifting orbit around the besieged planet. The cafeteria compartment was now full of injured crew, and the unconscious Yolunu's broken leg was low priority to the mercenary trying to save his friend's lives.

"Red dog leader calling anyone, we're planning a revival at Bootleg Hill. Copy?" Panic and fear could be heard in the voice that pierced through the static.

"Kid needs help," someone said from the hallway.

The captain of the vessel nodded his head in grim agreement.

"Anyone know where Bootleg Hill is?" Jeff asked in a subdued voice.

"Yeah, old code Tim used. It's over on the Southern Continent. Suicide, man." A different human woman braced herself against the hatchway and offered her hand to the pilot.

"If you decouple and drift free they might not notice. We'll wait as long as we can." The captain shook hands with first Jeff, and then the woman who tacitly agreed to join him.

#

The small shuttle craft drifted for several hours, its occupants chilled thoroughly in the dead air of the cabin.

"Going to have to turn the air on soon. Might as will make the run now. You sure of the exact spot?" Jeff asked again as he prepped several panels of switches.

"Yeah, lot of ground to cover though." The woman's numb fingers fumbled with the buckles of her drop harness.

"Great. Well, who wants to live forever?" and he hit the switches all at once.

The engines roared to life and frozen air crystals blasted from the vents at the same moment.

Jeff steered the vehicle's nose toward the planet, and they were pressed against their seats.

The various noises masked the woman's intense "I do."

#

"You need to rest," Enrico said to Neavillii who was still carrying him. They were on the outskirts of the city and moving on foot.

"I will continue, I must." Neavillii barely had breath to run, and Enrico saw her waste a precious amount trying to reassure him.

Tadesde aircars continued to make bombing runs on the city, and they were still far from the foothills that encircled the valley the city was built within.

"We would be honored to carry your companion, my Lady." The native, who first offered them escape, jogged easily beside Neavillii.

They had gone farther into the building and left behind those who milled aimlessly in the audience chamber. An underground thoroughfare led them out of the building and nearly out of the city.

"I am even further in your debt, thank you," she gasped as she gulped air, and Enrico knew he was a burden. Two of the natives took him in a chair carry before all began running again.

Amigo darted back and smiled at Enrico.

"Angry people, let us go there." Amigo pointed down a smaller street that branched off of the main road they were following. Without waiting for a reply, she ran down the alley and out of sight.

Neavillii cursed silently, still struggling for breath, and turned down the alley.

A vehicle could be heard on the street in front of them as the natives moved into the alley.

"Trapped!" Amigo cried from her vantage place at the lead.

"We will see," Neavillii grunted as she fired her sidearm at the ground car that entered the alley.

Its front burst into flames and two Sansheren jumped free of it moments before it exploded.

"My Lady, this way." The two natives who were not carrying Enrico held up the lid to an entrance into the sewer system.

Neavillii was pinned down in a doorway by fire from the two Sansheren who were using their burning car as cover. Another ground car moved its nose halfway into the alley before its occupants climbed free and started shooting.

The natives carrying Enrico dropped him down the rank hole and jumped in after him.

"-my Lady!"

Enrico's voice blended with the impassioned plea of the Bystocc still above ground.

Neavillii held the native's gaze for barely a second before turning her attention back to the ones shooting at them.

"We have to help her." Enrico tried to free himself from the restraining hands of the sympathetic natives.

"It is she who is helping us. I would rather her sacrifice were not in vain," the last native said from the top of the ladder while pulling the lid closed.

The remaining light from the hole was blocked as Amigo dove through and into the grieving Enrico's arms.

She was covered with blood, but he could see no injury.

"We go now," she whispered.

Enrico felt something inside him die with the light, and he was left standing alone in the dark, empty.

The natives moved silently in the dark, and Enrico was startled when one of them picked him up and they began to walk.

"You can see in the dark?" he asked while still holding the clinging Amigo.

"We are a nocturnal race, my patron. It would help greatly if your friend could be carried by another." The native was already breathing heavily when it paused to allow another to reach for Amigo.

"I can run," Amigo said a bit too loud, and Enrico realized that, since the first contact in the audience room, everyone was speaking English.

"Do you know where the rendezvous spot is?" he asked, again feeling like a burden.

"Yes," was the short reply.

Enrico felt disoriented as the darkness grew behind his eyes and the silence was broken by the struggles for breath fought by the one carrying him. Seemingly hours later, he was jostled and passed to another. And the run continued.

\#

168

"We are under radar and flying fast. Let's hope the boy is waiting for us," Jeff called out over the howl of the engines.

"If you land in the ravine, I'll scout for them." The woman held tight to her harness as the craft swung violently to the left and began following surface terrain.

"Roger that." The pilot kept his eyes on the horizon less than a mile away as they slowed to the speed of sound.

#

"Ouch," Amigo said as she brought her hands to her ears, too late to block the loud booming that echoed through the valley they were climbing out of. The sewer tunnel had taken them as far as a treatment plant several miles clear of the now-smoking city.

They were forced to hike into the steep hills from there, and Enrico insisted on walking with the aid of his cane.

The natives were exhausted and made no better time than him.

"That will be our ride. How far now?" he turned to address the natives.

"The other side of that ridge. I wish you luck, young master." The native bowed low.

"Are you coming?" he asked as the other natives walked back down the ridge they just climbed.

"No," the lead native still bowed.

"Why?" Enrico stepped forward, raised the other's head, and stared into eyes filled with pain.

"This is our planet."

Enrico felt his hand fall as the native moved to follow its companions.

"I am in your debt, and it will be my honor to see your planet free," he found himself whispering in Sansheren.

Amigo tugged on his free hand, pulling him up the last of the hill.

The shuttle was parked beyond; a human adult was running toward them, all the while scanning the sky.

"Buckle up, boys. This one's going to be a fun one," the pilot called out even as the ship lifted.

The hatchway automatically secured itself, barely missing the co-pilot's foot.

Enrico struggled to strap Amigo into the adult sized chair while listening as the co-pilot cursed. The forward motion of the craft threw Enrico backwards and into the next tier of seats.

"Straight up. Next stop, free fall," Jeff shouted, and Enrico had the distinct impression that the pilot was having fun.

"This is the right reverend red dog leader calling all you apostles. Prepare for a sermon on the mount. Repeat, prepare for a sermon on the mount," Jeff closed the mike and eased the vehicle into an arced path that pointed it directly at the planet's largest Moon.

"I thought this thing couldn't break orbit," the co-pilot said.

Enrico nodded in agreement. "You're right. Sermon on the Mount is code for a high orbital pickup. Tadesde broke that one," Enrico added to the pilot.

"Then let's just hope no one's listening, cause we ain't gonna get a second chance." Jeff didn't bother his passengers with information concerning reactor temperature and coolant levels. The pilot kept a tight grip on the controls and was unaware of the skeletal grin that played across his face.

"Red dog leader, confirm Sermon on the Mount. Be warned of a three-point-eight second window. Pursuit is rising from the ground as we speak." The captain's voice was a tinny echo, and Enrico grabbed his release button as the mercenary ship filled their port window.

"Confirmed. And on my mark. Mark!"

The two vehicles matched speeds and connected in what was not a crash only by definition of damage.

Enrico lunged forward and pulled Amigo free of the straps without bothering to unsnap them.

The copilot activated the hatch.

Jeff did not move from the pilot's seat as he worked the controls.

"Let's go," Enrico called from the airlock of the larger ship.

"Negative. Right now I think a bit of a distraction is in order, sonny boy," Jeff shouted, and Enrico's protest was cut off when the pilot hit the airlock override.

The hatch slammed shut in Enrico's face, and a precious

second passed as the airlock control panel confirmed the seal, then the couplers blew free with the shuttle. And Jeff aimed his shuttle straight at the rapidly approaching enemy fighter. "Geronimo" echoed through the mercenary ship's intercom a moment after impact.

Enrico and the copilot made no move to leave the airlock as they stared at each other in shock.

"Yolunu," Amigo said, sniffing the blood she wiped from the wall of the corridor.

"Come on." The co-pilot was the first to move, and led Enrico down the corridor to where Yolunu lay strapped to a table, her foot twisted sideways; the leg was bloated well above the knee.

He could detect no rise or fall of her chest.

"The tourniquet just ain't holding," someone said in response to Enrico's questioning look.

"She dies." Amigo stood in the hatchway, refusing to enter the room.

Enrico felt her fear echo through him.

"We have to space her. Now." He felt a strong hand on his arm, stilling him when he would have moved closer to his friend.

"Listen here. I don't care what species it is, I ain't allowing no bigot to space an injured person. The captain won't either." A tall, black adult held him.

"You don't understand, we'll all be killed. We have to get her into the airlock. Help me." He looked from one person to the next, only to be met with the same hostile stare.

"She'll give birth soon. We'll all be killed." Enrico looked to the doorway to find that Amigo was nowhere to be seen.

"You saying that's pregnant? Man, I've seen one of their kids. Get out of the way, Jake." The small adult pushed through and shared Enrico's look of fear.

"You sure?" the one called Jake released Enrico's arm grudgingly before picking up Yolunu and moving toward the corridor. He was forced to turn sideways to clear the hatchway, and those in the room could see the swelling of Yolunu's abdomen.

"Hurry!" Enrico followed the other into the corridor.

Jake shoved Yolunu's body into the airlock and was still pulling the door closed when a burst of green blood splattered out. He continued to pull the door shut and secured it. The corridor was silent as he turned his bloody face to Enrico.

Nothing was said between the two of them as others passed and stared through the airlock window.

"I need to speak with the captain," Enrico said to no one as he turned away and limped toward the front of the ship.

"Hey. How long can they survive when they run out of food?" Jake still held his position.

"I don't know," he said over his shoulder.

Amigo crept out of the small hole in the deck plating and took Enrico's hand.

Chapter Twenty - Wergol - 2012

"Damn it! Where is he?" Morgan turned to Banessa, only to realize she spoke in English.

"Your family doctor will arrive soon," Banessa said from where she leaned against the wall. The Sansheren, still bleeding lightly from her side wound, anticipated her leader's source of impatience.

"In there!" Denise's high-pitched voice announced Isaacs's arrival.

"What took you so long?" Morgan demanded, even as she moved of out of his way.

"Get her out of here," Isaac said in Sansheren, without ever acknowledging Morgan.

Banessa and Greg moved to lead the unresisting Morgan out of the room and down the stairs. Her last glimpse of the room showed Tim's pale face, Isaac opening his bag, and Denise sitting on the far edge of the bed.

"Why! On whose authority?" Morgan challenged from where the stairwell emptied into the bar commons. Morgan found herself staring across the room at the captured Tadesde spacers; anger and hatred swelled up to replace the worry and fear that threatened to overwhelm her.

"In accordance with the neutrality pact signed by your love Neadesto, I must humbly request that I and my wives be returned to our ship," the conscious prisoner said, and held her head proud, staring ahead, refusing to meet anyone's gaze.

Morgan struck her, hard across the face after she finished her request. "I no longer wear Neadesto's banner! " Morgan spat out with contempt. She tugged at her own House banner before turning her back on the prisoner and moving toward the injured woman who had tried to warn Tim. "How is she?"

"An explosive charge detonated within her maternal nest. She will die without another child," Tansea said as she placed her small hand on the arm of the crying wife.

"But, she has not given life to even one. How can she die without children? Who will remember her face? Who will speak her name? Why couldn't it have been me? At least I have given twins to a loving father. But, why?" Few in the room could meet the distraught wife's gaze as she struggled to accept the news.

"I would speak with her a moment," Morgan said.

Tansea, knowing some Sansheren custom, helped the crying woman walk a few feet to the bar. Everyone in the room was silent as they watched Morgan approach the dying spacer.

"You have done me an honor, and I am in your debt. I would discharge this debt before your death, my Lady," and with that, Morgan leaned over the still form and whispered a single word into her ear.

"What's happening?" Greg whispered to Tansea as all eyes remained on Morgan.

"The debt at death is held over and granted each of the deceased's children. This woman has no children, Morgan could've waited a few moments and then been free of the debt," Tansea whispered back.

Morgan heard their exchange without response; she realized that she was giving the dying woman a gift whose value was beyond belief to the Sansheren and beyond the comprehension for the humans present. Morgan gave her peerage in the form of the name of the Tenth rank of Sansadee.

"My thanks, my love." The dying spacer struggled to maintain consciousness long enough to open her eyes and acknowledge the gift. Her eyes never opened, but Morgan and those close by could hear her whispered words. The silence grew as her breathing quieted until it was apparent she was no longer struggling.

"Let it be for ever recorded in the records of the Sansheren that this person gave not only her own life but the lives of all of her descendants to save a member of my family. Let it also be recorded that she died my equal."

As Morgan unfastened the banner that covered her left breast, the captured spacer gasped and then began to struggle against her bonds. Banessa struck her quiet.

"I publicly acknowledge a debt of honor to her spouse, and if she will accept, I would ask her to enter my House, my family, and my home." Morgan still had not raised her eyes as she draped the banner across the chest of the dead.

"Oh, my Lady…" the crying wife moved forward and tried to kneel, but Morgan held her shoulders and forced her to remain standing before enveloping her in a hug.

"If you would take a berth upon my ship the Yonxine, I would be grateful," Morgan's voice was soft and tender, her eyes held wide open, as she spoke to her new wife.

"How was I to know she was a member of your family, my Lady? My Lady? There are so many of your lovely species on this planet, which ones are family to you if they do not look like you? How were we to know?" The captured spacer was staring around the room, trying to make eye contact with any of Morgan's people.

"Do you think I would defend just anyone? Do you think I am so easy in my allegiances? I named him family to a member of my own personal family; I would think that would give you warning. If you were smart enough to take it," Morgan said over her shoulder, her voice tense and angry.

"My Lady is correct; a fool as ignorant as I is so far beneath her as to be without value. I would offer my life to feed your children. I am yours to destroy," the woman whispered with her head bowed, and Morgan thought she was bereft of hope or honor.

"Tansea. Attend my new possessions." Morgan waved Tansea to the injured attackers who were lying guarded on the bar floor.

"Surely you do not hold my wives responsible for my ignorance? My Lady, you're a just and noble person, please spare their lives." Even as hope left her, Morgan could still see her love for her spouses.

"Do not judge me by your own corrupt standards; I have no need for the lives of your spouses. You are without value; I would not feed my children your bones. The stench of your dishonor would contaminate them," Morgan said before she again turned her back, a move Banessa interpreted as an end to the audience, and she again struck the prisoner silent.

"Tansea?" Morgan walked to stand beside the small medic who

was just finishing stitching a long cut on one of the captive's foreheads.

"Oh, they will live. This one will be forced to live on the charity of her family, though. The other one will be fine in a week or two. Neither of them will be able to ship off planet for at least a month." Tansea finished her work with more concern than Morgan felt any survivor of Bystocc should show for Tadesde's retainers.

"But we must ship out in four days or we are stranded." The captive kept speaking through Banessa's next blow.

"You must not do anything. Have you forgotten your debt to me so soon? You were stranded the hour you decided to attack my family. If any further damage comes to him, or to any other member of my family on this planet, I will hold you and your family personally responsible. The records of the Home world do not contain accounts of blood feuds as severe as I will pursue against your face. Take your spouses and leave this establishment. You may take residence at the Brigada. Leave." Morgan turned away in time to see Tim being helped down the stairs by Isaac.

"Why is he cutting him free? He has to wait for the Sansheren authorities to come for mediation." Tim's voice was weak, but Morgan saw his anger and confusion.

"As the highest ranking Sansheren currently on the planet, I am the authority. They have been instructed that if anything happens to you or anyone else I know, they'll be punished severely." Morgan moved toward Tim but his expression of hostility confused and frightened her, and she shifted to the bar instead.

"So that's it? No jail, no nothing? Just be good and stay out of trouble?" Tim asked with a scornful laugh.

"I have stripped them of House and family, they will live on the charity of strangers on an alien planet. I thought it was enough." Morgan interpreted the scorn in Tim's voice as a challenge and turned to face him.

Tim's eyes held hers before they slid down toward her bared breast and then danced about the room.

"Your banner," Tim whispered, and moved to the dead spacer and her spouse.

"I wanted to honor her." Morgan's voice softened, and she

176

moved to stand beside the still grieving wife.

"He... He kept trying to tell me something. I didn't understand. He grabbed my arm and shouted something. I didn't understand. When he jumped up and ran after me, I put my back to the wall and drew my gun."

Everyone in the room listened to Tim's quiet voice.

"He smiled when I pointed my gun at him; in that pinched face routine of theirs. I was going to shoot him when I heard sounds down the alley. They all came running forward at once. He jumped in front of me, the dumb fuck. I could've shot at least one of them if he hadn't got in front of me. The shot almost ripped him in half, but you know he looked happy when he fell, like saving me was important to him. Someone want to explain this to me?" Tim looked up from the dead spacer's face with tears in his eyes.

"You're important to Morgan, so you're important to them." Greg gestured at the Sansheren in the room.

"He was wearing Tadesde colors. Are you telling me Morgan is a friend of Tadesde?" Tim's voice became hard, cold.

"The opposite. These two wanted to defect to Morgan. Saving your ass was the best offer of personal value they could present her."

As Greg finished speaking, Tim turned to Morgan, a host of questions seen on his face.

"They decided you were a member of my family and one tried to warn you while the other ran for help. It was a noble gesture, don't you think. Neither one spoke English and they had no weapons. She was happy to give her life for yours because it meant her wife would be guaranteed a place with me. And she is. I've taken her wife to be my own." Morgan smiled down at the one she spoke of, and missed the confused expression on the faces of the other humans in the bar.

"You mean that's female too?" Tim pointed at the widow in disbelief.

"Of course." Morgan was confused.

"I told you they were a race of fags and dykes," Tim said to Greg, who refused to meet his gaze.

"I don't understand. All Sansheren are female. I told you." Morgan looked from Tim to Denise and then to Greg.

"Just what the universe needs, a race of lesbians, I'd hate to live with a group of them. Permanent PMS. So tell me, where do babies come from?" Tim elbowed an embarrassed Greg in the side with a forced, bitter laugh.

"Sansheren reproduction is asexual," Morgan said in a near whisper through the fear that turned to anger and built within her.

"No wonder you're so screwed up." Tim shook his head and limped to the stairs.

Denise kept her head down as she started to wipe the blood off of the table.

Greg refused to meet Morgan's eyes, and he followed Tim up the stairs.

"Take my new wife and her deceased back to our rooms; make arrangements for transportation of her genetics back to the home world. I want her archetype recorded with honors." Morgan struggled to control her voice as she gave Banessa the orders.

Banessa moved to get everyone out of the bar, leaving behind two of her best people as guards inside the bar.

Tansea placed her hand on Morgan's as she walked to the bar.

Isaac sighed as he moved to the stairway.

"It's empty." Morgan said as she picked up a wine glass from the bar.

"Here." Denise moved behind the bar and took the glass from Morgan's unresponsive fingers. Nothing was said between the two women as Denise filled a clean wine glass. She set the bottle in front of Morgan, and moved to sit beside Sam at the far side of the room.

"He's judging us by what he saw from Tadesde. That dishonorable, nameless bitch," Morgan said to no one; Tansea was the only one close enough to hear.

"He can only relate to what he knows. You cannot expect him to forget so much pain quickly." Tansea moved closer to Morgan and refilled her glass from the wine bottle.

"But we're not like Tadesde. She's insane, why can't he see that? They say she hunted her own child once. She's evil," Morgan said in monotone English. She never raised her gaze from her glass.

"Someone will stop Tadesde. You must worry about your family and your friends." Tansea took the small sip from her own glass.

"With Sansheren our friends are our family. You're right, someone will stop Tadesde - I will. It's time I quit living off the charity of my beloved Neadesto and made a place for myself." Morgan drank her glass of wine without tasting it and poured a refill, which she also downed.

"You have made a place for yourself: Bystocc. Your future is secured. If Tim is to be a part of it, he must learn to accept you as you are. Tadesde is a member of the Twelfth rank; she is beyond your reach. Forget her," Tansea said, and Morgan decided to launch a personal attack against Tadesde. A suicide plan, that as simple as it was, gave her comfort.

"Tim won't accept me because he thinks we're all as bad as Tadesde. If I kill her maybe he will forgive me for the harm she has done. Maybe." Morgan looked at Denise and called for a writing board.

Denise did not respond, and Morgan realized she and Tansea were speaking in Sansheren when a member of the security detachment crossed the room to hand her the requested implement.

"Child, you're upset. Let it wait until morning. Speak with him then. He'll grow to understand. It was a shock and it takes time." Tansea filled the empty wine glass one last time before moving across the room to sit with Sam and Denise.

\#

"How dare you treat her that way!" Isaac shouted. "Of course she went native. She's had no human contact for over fifteen years. It's a miracle she held on to her humanity at all. And then you come along: the Almighty from her childhood, and tell her she's screwed up!" Isaac did not release Tim's eyes as he paused for breath.

"She quit thinking in English years ago, as a human being she's no older than twelve or thirteen. And she still has a crush on you. You're an idiot and worse. She was rescued by a race that is both male and female at the same time: she was neutered by an alien doctor, and you feel you have the right to tell her she's screwed up? Of course she's screwed up, how could she be anything but? After what she went through, it's a wonder she's sane, let alone the ruler of a planet with tens of thousands begging to be her subjects." Isaac continued to stare at Tim long after his words fled the room.

"What do you mean she was neutered? I knew the Sansheren were barbaric, but, why?" Tim tried to sit forward in the bed but discovered himself exhausted.

"The Sansheren didn't do it," Isaac said in disgust. "She was dumped on Faldebbia. Their doctors had never dealt with the human female before. They didn't understand her menstrual cycle. She was just a kid. No one had explained it to her. They didn't understand the bleeding would stop on its own, so they removed her uterus and ovaries. Without them, she couldn't develop physically. I met her at about the same time she found Sam. I offered to start her on hormone replacements, but she didn't agree until she discovered there was a chance you were alive. Of course she's a little screwed up! That kid's in love with you!" Isaac said and didn't wait for a response to his explanation. He stormed out of the room, and his momentum carried him down the stairs. He stood in the doorway watching Morgan for a few minutes without her noticing. She looked defeated, and he watched as she smeared a tear through her makeup and continued writing.

"She's getting drunk and trying to write a suicide note." Tansea crossed the room and whispered to him.

"Is there a real danger?" Isaac could not take his eyes off of the beautiful woman that Morgan had become, as she erased the writing board and started again.

"She thinks she'll challenge Tadesde," Tansea said with a shrug.

Denise moved back to the bar and poured Morgan a drink from a new bottle. "I'll always love him too," Denise said, and poured her own drink as she spoke.

Morgan made eye contact with her as they both drank.

"Well at least she can't try tonight." Isaac motioned Tansea to lead the way out of the bar.

\#

"She had lilacs in her hair. Do you remember?" Tim was still staring at the door Isaac had left through minutes before.

"Do you still have them?" Greg's voice was quiet, with no inflection. They both knew the answer, even as Tim smiled and reached into his pocket for a small pouch.

"I want to keep remembering her the way she was. She's so hard now. She doesn't need me. Hell, she doesn't need anyone," Tim said as he opened the pouch and rubbed his finger against the small mound of dust in the bottom.

"Maybe she needs to think she needs someone. Maybe she needs to be a girl, a woman, with someone," Greg said without looking at Tim. He didn't alter his gaze when no response came to his comment, and the silence built.

#

"Honey if you really want him, just go up and get him." Denise leaned forward across the bar.

Morgan was too drunk to notice how intoxicated Denise had become. "I wouldn't know what to do," Morgan said in an audible voice as she stared into her wine glass.

"Aw hell. You don't have to do anything. Just march up those stairs and climb in bed with him. He won't kick you out." Denise giggled as she poured them both yet another drink.

"Do I look okay?" Morgan tried to focus on her image in the wall mirror behind Denise.

"Here, let me help," Denise said and moved between Morgan and the blurry mirror.

"Hand me a wash rag, please. He didn't like my makeup." Morgan started to wash her face and neck.

Denise moved her hand to Morgan's face. Placing her hand against Morgan's cheek, she felt an overwhelming urge to cry.

"Wear your hair down, child. Now go." Denise said, and turned away from Morgan, leaving her to finish her preparations alone.

Morgan stared at the blurring mirror as she unfastened the tie that held her long black hair back. In the mirror, she saw herself un-aged, frozen at twelve years old, small red lips standing out from her pale olive skin. The river of black crossed over her shoulder, and she tried to steer her hair to cover her small, bannerless breast. It just reached the bottom, but the hair insisted on parting around the peak and giving teasing glimpses with every move. She looked at herself one last time, shrugged, gulped the last of her wine, and pushed herself away from the bar.

As she moved across the tavern room, gravity seemed to pull her to the stairwell. Morgan walked to the stairs and began to climb.

Holding onto the banister, Morgan paused to stifle a laugh that threatened to escape her control. She stood, trying to remember why she was in the stairwell, but the urge to laugh remained. Drunk and tired, she decided she was climbing the stairs to go sleep off the effects of the alcohol she could vaguely remember drinking.

"Aw hell. You don't have to do anything. Just march up those stairs and climb in the bed..." the image of Denise overwhelmed her sense of time. She knew Denise had been trying to tell her something else, but she couldn't focus on her words any longer. The laughter was swelling up within her, and she decided to give in to it. A single tear slid down her cheek as the laughter evaporated.

Morgan stood at the top of the staircase and looked down the long hallway before her. One doorway, the second to the left, beckoned her. A sense of unease and sorrow hit her unprepared as she approached it.

Tim was there, she remembered. She knew why she had come up the stairs and what Denise had told her. Still she stood, poised with her hand on the doorknob, and she felt a second tear join the first in its slow journey down her face.

"Hi." The door was open. She couldn't remember turning the knob, but she realized she had been standing in the doorway for some time, and tried to say something in explanation. She wanted to explain to Tim how she felt, why she was there - not for the reason Denise suggested, but just to talk. To try to explain everything that had happened to her; to hear everything that had happened to him. To talk and to see him, just to be in the room with him and watch him speak, was all she wanted.

"Hi," was what came out of the overwhelming desire she felt.

"Hi yourself, kid." Tim smiled, before turning his gaze from her and nodding to Greg.

Greg smiled, in a sad but hopeful manner, before he stood and walked toward the door. He took Morgan's hand from the door knob, and with his other hand on her shoulder, he pushed her further into the room as he left.

The door closed with little sound to disturb the tableau that was building in the room.

It was a small, dirty room. The walls were brown, the floor had once been white, and an uncurtained window showed the wall of the building across the alley. Tim lay in the middle of a soft looking cushion that was placed on top of a raised platform, a bed, Morgan thought, and for a brief moment the laughter threatened to return. The blankets that covered him were deep emerald green, and Morgan was surprised to find herself noticing how clean and inviting the entire bed looked.

She walked across the room, but stopped when she got to the bed. Afraid to sit and embarrassed to be standing beside him, she knelt at the head of the bed; her face came even with his.

"Shit," Tim whispered, and Morgan bowed her head in response. Her hair covered her face and blocked the light for her.

"I'm sorry," she whispered.

Tim reached forward and moved the hair from about the left side of her face.

"You'll always be beautiful," Tim said with his hand on the back of her neck; he pulled her closer and tilted her face to him.

"I didn't keep my promise, I took a wife." Morgan looked deep into his eyes and didn't understand the smile she watched fade into pain.

"So did I, so did I." The pain in Tim's eyes faded away as he pulled her to him and kissed her closed lips gently. His hand on her neck, he guided her forward until she was leaning over him and he was lying flat on the bed.

Long after the kiss ended, she moved away and stood before him. Without breaking his eye contact, she reached behind her and unfastened her remaining banner. It fell to the floor and was joined by her pants.

Tim ran his gaze down her body and back to her eyes before lifting the bed covers aside and holding his hand up to her.

Morgan paused to remove her sandals.

\#

"I would bear your children, my love," Morgan said several

hours later as she lay curled against Tim's side. The sweat had cooled from her body, but not the pain.

"Hey, don't worry about it. It's just as well; children can be very complicated off Earth." Tim's voice was brusque, and she felt herself near to tears over the pain she imagined he had endured.

"Let's just sleep together now," he said and moved her face to his and kissed her once more.

#

"I love you," Tim whispered as he woke up. He reached beside him to discover he spoke to an empty bed.

"Hey, sleepy head. These just came for you." Denise waved to Tim as he exited the stairway. The items in question were a vase of bluish green flowers. The bar was filled with the overpowering odor of lilacs.

"Read the note." Sam pointed to a writing board clipped to the side of the vase.

It was never my intention to complicate your life. I have to leave. I hope I can see you again when I have a chance to return to Wergol. Right now my honor demands I address the insults Tadesde has done my family. I have been informed that she is at this moment petitioning for a hearing by the council of the Great Houses. She claims bias in the Arbitration, and I must attend the council. I am sorry to have disrupted your life.

Your humble servant,
Morgan

"Damn," Tim slammed the writing board down and stalked out of the bar; shoving past a surprised Greg.

"Here," was Denise's response to Greg's puzzled look.

Greg read the note out loud to the silent room before rushing out to find Tim.

Chapter Twenty One - Earth 1998

Turning her head to get the sun out of her eyes, Morgan noticed them. They were marching across the sidewalk, down the small hill, and onto her plate of uneaten food before retracing their path. Morgan reached forward and killed one of the small black ants. She focused her entire mind on the crunch of squishing the ants. She did not let her attention drift even after she had killed all those within her reach.

The ants milled about in a cluster – not willing to take the now deadly route - and worked their way farther down the blanket until they found the small styrofoam bowl of sun-stale coleslaw.

As Morgan watched the ants, the sounds of Greg and Sam tossing a football faded from her mind.

"Way thanks, man," Sam said, as Greg's throw slid to a stop on the towel of a sunbathing girl. She lifted herself up from the towel with one hand, and Sam was treated to a tantalizing view of her oiled breasts as he smiled and bent to pick up the errant ball.

"Sorry, ma'am. My friend's a bit spastic today. It won't happen again," Sam said in his best sexy voice before standing and turning away with a blinding grin on his face. Throwing the ball back towards Greg, he deliberately nailed a small brown poodle that was about to mark a tree. The dog yelped, and the rather large woman at the other end of the leash frowned the entire time it took her to walk down the hill.

Greg found another target for their game. He threw the ball wide of Sam and it struck Denise. She and Tim were trying to use a small cluster of hedge bushes for concealment.

"Quit fucking around, ass holes." Tim sat up from beneath Denise, and stabbed the offending football with his pocketknife, before throwing it back in their direction.

Denise made a point of rubbing her bottom before smiling

coyly in their direction, and then lowered herself back down behind the bushes.

"He shouldn't do that around the kid," Sam said quietly to Greg as he picked up the deflated football.

"Why not? It's not like she ain't seen it on the TV," Greg said in a puzzled voice. They'd moved back up the hill to the picnic spot where Morgan was again killing unsuspecting ants.

"She has a crush on him." Sam stopped moving once Greg caught up.

"Hell, everyone has a crush on Tim. Why'd you think we stick around this crazy setup?" Greg grinned and punched Sam in the arm to distract from the pain in his voice. They both laughed and continued up the hill. Neither one noticed Morgan pause in killing the ants.

"The lovebirds are done." Greg nodded down the hill to where Tim was standing up behind the bushes and buttoning his pants.

Denise came into view, and looked around blushing as she straightened her dress. Tim said something to her as he started walking up the hill toward the others, and Denise blushed even redder.

She moved to follow him, picking twigs and such from her hair, and caught up with Tim when he paused to pick a half-bloomed stem of lilacs from one of the bushes that helped conceal them. She smiled and started to straighten her hair as they crossed the open space up the hill.

"Here, kid," Tim said, kneeling beside Morgan.

Morgan felt her face grow warm. She tried to break eye contact with Tim as he leaned close and slid the lilac into her hair just above her ear.

"Shit." Denise threw herself onto the ground between Greg and Tim and continued to comb her fingers through her own tangled hair.

Morgan sat, still holding Tim's eye, with her back against a tree. The smell of the flowers made her dizzy, and the only escape she could find from Tim's gaze was to close her eyes. She felt herself drifting toward sleep. She could feel the sun, hot against her legs, and hear the others talking. She thought that the day should last forever.

"Sometimes I'd swear you care more for her than you do for

me." Denise wasn't quite whining, but Morgan could hear the pout in her voice.

"Yeah, so? What's your point?" Tim's laughter was joined by Sam and Greg.

"You can't love her, she's only twelve years old. That would be sick." Denise sat upright and glared at Tim.

"It's not sick. At least I don't think it is. I've waited a year so far. I'm willing to wait until she's legal. Hell, I'll wait forever for her. She's the most beautiful thing you'll ever see. I've been in love with her since the first time I saw her. I'll always love her." Tim was smiling at Morgan's slumped form and didn't see the pain on Denise's face.

"You're just making time with me until you can have her, you bastard." Denise stood up. Tears filled her eyes, and she turned and ran before the silent men could see them.

Morgan felt a smile build within her, and she allowed her body to fall toward Tim.

Tim caught her as she drifted down, and offered his leg for her head to rest on.

Morgan squirmed about, looking for a comfortable spot.

"God damn. I thought I just took care of that problem." Tim chuckled to the uncomfortable laughter of the other men.

"So, how did you meet her?" Sam asked from his reclined position.

"Meet the burglar man." Greg theatrically waved his hand toward the smiling Tim.

"No shit, how did you meet her?" Sam held his smile as he asked his question again.

"No shit. I broke in. Tuesday, 1:00 AM, no lights on, TV playing with the sound way down. I figured whoever was home was fast asleep. She was on the couch, swallowed up by the cushions and hidden in the blankets. By the light of the TV set, she looked like a doll. One of the finest porcelain dolls you could imagine." Tim stared down at Morgan's still form as he talked, and she listened to him.

"The burglar." Sam shook his head in disbelief.

"Yeah. I turned the TV off, and this soft little voice said; 'turn it back on'."

Morgan drifted off to sleep.

#

"Did my little sister change lovers?"

Morgan heard her brother's voice and didn't realize she was awake until Tim tensed beneath her.

"Get lost, asshole." Greg rose and moved down the hill toward the group of Asian youths, who stood laughing on the trail below.

"She's the world's youngest nymphomaniac, that's what she is," her brother said, and Tim raised Morgan's head and placed a coat beneath her.

"The man said get lost, asshole," Tim said, moving to stand beside Greg.

Sam was already there.

"Does she keep you well? Her little sex slaves," her brother said with a callous laugh, and Morgan sat up to look where her brother and his four friends were moving apart.

They were putting a few feet between themselves, and Morgan could see a knife shine in her brother's hand.

"Damn you," Tim said, and he drew his own knife. The two groups eyed each other as they maneuvered to find the best advantage, each waiting for the other to make a mistake.

"I wonder if our father would like to know that you're paying someone to go to school for you," Morgan said in Chinese from behind Tim.

"Fuck you," her brother said in English, without meeting her eyes.

"Is everything OK here?"

Two police officers stopped their bikes ten feet away from the groups and waited for an answer.

"No problem, sir, they were just leaving." Greg said while continuing to stare at the five in front of him.

"Yeah, right." Morgan's brother laughed and walked away. The laughter of the group echoed off the hill.

"Is that your brother?"

Morgan looked at the female officer in front of her and recognized her from three years prior. "Yes," Morgan said and dropped her gaze.

"I've dealt with him before," the officer said to her partner. "I'm sorry kid. Good luck."

188

Morgan held her arms tight about her as the two officers rode away.

"Put your coat on," Greg said to Morgan with a frown, to fill the silence that built as the cops rode away.

The sun was behind buildings to the west of the park, and it was beginning to get chilly in the artificial twilight.

Morgan turned and walked to where they had been sitting. Her coat was in the pile with several others. As she picked it up, she noticed Denise's coat. "She'll come back," Morgan said as she held up the sleeve of Denise's coat for the others to see.

"Hey baby doll, they always come back," Tim joked.

Greg made eye contact with Sam, and smiled sourly as he grabbed his own jacket.

"It won't hurt to take Fifth Street out and head down Grand. If she's on her way here from her home we'll catch her," Sam said, as they walked down the hill. Like Tim, he wore no coat. He had a faded BDU shirt on, his name tape still in place over the pocket, though no rank or service tapes remained.

Tim wore a black cotton sweatshirt with "VISUALIZE WORLD POLICE" barely readable in peeling press-on letters.

"Have to turn when Grand meets Thirty-eighth. I'll be damned if I'll go any farther out of my way for a pouting girl." Tim took the lead as they exited the park and started walking down the busy avenue.

Morgan always marveled at how calm it could be within the tree enclosed park, and how busy it was on the street.

"I hear you man." Greg grinned now, the reflexive, angry smile that always made Morgan just a little afraid of the tall, black man.

Morgan stared at Greg as they walked. She moved to put her hand in his and was rewarded with a gentle smile. The sincere expression transformed his face from hostile and withdrawn into one of pleasant surprise.

"What time is ShaTilla coming tonight?" Morgan asked Greg.

"She isn't." The angry pain was back in his eyes.

Morgan peered at him and watched as he stared down several youths who lounged in possession of the corner they were approaching.

"Genevieve is going out of town this weekend." Greg never paused as he approached the intersection, and the walk signal blinked on just as Morgan stepped off the curb.

"ShaTilla could stay the weekend with us." Morgan turned her attention from Greg, and watched as Tim helped himself to the contents of an unsuspecting woman's purse.

She was short, at least a foot beneath Tim's five foot ten inches, with bleached, brittle looking hair sticking up over six inches. Her thick makeup reminded Morgan of a program she had watched on burial preparations.

Tim winked at Morgan as he finished his inventory, and then placed something into her bag, before walking off, whistling.

"I'm working doubles all week long, but if you don't mind, I think I'll tell the bitch to drop her off before she leaves. Thanks." Greg smiled down at Morgan's head as they walked past the targeted woman.

A few feet ahead of them, Tim hung up a pay phone and turned to lean against the wall. He pulled out the smallest of his pocket knives and started to clean his fingernails. Tim nodded toward the woman in answer to Greg and Sam's questioning looks.

She was approaching the front doors of a large bank.

"Remember that pea-shooter I copped off that vine dealer last week?" Tim continued to stare it his fingernails, a feral grin haunted his face.

"The one I told you to throw in the river? Man I told you not to be holding no damn gun around me. I ain't going down on some Federal crap. I don't care how much it's worth on the street!" Greg growled at Tim.

"Neither am I. On the other hand, I've been hearing tell about some upstreet, liberal bitch who's doing a lot of banking for the Vinetta cartel. I think she's about to be introduced to a few feds herself." Tim nodded his head toward the chaos at the entry to the bank.

The woman walked through the first of the doors, only to find the second would not budge. The entry doors locked with a very audible click, and she was pounding on them hysterically. Her makeup was running down her face, and as Tim pointed her out, several police cars pulled to a stop in front of the building.

"Are you sure she's the one?" Sam asked as they turned and continued down the sidewalk.

"Damn straight." Tim grinned and showed Sam a bank deposit

bag. It bore the distinctive logo of a laundromat not too far from their apartment complex. It was common knowledge on the street that the business was a cover for drug traffic.

#

"Let's go home." Morgan was sitting on a bus bench on the corner of Grand Avenue and Thirty-Eighth Street.

Tim was staring in the window of the adult bookstore Greg and Sam were leaving.

"Sure, sweetheart," Sam said as the three men exchanged grins before heading down the next alleyway toward home.

Denise was entering the alley from the opposite opening and Tim sped up to meet her.

There was no bright light, or loud sound, only a growing darkness that obscured Denise and then Tim.

Before Morgan could stop her forward foot from touching the ground, she was within the darkness.

#

When the darkness left there was only pain.

"It's a dream," Morgan heard her own voice say as she sat up and looked about her.

The room was small. Tim was lying on top of Denise. Morgan was sprawled across both Greg and Sam. Sam was sitting with his back to a wall. Greg was moaning under his breath, but his face was turned away from her. Tim propped himself up on one elbow and tried to wake Denise.

Morgan continued staring about at the white glowing walls as Denise gasped, then grabbed Tim, and began to cry. The room was no more than an eight foot box she decided. A recessed circular hatch drew her attention to the ceiling above them. Sam followed her gaze and stood to reach for it. Tim was bumped in the shuffle, and shrugged off Denise to try and help turn the obvious handle. Greg sat up, and Morgan gasped when she noticed the deep gash on his cheek. A clear, dry coating covered more than half of his face, but the purple of a forming bruise could be seen.

"Some fucking dream. I sure hope you wake up soon because

your fucking dream punched me." Greg shifted away from Tim and Sam, to lean into one of the corners.

"Shit! Now your damn dream is pissing my pants for me." Greg started to jump up from where he had chosen to sit; Morgan watched his face turn pale as he settled for sliding along the wall away from the corner. The corner he leaned against contained a small fountain of water that shot up less than a foot, before splashing onto the floor and pooling in a mesh covered hole.

"Give it up, it ain't moving," Greg said to Tim, and moved to a drier spot.

"Never. You okay, man?" Tim turned toward Greg.

"I wanna go home, please. Just let me go home," Denise cried in a plaintive whine.

"Yeah, I'm alive, for now." The depressed looking Greg slid to the floor and wrapped his arms around his knees. His face was obscured from Tim's quizzical look.

"I want to go home. I don't want to be here. Please Tim, let me go home." Denise continued to cry as Morgan put her arms around her, and brought the distraught older girl's head onto her lap. The whine in her voice was replaced by a quieter sobbing.

"Thanks, kid." Tim's smile was forced.

"Hey, one more try, man. I thought I felt it give." Sam was still trying to move the hatch handle.

Morgan felt a scream begin inside her as she watched first Sam's, and then Tim's outstretched hands disappear into darkness.

#

The darkness was quicker than her scream, and she woke up as it erupted from her throat.

"That'll be the five AM wake-up call. C'mon folks, breakfast time." Greg said leaning against a wall, the bruise on his face even bigger.

"Food?" Denise sat up; Tim lay beneath her, frowning at the placement of her elbow.

"I lied. Plenty of water, though." Greg gestured toward the corner the unconscious Sam lay in. The small fountain now fell from the top of a wall and was pooling around Sam's legs. The hatch was on the opposite wall.

"He's alive. Nasty bump though."

Greg's cavalier attitude was beginning to irritate Morgan, and she could see that it was angering Tim.

"You could have moved him." Tim moved toward Sam.

"Where?" Greg gestured about the box, and Morgan realized that, until Tim stood, he and Denise had blocked off the center of the room, leaving her alone in the small open area.

"Forget it, let's move him now." Tim reached toward Sam's inert form.

"What about his neck or back?" Morgan asked in a whisper.

"Shit," Tim said, and straightened up without touching Sam.

"The damage is beyond done." Greg never moved from where he sat.

"Just what is your attitude, asshole?" Tim lunged toward Greg, even as the darkness began to build.

Morgan saw Greg smile as Tim fell to his feet, and then the darkness and the pain returned.

#

Morgan woke to find her head resting on Greg's lap. "You saw them, didn't you?" She asked in a whisper.

"Yeah. You too?" his voice was hopeful as he wiped tears from his face, and handed Morgan the wilted lilacs she had forgotten.

"No. But the darkness lasts longest for Sam, and then Tim and Denise. You're always awake before me. And they hit you." She reached a hand up and touched the bruise that had spread to cover the entire side of his face underneath the protective coating.

"Yeah, well, remind me not to be a hero next time." Greg took Morgan's small hand in his larger one, and helped her to sit up.

"I don't recall you being a hero the first or second time. Asshole," Tim said as he moved toward the still form of Sam.

"Fifth," was Greg's response as he moved his legs to allow Tim to lay Sam flat.

"What?" Denise sat up, rubbing her neck with one hand, and smearing what was left of her mascara with the other.

"I've woken up five times so far. Each time the door is somewhere else and we're in a tangle. I was half conscious one time. The pain and pressure made me wish I had ridden through like you sleeping beauties." Greg reached beside him, and cupped some water from the fountain that now poured out one wall several inches up from the corner and pooled at the bottom.

"What did they look like?" Morgan asked, loud enough to silence Tim.

"Short, gray robes. And tentacles, or ropes. It doesn't matter." Greg shrugged as he wet Sam's lips.

"Tentacles?" Denise looked around the room as if expecting THEM to appear in every corner.

"Oh, come on. This is too much," Tim said as he stepped over Sam's body and reached for the hatch.

"It ain't budging man." Greg never looked in Tim's direction as he continued to trickle water into Sam's open mouth.

"Well, maybe if you got off your self-pitying ass, we might have a chance." Tim again glared at Greg.

"Don't have to. We're not the first." Greg pointed to the farthest wall from him, and Denise directed her frightened gaze that way.

"DBS93? What does it mean, Tim?" Denise sat rubbing her finger over the scratches in the wall.

"MAT-89, RIC+DEB77. And my favorite, SEX69. It means we ain't the first, baby. If they didn't get out, what makes you think we will?" Greg pointed at different marks on the wall as he spoke.

"Because maybe they all had your defeatist attitude. Think about it."

Morgan watched Tim as he spoke.

"Hey, keep your voice down," Sam muttered as he tried to sit up.

"If you're going to heave man, aim over here," Greg said as he quickly moved away from the water corner.

"I'm okay," Sam said, before his stomach disagreed and he began vomiting in the wrong direction.

"Oh, shit. Ain't we just a barrel of monkeys?" Greg snorted in disgust as Denise began to whine once more.

"Shut up Greg. He must have a concussion. He needs a doctor," Morgan said as she pulled Sam's hair back off of his face.

"Well, I'll tell you what. Why don't you just knock on the door and tell our Martian friends? I'm sure they'll just take care of everything for us." Greg turned away from the others in the room.

"I'm okay," Sam whispered as he wiped the last acidic drops from his lips.

"Tim, I want to go home." Denise was just staring about the room, her eyes wide as she spotted each successive scratched message.

"Is your watch working?" Morgan's quiet voice was barely heard over Denise's resumed crying.

"Yeah man. Is it teatime?" Greg began to laugh.

"It's six thirty. AM. Shit." Tim sat down as the information penetrated, and confirmed their situation.

"Fourteen hours, or thirty eight?" Morgan moved away from Denise and sat between Tim and Sam.

"Fourteen. Tentacles, huh?" Tim made eye contact with Greg, and they both smiled.

"Yeah man." Greg leaned over the mess Sam made, and he and Tim shook hands, once.

This time the darkness did not surprise Morgan.

\#

"Well, there are some benefits to waking up first," Greg said with an embarrassed laugh as he refastened his pants.

"Please move," was Morgan's response as she realized that she needed to follow Greg's example and relieve herself. The water once again spurted up and drained into the corner.

"I'll check on Sam." Greg turned away and made himself busy.

"How is he, man?" Tim sat up slowly.

"How the hell should I know? He doesn't look worse." Greg offered Tim a lopsided grin.

"Tim?" Denise whispered as she sat up.

"I can't take you home, kid," Tim said to the frightened girl.

"I know. It's just that I'm hungry, and I have to pee," she continued to whisper, even as tears welled up in her eyes and threatened to overwhelm her once more.

"Yeah. We're all hungry." Tim moved closer to her and put his hand on her shoulder.

"You can pee in the corner," Morgan offered.

"Oh. I…" Denise looked around at the small room, a blush spreading across her face.

"We won't look." Tim removed his hand from her shoulder and sat with his back to a wall.

"I know.., I don't know. I'll try." Denise stepped over Sam's body and stood in the water corner, looking about the room once more.

"Yeah, yeah. We get the hint." Tim laughed as he stood and reached for the hatch.

Greg snorted in disgust before standing to join him.

Morgan was forced to kneel in a corner, straddling Sam's feet to keep clear of them.

"I don't have to anymore," Denise said from the corner, much louder than she planned.

"Bull shit. Keep trying," Greg muttered, without turning toward her.

"Don't think about peeing. Think about relaxing, and just let go."

Denise met Morgan's eyes as the younger girl spoke.

"I don't think I can," Denise said, the tears once more beginning to form.

"If you don't do it now, you're going to wake up to pissing your panties," Tim said to the wall.

"Just relax, think about gravity. Pushing down through you. Or walking into the ocean. The water coming up your legs," Morgan said in what she thought was a soothing voice.

"Keep that up, and I'm going to beat her to the punch line," Tim said as he and Greg began to laugh. Their laughter covered up the sound of Denise's success.

It didn't disguise the sharp odor.

"How did you wipe?" Denise turned her gaze back to Morgan.

"Your scarf." Morgan pointed to the cloth lying on the floor, just clearing the water pool.

"Can we turn yet?" Greg asked impatiently.

"No! Not yet," Denise squealed, even as Tim turned and leered at her.

"Not nice man. Give the same courtesy you expect." Greg grinned at Tim.

"I don't need no fucking courtesy," Tim said as he stepped over Sam and offered a blushing and angry Denise his hand.

"Then you won't mind if I watch?" Denise asked in a bitter

dare.

"Hell. You can hold it if you want," Tim said with a wink to Greg as he reached inside his pants.

"Kneel down, or you'll splash everywhere," Greg said as he turned a smile to Morgan.

Tim followed Greg's gaze. "I was just trying for a freebie," Tim said with a weak laugh as he grinned at the irritated Denise, and pulled his empty hand away from his pants.

"I won't watch," Morgan said as she realized Tim's bravado.

"And I won't laugh," Denise said, and she moved to sit beside Sam; pulling his head onto her lap.

"He's not hot. That's good, right?" Denise asked the room, as much for reassurance as to ignore Tim.

"Yeah. I think so." Greg was once more sitting against the wall, and he motioned Morgan to join him.

"How's his pulse? Is it strong? Morgan asked as she sat down.

"Yeah. I think so. I had a concussion once, when I was ten. The hospital sent me home. My mom kept checking my eyes. She said I could sleep as long as they matched. I was in bed for two days," Denise whispered with an unfocused look.

"I'll be fine." Sam's eyes remained closed as he spoke.

"How long you been playing 'possum man?" Greg asked, a relieved laugh entering his voice.

"Since Denise was in the corner. I figured she would want the privacy." Sam looked up and smiled weakly at the blushing girl.

"Always the gentleman," Tim joked as he began to urinate.

"Believe it, man. Hurry up. I don't want to add to the stench, again." Sam moved to rise. Evidence of his concentration was etched into his face.

"Sure thing. It's all yours." Tim gave a sweeping bow toward the corner, and moved to turn away.

"Thanks, don't worry about kissing wall. I lost my modesty in The Corps." Sam shuffled forward on his knees until he was in the corner.

"That's what they all say." Greg started with a laugh.

"No, seriously. The easiest way to break a person is to make them piss their pants. The Marines teach you how to break yourself, and then rebuild you." Sam finished his job long before his speech, and was cupping water to drink and wash his face with.

"More of that military brainwashing crap," Tim said as he shook his head.

"It doesn't stink," Morgan interjected as Sam turn towards Tim.

"We just got used to it," Greg offered the room.

"No. She's right," Tim said.

"You guys figure it out. My head hurts too bad to think," Sam said as he moved away from the corner and sat.

"Well, one thing's for sure, they ain't coming in here when we're asleep and cleaning things up." Greg pulled his knees into his chest as he spoke.

"How do you know?" Morgan asked.

"True. Any other ideas…" Tim slumped forward as he spoke.

The last word stretching out into the darkness as Morgan made eye contact with Greg.

#

"Course corrections," Morgan said into the near silence of the small room. The only sound came from the drinking fountain that was now once again pouring from the ceiling, this time the waste drain was at the top of the wall.

"That would make sense," Tim said from where he stood in one corner, trying to shield Morgan from the spray of the fountain.

The water already covered their feet.

"When do you think they'll make another one?" Sam asked. He sat, leaning against the wall, in the driest corner. His unfocused eyes betrayed his lack of hope.

"It's been hours. What if they don't?" Denise looked in panic from Tim to Morgan.

"They will," Morgan answered.

"Says who?" Denise tried to keep the ever present panic from her voice.

"The Man has too much invested in his cargo to let it die." Greg gave a bitter laugh, before noticing the questioning look from the two girls.

"Don't worry about it," Tim said when Greg opened his mouth to continue talking.

Greg shrugged, and shifted away from the falling water and

closer to Denise.

"How long?" Sam asked into the renewed silence.

"Two and a half hours, this time. Four days, so far," Tim answered, and then glanced at his watch to check.

"I'm hungry," Denise whispered.

"Have a drink of water." Tim's comment brought bitter laughter from the other men and an elbow to his hip from Morgan.

"You're being mean to Denise again," Morgan said, not looking up at Tim.

"Sorry," Tim said to Morgan.

"And now to the next nasty subject," Greg said, and Morgan saw Sam slump.

She watched Greg wince as he realized his bad news would have to wait until after the new blackout faded.

#

"What was your bad news?" Morgan asked when she knew she was awake.

The fountain was still on the ceiling, but the drain was beneath it once more. Tim lay propped up in a still damp corner, and Morgan found herself sprawled across his legs. As uncomfortable as she was, she didn't move.

"Moot point. He alive?" Greg asked.

Morgan twisted about so that her head and shoulders remained on Tim's lap, and raised her hand to his face to check.

"Yeah. What was it though? Drowning?" she turned again as she spoke, and stared at Greg.

"It didn't happen. That was a rough one though. They'll be out for a while. You okay?" Greg finished checking pulses and straightening out the other two.

"Yeah. I'm just tired. Do you mind if I sleep?" Morgan closed her eyes as she spoke.

"Sure thing, sweetheart," Greg said as he smiled toward her.

She squinted and watched his gaze drift from her face to the crushed wilted bunch of lilacs he found in the drain.

"I think you want these." Greg leaned over the still unconscious Denise and offered Tim the flowers.

"Thanks man," Tim said as he wiped a hand across his face and then stared down at Morgan before reaching out. "She okay?"

"Just sleeping," Morgan heard Greg say. "How long's it been?" Greg moved back against the wall and Morgan didn't open her eyes as she heard Sam sit up with a groan.

"Eighteen hours. Nearly six days." Tim continued to stare at Morgan as he held the lilacs to his nose.

"I don't suppose somebody left a cheeseburger behind this time?" Sam asked, but Morgan heard no hope in his voice.

"De nada," Greg said as he watched Tim caress the flowers.

"Hey, put them in here, man." Sam took a small leather pouch from about his neck and handed it to Tim.

"I thought that was your grandfather's?" Greg asked.

"Naw. I grew up in Foster Care. I bought that to join the Corps with." Sam didn't blush as he denied an involved history he had woven.

"Thanks." Tim opened the pouch and poured its contents into the palm of his hand. Four kernels of corn: two red streaked ones and two bluish purple; a dried twig of sage that filled the room with its musty odor; and a small nugget of gold.

"Just dump it, man, it was all bullshit anyway," Sam said, and he didn't look at Tim.

"I'll keep it." Tim smiled at his friend as he poured the few items back into the pouch, and then broke most of the stem off to force the flowers in.

"Yeah, thanks. I am an Indian. At least that's what the note said. Choctaw. Six months old and almost dead from starvation. She must've had her reasons." Sam continued to stare at the floor as Tim and Greg exchanged looks before Greg reached a hand to Sam.

"Man, I was four years old when mine dumped me on the state," Greg said. "Two days after Christmas. The bitch didn't even let me bring my new truck."

"Why did you leave home?" Denise said, and Morgan looked up in time to see Tim meet Denise's gaze.

"For a really lame reason," Tim said and Morgan thought he sounded sad.

"This I gotta hear," Greg said as he offered Denise a place to sit beside him and Tim.

"It ain't worth worrying about. What do you think we should

carve into the wall?" Tim said much too loudly.

"Now I want to hear," Sam said, looking up from his feet.

"So my dad didn't like my music, okay?" Tim said with a sigh. "What do you want to carve in the wall?" he added in a rush that did not prevent the others from laughing.

"I left for you," Denise said as the laughter subsided.

The sound of the corner fountain filled the room, and no one spoke for a long time.

"What did Greg mean by cargo?" Denise asked; the loudness of her voice startled Morgan.

"Just that," Greg said more in answer to Tim's look of warning.

"I don't understand. You make it sound like we're a thing, or food." Denise sat forward, and her voice rose in panic.

"Denise baby, you ain't that slow. What color is my skin?" Greg shrugged off the angry look Tim was giving him, and spoke to Denise.

"Oh." Her small, pathetic word ended all conversation as each thought about the ramifications.

Morgan, still lying on Tim's lap, bit her lip to keep from crying.

"What are you carving?" Morgan asked finally as she tried to twist her body to see Tim's work, without leaving his lap.

"Watch the elbow," Tim said with a self-conscious laugh, and then placed his back against his finished project.

"I'm sorry," Morgan whispered as she quit trying to see behind Tim, and focused her attention on the room.

"Hey, does anyone else feel that?" Greg leaned away from the wall as he spoke.

"Yes," Morgan answered for the rest. The room was vibrating slightly, a hum building with the motion.

"How long has it been?" Sam placed his hand flat against the floor as the vibration built in intensity.

"Seven and a half days. The water's off." Tim pointed to the corner.

"We're here, aren't we? Tim?" Denise asked, her voice rising as panic set in.

"Yeah. Hey, we probably aren't going to be given much choice in things. Just..," and Tim's voice was cut off by the darkness.

Chapter Twenty-Two - Bystocc - 2012

Neavillii lay on the floor of a barren room. She stared at a dirty spot on the ceiling and tried to block out the distant screams that echoed. With a sigh, she tried once more to rise; falling back when her body exploded in pain. One of her arms ended in a bound stump at the elbow, and she feared a seeping injury in her spine.

The shot that had disabled her had also robbed her of her consciousness, and thus her ability to choose her moment of death. Now she lay, beaten, waiting for her captors to return. Her only satisfaction lay in the fact that Tadesde's retainers had not recognized her. She was being forced to die alone, but she wasn't being tortured.

Neavillii was startled out of her misery and depression when the door opened, and a tall, thin Sansheren strode into the room. She wore a single banner of order, and for a moment Neavillii thought she was hallucinating her first days on the planet when she recognized the young soldier as the leader who had escorted her and Morgan for the Arbitration.

"I was told it was the great Neavillii. Subservient spouse to an alien monster. Tell me, what is it like to bed something so bald?" the interrogator punctuated her sentences by kicking Neavillii in the side.

Neavillii felt her body driven along the floor until she was brought up against the wall.

"I contacted my Lady Tadesde the moment I heard your name whispered among our troops. It is a pity she will not be here in time for your death; it is a spectacle I intend to enjoy."

Neavillii felt bones cracking under the continued onslaught.

"But I will be here, and I find it no pity that you will not. Your

202

familiarity grows tiresome." Tadesde stood in the door of the room, pointing a weapon in their direction.

The interrogator froze at her leader's voice, and did not move until well after Tadesde's shot pierced the back of her head and exploded.

Neavillii stared up as the face disappeared in a flash and the body tumbled onto her.

"Remove this carrion, and tend my children." Tadesde moved to one side as her aides ran into the room and grabbed the dead body.

Neavillii noticed with a light-headed giggle that the body continued to bleed.

"Child, you're injured. Where is my personal doctor? She must have the best care. Hurry, hurry." Tadesde bent over Neavillii and wiped at the blood that now covered her face.

Neavillii cringed in horror when Tadesde, standing to make room for the medics, absent-mindedly brought her blood soaked fingers to her mouth.

"You're crazy," Neavillii whispered.

Tadesde did not seem to hear as she walked out of the room, laughing.

The medics did, and Neavillii could see agreement in their eyes.

"We have sent word to the Houses. You will be ransomed, my Lady." A young retainer bent over Neavillii after the medics left and whispered her encouragement.

"Who defected?" Neavillii asked the question she had not dared pose to the terrified medics who attended her injuries.

"Her first wife declared peerage. And her Gulardee of the Twelfth, she whom you just saw die, claimed the loyalty of her fleet and demanded marriage." A loud noise outside the room brought the terrified retainer's gaze to the wall, and a long moment passed before she relaxed enough to look back at Neavillii.

"Tadesde will leave for the Western Continent. You must have faith and patience. This ordeal will be over one day and you will tell your children of it." The retainer gave Neavillii a brief pat to her uninjured hand.

"My children are in a nursery on the Western Continent," Neavillii said without looking at her sympathizer.

"They have not been found, my Lady. There is yet hope."
Another pat and the retainer stood and slipped from the room.

#

"What do you want?" Tadesde lay reclined on a platform in
what was the Administration building's cafeteria. It was the same
room Neavillii had granted her first audiences in.

An aide cowered halfway across the room, not daring to come
closer. "Most beautiful of patrons. If it pleases you, we have
your meal prepared." The aide did not step closer as she spoke,
but instead, shoved a young apprentice forward.

Tadesde jumped up and crossed the room, startling all present.
"This swill is overcooked," she shouted, flinging a chunk of meat
in the apprentice's face.

The cook's apprentice nodded her head in agreement and ran
from the room, not daring to wipe away the clotted blood that
dripped where the meat hit her.

"Is there anything else?" Tadesde paced in a circle as she
waited for the aide to gather her courage.

"It has come to our attention that someone is broadcasting off
planet. It is possible that Morganea has–" the aide darted out of
Tadesde's way as she rushed to the door of the room.

"Where is Ferseca? I must speak with my wife. Where is
she?" Tadesde traveled down the hallway shouting in growing
panic.

"I am here, my love. Come, we will speak in private." Ferseca
was older than anyone else still in Tadesde's camp.

"There is a traitor. Morganea has been warned. What will we
do?" Tadesde collapsed at Ferseca's feet as her older spouse sat
in a chair.

"We are safe, my love. I know Morganea has been warned.
We've been trying to find the traitor for a week now." Ferseca
stroked Tadesde's hair, noticing not for the first time the streaks
of green that were becoming dominant.

"But if Morganea knows, she will pledge a debt of honor
against me. She will hunt us." Tadesde clutched at her spouse's
knees, not caring of the blood she was drawing.

"Hush, love. Morganea does not know we anticipate her

arrival. We will set a trap. An ambush. All will be well, my love." Ferseca, too, ignored the blood that dripped from her knees. She lifted Tadesde's head and saw reason creep back into her bloodshot eyes.

#

"The meat goes rancid, my Lady." Nogina stood in the doorway of the nursery viewing rooms where Numane's death children prowled behind the glass.

"I know, and yet we dare not use the generator. That would be too great an invitation. So, tell me my friend. Whom do we abandon?" Aldera held her hand up to her exhausted aide and pulled the other onto her lounge.

"Of the older children, only seven have achieved the point of reasoning. It would be a place to start." Nogina leaned back against the headrest as she spoke.

"There is a priority list in my office, we will use the last of the meat and then wait. We will offer to clear the escape passage to any who would leave." Aldera shifted her position until she was reclined on the lounge, her head resting on Nogina's lap. The children behind the glass continued their restless prowl as she lay silently.

"My Lady, we…" The young aide was cut off by Nogina's raised hand. Walking further into the room, she saw Aldera reclined with eyes closed against the candlelight.

"The sound of digging can be heard at the main tunnel. The staff is afraid," the young aide admitted.

"Gather everyone in the lunchroom. We will be there soon," Nogina said while shifting Aldera's head forward on her knees.

"It seems your list will never be read my Lady. Someone is digging us out. Your staff awaits you in the lunchroom," Nogina said to Aldera.

"Strange. Regardless of who is coming, I am relieved." Aldera walked to the glass and reached out before turning sharply and leaving the room.

Nogina rushed to catch up.

"Power up the generators. We will want light. If it is Tadesde's forces, I would suggest we open the nurseries. Any comments?" Aldera asked with the same fatal calmness she had felt through the entire crisis.

"If it is not Tadesde and we power up?" The question hung in the air.

"If it is not Tadesde, we leave. The meat is gone; our air will run dry soon. We do no one honor in a lingering death." Aldera nodded to Nogina, who entered the room just as the lights flooded back on. The candles that lit the room flickered as everyone struggled to adapt to the light.

"My friend, bring the seven you spoke of to the first bend in the tunnel. Everyone else, gather your personal journals and join them." Aldera moved to the door.

"What about you, my love?" Nogina silenced the room with her question.

"I will be in my office, setting the main overrides to open the nurseries when the primary seals are blown. As you said, the generator will draw Tadesde's people." Aldera left the stunned room and ran down the corridor. In her office, she set the codes and retrieved a parcel of emergency explosives. She paused to smile at a small toy that Amigo had made for her.

Aldera stood in the doorway of her children's viewing room when she heard two explosions coming from different parts of the complex. She slammed the door closed even as she saw the glass drop. Running down the corridor, she heard shouting behind her but never paused to look back. The escape tunnel lay before her when she skidded to a stop. The noises behind her turned to screams, and she allowed herself a grim smile as she set the explosive she had brought from her office. A blur of green caught her eye as she pressed the detonator.

#

"And how are you today, my beautiful friend?" Tadesde entered Neavillii's room, not bothering to hold the door for her aides, who were forced to reopen the heavy door.

"Better than you, I see." Neavillii grinned at Tadesde in reference to her captor's green fur.

"Such insolence. And from one I have treated as my very own. Have you no gratitude for the one who saved your life?" Tadesde crossed the room and reached her hand for Neavillii's face

Neavillii pulled back, in obvious disdain.

Tadesde curled her claws into her palm and struck Neavillii across the face, hard. "May I assume that you will not even consider the honor I would bestow you?" Tadesde fingered Neavillii's bonds.

"There is no honor you could offer me, except it be the viewing of your death." Neavillii finished speaking and spat the blood that filled her mouth at Tadesde.

"I had intended to accept a marriage proposal from you. But I see now that you're far beneath my notice." Tadesde struck her several times as she spoke.

"It gladdens me to be beneath your notice. It frees me from speaking to you." Neavillii forced a laugh as another blow struck her. She felt a throbbing in her back.

"You will tell me when Morganea will return!" Tadesde screamed as she knelt in front of Neavillii.

Neavillii closed her eyes and held her tight smile.

"You cannot deny me!" Tadesde jumped to her feet and glared down at the defiant Neavillii.

"Tell me, when will your whore return!" Tadesde punctuated her demand with a sharp blow to Neavillii's already bleeding face.

Silence was Neavillii's response, and it grew as Tadesde paced within the confines of the small room.

Her two aides were forced to dodge to avoid her. "She has abandoned you and this rock, has she not?"

The growing panic in Tadesde's voice gave Neavillii hope as her tormentor walked toward the door of the cell. And fear of dying alone gave her courage.

"You are the one who has been abandoned. I heard you are without family now. You have my sincere condolences." Neavillii bared her teeth in a grimace as she spoke.

Tadesde froze before the open door as Neavillii spoke, and continued to stand even as the silence became awkward. The two retainers began to fidget.

"Your people are afraid you will destroy them with your dishonor."

As Neavillii spoke, Tadesde strode toward her. Neavillii was still smiling in defiance when the mad leader struck her. The impact of the blow threw her across the room, still shackled in her chair.

The two retainers were silent as one moved to check Neavillii's condition.

"She dies. Call for the maternity team." Ferseca growled to the room as she placed a hand on Neavillii's stomach and the maternal nest it contained.

"Who would tell her of my temporary troubles? Who would disgrace me so?" Tadesde muttered under her breath as she walked toward the still form of Neavillii.

"She dies, my Lady. We must have a maternity team in here to revive her." Ferseca met Tadesde's eyes and saw a moment of recognition.

"No one loyal to you, my lady, would have dreamed of telling this creature of your dishonor. I assure you," Kihani said from the door. And Ferseca turned to stare at her choice of words.

"You are right, no one loyal to My Lady," Ferseca said with deliberate inflection, and Tadesde turned her unfocused gaze to the young retainer still standing beside the door.

"What do you mean, she is dying?" Tadesde demanded. "Now Morganea has a debt of blood, a debt of family, and a debt of honor against me. So it is to be war. I knew as much when I first saw her. Come, we must prepare." Tadesde continued to speak without emotion as she moved to the door.

"It could be prevented. The maternity team might still revive her, my Lady. You would be responsible for her children. Morganea would be your kin." Ferseca stood and moved to follow Tadesde, who continued to speak to herself.

"What? No, this will serve my purpose better." Tadesde waved Ferseca through the doorway as she smiled in the dying Neavillii's direction.

And closed the door in Kihani's face.

"My Lady!" Kihani cried out, and Tadesde's laugh could be heard through the door.

"I always feared dying alone, but somehow this is worse. I am sorry, my friend," Neavillii whispered to the sobbing retainer who had comforted her before.

"Is it soon?" the young retainer asked, and smeared tears across her face before she moved to release Neavillii's bonds.

"Yes. Do not unfasten me. I think it is the only thing holding the bones together. Have you any children?" Neavillii could not see the one she whispered to, the darkness behind her eyes was too intense.

"I have not yet reached the age of fertility. There will be no one to wear my face. You are wrong though, this is better than dying alone." Kihani lay down and placed her arm over the trapped Neavillii's shoulder.

"Thank you. The moment comes; sweeter than the hands of the lover is your embrace. I only wish there was someone to record your honor." Neavillii relaxed into Kihani's arms.

"Perhaps when your wife returns," Kihani said as she unfastened the straps and allowed Neavillii to fall into her arms.

"Indeed," Neavillii whispered as she felt the pressure build. The blackness was joined by a rushing sound that obscured any final words Kihani might have said.

Chapter Twenty-Three - Sheresuan - 2012

"My daughter! And how was your search for family?" Neadesto asked as Morgan strode into the small audience chamber unannounced.

"Successful. They remain on Wergol. Tell me, when will the council meet?" Morgan bowed when she completed the distance between herself and the raised lounge Neadesto shared with Iedonea. The few retainers present were old friends and confidants and only those trusted to watch Neadesto sleep knew the location of the private hall.

"It will not. Council has rejected Tadesde's claim. She did not even present it in person. One might think she herself did not feel it had merit," Iedonea replied, and held her hand out to Morgan in an invitation to sit.

Morgan continued standing without acknowledging the gesture.

"Tell me the joy of meeting your family once more." Neadesto interrupted Morgan before she had a chance to respond to Iedonea's information.

"There was little joy to recount. Tadesde killed the wife of the one I searched for. He holds all Sansheren at fault for Tadesde's unfortunate birth. And I'm forced to wonder how many other species judge us poorly because of this one indulgence." Morgan clenched her fists in frustration.

"Indeed. It is a shame then that no House has the courage to stand against her," Iedonea said, her hand upon Neadesto's leg when the older woman would have spoken.

"I agree, my aunt. Tell me, what has the House discerned about Tadesde's strength?" Morgan moved closer and lowered her voice.

"My House has always honored its pledge of neutrality. If your newly formed House would be so kind as to put in its intelligence request formally, I am certain they will be answered with all due haste," Neadesto said a disapproving frown hard upon her face.

Iedonea echoed the frown as she turned sideways to see her father and wife.

"That is not necessary, I have decided. I, Morganea, hereby pledge before witnesses, my House, my resources, and my life to the destruction of the person of Tadesde. She has committed acts against my family and my blood. I do not hold her House, nor her retainers responsible, save those that actively resist me." As Morgan paused to draw a breath, she thought again of her resolve to infiltrate Tadesde's home planet and assassinate the insane leader.

"And I will pledge myself, and any who would follow me, to your glorious banner. Not since the days of Mesine has there been so noble a cause." Iedonea stood and knelt in front of the stunned Morgan who looked from Iedonea's serious expression to Neadesto's bemused look before moving forward to offer her hands to Iedonea.

"My aunt, I have no words for the honor you do me," Morgan said, and also knelt.

"That was eloquent enough, I think. Do you not, my love?" Neadesto chuckled as she spoke.

"Very eloquent. Come, there are arrangements to be made. I must poll my people. Any who wish to stay with the most loved Neadesto will be allowed to." It was Iedonea who helped Morgan to stand.

"You rush; I would be allowed the opportunity to contribute to this honorable event." Neadesto stood and faced Morgan as she chastised Iedonea with a smile.

"I would not dream of infringing on your neutrality, my parent," Morgan began, to be silenced by Neadesto reaching fingers up to her lips. The claw tips were still razor sharp, she noted, and it seemed to heighten her sense of surrealism.

"It would be my honor to bear your children, my beautiful apprentice." Neadesto began to kneel only to be forced to move out of the way of the fainting Morgan.

"I had heard her species did that. A reflex to play dead when things become too overwhelming. Well, where is her doctor?" Iedonea moved to stand above Morgan.

"Overwhelming, you say. I suppose one might consider that a compliment." Neadesto looked from where she knelt beside Morgan and exchanged a smile with Iedonea.

"Indeed, one might."

Chapter Twenty-Four - Earth – 1995

"Class, we have a new student today." The teacher placed her hand on Lui Moih-Gan's shoulder and turned her toward the room full of curious children.

"What's your name?" one of the children shouted. The room grew silent waiting for the answer.

The teacher removed her hand from Lui Moih-Gan's shoulder and studied the enrollment paperwork, again.

"Does she speak English?" another child asked from beside Lui Moih-Gan.

"Moegan," Lui Moih-Gan whispered as the teacher continued to stare at the papers and her hand.

"Morgan is a nice name, yes ShaTilla, she does speak some English. Now why don't you show her the art project we're working on while I go talk to Mrs. Everston about music." The teacher smiled down at both girls, once, and then turned away.

"My name's ShaTilla, that has a double L, not a Y or anything. What's your name? Mrs. Jameson couldn't say it, could she? She couldn't say my name when school started. She said the l's." The girl beside Morgan was taller, even sitting down.

Morgan kept her eyes on the table, seeing only the other's dark hands.

"You do speak English, don't you?" ShaTilla asked after a small silence passed.

"Yes." Morgan didn't whisper, she just didn't try very hard to be heard.

"Scared, aren't ya? Nobody will hit you here. I promise." ShaTilla leaned closer and put her arm around Morgan protectively.

Morgan held very still and waited for the other girl to move away. Her shoulders ached from the pressure on her bruises.

"My dad hits me, too." An older boy, sitting across from Morgan and ShaTilla, said in a hushed voice, and Morgan looked into his eyes to see the pain she was feeling. "If you tell the teacher, the state will move you to a Foster home for a while. Sometimes that's better."

"I can't, they'll send me back to Taiwan," Morgan said before dropping her eyes again.

"Unjust," the boy said, and then return to the picture he was drawing on his notebook.

"You can come over to my place anytime you want. I live with my mom and her stupid, new boyfriend. He's real dumb, but he don't hit or anything." ShaTilla dropped her arm from Morgan's shoulders and picked up a colored pen.

"I live with my brother," Morgan said.

"I used to visit my dad a lot, but now he lives with some old home boys and he don't want me around them," ShaTilla said. The older girl reached to the center of the table and chose a picture for Morgan to color.

"He is ashamed of them?" Morgan asked, accepting a blue pen from her new friend.

"Afraid's more like it. He wouldn't be hanging there if mom hadn't told the state on him." ShaTilla traded pens as she spoke.

"Told the state?" Morgan retrieved the green pen the other discarded.

"Child support, you know, it takes all his money. Hey, wanna meet him? My dad? He's gonna take me to the park after school. You could come." ShaTilla paused in her coloring and Morgan looked up in time to see her smile.

"I would be honored," Morgan said with her own hesitant smile.

Through the morning, her thoughts turned back to the father being forced to live with bad people because he couldn't afford anything else, and a determination not to spend another night in her brother's house. By lunchtime, she was ready to mention her plan to her new friends.

"Rent costs lots of money," JC, the boy from across the table, said a third time.

"I have some money," Morgan answered again.

"How much?" JC challenged with a look in his eyes that sent a shiver through Morgan.

"Nothing right now," Morgan lied, remembering the flight hostess and her fear of showing money.

"Oh," JC said, and Morgan saw his disappointment. "Well, rent costs money, as you'll have to get some." That said, the older boy stood, and walked away from their table.

"I do have enough money, I think," Morgan whispered to ShaTilla.

"I don't know. There are laws and stuff. He probably won't agree." ShaTilla picked up her lunch tray and stood waiting for Morgan to join her.

"I won't go back there," Morgan said in a voice drained of emotion before standing and picking up her own, still full, tray. The rest of the day passed slowly.

#

"You're dreaming child." ShaTilla's father was a tall black man who wore his hat backwards and smelled of greasy food.

"I have nine hundred dollars a month," Morgan said, and waited for him to meet her eyes.

His face was slow in turning, and she was afraid she would see JC's expression. The look he gave her was so filled with pity and sadness it forced her eyes down.

"You want to tell me what he did to you?" he asked finally.

"No. I want to share an apartment with you." Morgan kept her eyes on ShaTilla, sitting at the next bench over.

"Okay, let's go get your stuff." He offered Morgan his hand.

"There's nothing I want from there," Morgan said and stood without help.

"Fine by me, never did like a confrontation. You sure he's not gonna call the cops?" they walked together toward ShaTilla.

"I'll call him. He won't say anything." Morgan smiled bitterly at her new friend.

"My name's Greg kid. Looks like you got yourself a deal." Greg held out his hand again.

Chapter Twenty-Five - Sheresuan – 2012

"Thank you." Morgan felt the dream fade as she opened her eyes.

"Shh, sleep child. My wife Iedonea will take care of everything." Neadesto lay beside Morgan in her own large bed.

"But, your House? Your neutrality?" Morgan struggled to sit, and settled for leaning on one elbow and facing Neadesto.

"Your House's neutrality, my love. I have joined to your banner. And as to my neutrality, your courage would have made it appear as cowardice, and rightly so. No, this is for the best." Neadesto patted her shoulder before lying flat on the bed.

"I have no desire to be called Ouosin. Besides, who would follow me?" Morgan stared down at Neadesto's frail form.

"You would be surprised. It was not I who fell stricken before the ceremony could be completed. Here, I would have given it to Iedonea, but many times she has refused to allow me to retire." Neadesto twisted to reach the edge of the bed, and the banner that lay folded on a table beside it. Turning back she showed the banner to Morgan. It was old, though well cared for, and Morgan recognized it from her history studies.

"I have no right to this, my Lady. A Sansheren should wear such a thing." Morgan felt tears swell up and wiped at them as she refused to accept the ancient banner. It was thought to be the banner worn by the first Sansheren to unify the first House. The first Sansheren of the Twelfth rank of the Sansadee, the ruling class.

"It is by every right you should wear this banner. We have always held that anyone could rise to the top, and you, an alien to our culture, have proven that. Take it, now." Neadesto pressed the banner against Morgan's chest and the young leader fell backwards until this time she lay flat on the bed, her head unsupported.

It was Neadesto who placed the call to the resuscitation team, and Morgan watched her put away the communication unit without realizing the implications of the act.

Morgan continued to stare at Neadesto even when her adopted parent closed her eyes and settled herself on the bed, awaiting death at Morgan's hand. Life would come with the resuscitation team.

#

"My Lady, the beautiful Iedonea wishes a moment of your time. When it is most convenient for you." An elderly aide bowed low at Morgan's feet.

"Tell her I will come immediately." Morgan turned away from the departing aide and spoke to the medic beside her. "Notify me the moment she awakens." Morgan straightened the covers about the sleeping Neadesto.

"I will, your Ladyship. With the exhausting production of four, it will doubtlessly be some time." The medic kept her head bowed as she spoke.

"I have been honored," Morgan whispered before turning to leave the room. The consummation of her marriage to Neadesto was completed, and now Morgan brought her thoughts back to Tadesde with a frown as she walked down the corridor. Her plans to infiltrate Tadesde's House as a mercenary were destroyed when Iedonea joined her House. The word of such a highly placed defection would spread to the other Houses as fast as ships could get clearance to depart. And with her marriage to Neadesto and the stewardship over House Sheresuan's neutrality, she was forced to consider calling out a personal challenge which she knew would be suicide; her human reflexes were no match to the average Sansheren, and Tadesde was young and crazy. Which left the ruse of war and forcing a space battle that would allow for a suicide attack of her ship against Tadesde's.

"They treat you like a god, you know," Isaac said as he hurried to keep pace with her.

"There is no Sansheren word for god. No religion at all. The highest entity is the most loved Sansheren," Morgan said disjointedly, her thoughts still on Tadesde's destruction.

"Close enough," Isaac said with a self-conscious laugh.

"I remember a story about a king who went naked in a parade, do you know it?" Morgan came to an abrupt halt as she waited for Isaac's response.

"The emperor has no clothes. A pessimistic thought, don't you think?" Isaac kept walking as he talked, not noticing Morgan's pause.

Morgan shrugged in answer to his question and then jogged to catch up. They approached Iedonea's offices together.

"I would have been happy to join you in the audience room, my Lady." Iedonea chided as she stepped out of her office and gestured to the rear entrance of the audience chamber.

Morgan followed her without speaking.

"The most revered Sansadee of the Twelfth and highest rank, Morganea."

Morgan repressed a jump of surprise when a young apprentice called out to the room. As she moved to Neadesto's lounge, she clenched her fists together and forced her face still. The room was packed with high level members of Neadesto's House. All bowing to her.

"Sit, please, my friends." Morgan paused as the crowd jostled about and everyone made themselves comfortable. With a frown, she offered her hand to Iedonea who knelt at her feet. Isaac and Nealoie knelt with her. Iedonea shook her head "no" with a smile and then a quick bow.

"It pleases me greatly to announce the honor our beloved Neadesto has granted this House. Even now she recuperates from the growth of four healthy children." Morgan did not raise her voice as she spoke, trusting that the acoustics designed into the room would carry her message. It also amplified the collective gasp, and then murmurs of approval, from the gathered delegates.

"Such an honor has rarely been recorded, my Lady. It also pleases me to announce that the declaration of war by both the House Sheresuan and the House America against Tadesde has been sent to the council of Houses. We await only intelligence reports of Tadesde's whereabouts to launch our offensive." Iedonea grinned to the cheering crowd, missing Morgan's brief look of confusion and panic.

"We must plan carefully, I will not risk this House in a private battle," Morgan tried to continue, but shouts of support soon made any speech impossible. Finally, she bowed in respect to her followers, a gesture that raised the cheers to a deafening level, and left.

"Your banner is unprecedented, though I suspect a few will leave after Tadesde is destroyed," Iedonea said as she, Isaac, and Nealoie followed Morgan into the corridor.

"I am a convenience to them, a means to destroy one whose existence has been an insult for too long," Morgan said in an offhand manner.

"You underestimate yourself, as usual, my niece. I said a few, only a few." Iedonea walked beside Morgan. Isaac and Nealoie followed close behind.

"Tadesde was born within the dead body of Dejymo's favorite wife. She should never have left the nursery. She has barely reached the age of fertility; Dejymo indulged herself by giving this favored child the name of the Twelfth rank. They follow me to destroy one who has become the monster she was born to be. And for no other reason." Morgan gave Iedonea a silencing look.

It didn't work.

"That Tadesde's Ouosin, all will agree. But it is you who have decided to destroy her, and it is you whom they follow." And Iedonea held Morgan's gaze for a moment before gesturing to Nealoie and taking a different corridor.

#

"This is the Sansheren ship Montana out of Bystocc, requesting an emergency orbit. We have a nursery situation in our primary airlock. Repeat, we have a nursery situation in our primary airlock and are requesting an emergency orbit," Enrico broadcast from where he sat strapped in next to the ship's captain.

Several fighter craft, dispatched from the orbiting station, continued to close with them. Still groggy from the shift, he tried his broadcast once more.

"This is the Sansheren ship Montana out of Bystocc, carrying a human crew and family to Morganea. We have a maternity situation in our primary airlock and request an emergency orbit."

He released the microphone and watched as the fighters narrowed the distance.

"This is escort craft Delta. Please repeat your..."

Enrico exchanged puzzled looks with the captain before thumbing his mike. "Say again? My grasp of your beautiful language is deficient and this moment hinders me even further." Enrico used his most stilted court accent.

The five small ships moved beside them, but did not seem to mind the captain's efforts to maneuver into an orbit approaching the space station.

"Obviously not enough, Montana. I asked by what right you claim kinship to the most beautiful and loved Morganea."

The captain continued trimming the ship's trajectory as Enrico answered. "I am named Enrico, adopted by Morganea on the fallen planet Bystocc," Enrico enunciated the Sansheren into the mic.

"They might not have heard it, boy. This is just about the fastest ship around. No brag intended," the captain finished with a grin as the station's computer signaled its desire to take control of the vehicle. The captain flipped covers onto several panels and leaned back in his seat, eyes still glued to his instruments.

"The Registrar confirms your lineage. What is the nature of your nursery situation? Do you require a resuscitation team?" a new voice asked.

The Delta pilot flared her engines, and soared out of Enrico's line of sight as their ship slid into the bowels of the station.

"Negative. The lovely Yolunu suffered a bone injury when Tadesde forces attacked this vessel unprovoked. Her children have been confined to our primary airlock the many days it has taken us to travel to this wonderful sanctuary of yours." Enrico felt the ship vibrate as it grated to a stop against a station airlock.

"Your compliments bring a blush to my unworthy face; a nursery team will clear your airlock. Please be ready to exit, I will await you there."

Enrico could hear several voices laughing in the background as the other finished speaking.

"What did you say to him?" The captain asked as they unbuckled and moved to join the rest of the survivors gathered in the hall.

"I don't know. I think she interpreted it as flirting." Enrico grinned before moving to get a position in front of the airlock hatch.

"Looks like they're gassing the little buggers." The captain pressed his face against the small window, trying to see through the dried blood splatters.

"They're cycling the hatch. Okay folks, the boy and I'll go first. I'll try and get supplies delivered; other than that, just hold your cool." The captain finished his address and opened the hatch.

Only the blood stains remained to show Enrico where his friend had been, and the infants had scraped and chewed clean those stains they could reach.

"I am station administrator Dafersi. It is an honor to meet one who is of our most beloved Morganea's species." The Ninth rank Sansadee bowed to the confused humans.

"I am Enrico; you grant me a false honor, my Lady." Enrico shifted his cane forward and moved to kneel. The captain, whom he had already instructed on Sansheren etiquette, was bowing his head over one knee.

"You are as humble as the beautiful Morganea. It is by right, if not by rank, that I grant you the respect that is due." The administrator dropped to both knees in an attempt to keep her head lower than Enrico's.

Enrico paused in his descent and then stood and offered his free hand to the prostrate stationer.

"I disagree, but we will research my right another time. Stand." He held his hand out until the other accepted it, and then nodded to the confused captain to stand.

"I would introduce the captain of the fast Montana," and he realized he had never heard the man's name.

"Frank Griffin, at your service," the captain filled in when Enrico looked at him.

"And I would introduce my foster child, the brilliant Amigo." Enrico turned to the airlock and Amigo poked her head out of the hatch, to be greeted by the gasp of the administrator.

"She no longer hunts, my Lady. There is no danger," Enrico rushed to assure the stationer who was backing away.

"It is my pleasure to meet one so wise and beautiful as yourself. I am humbled by your presence." Amigo stepped out of the airlock and kneeled on the floor.

"How old is she?" the frightened stationer stopped moving backwards but made no effort to regain the distance.

"Past four. She is safe, I assure you." Enrico placed his hand on top of Amigo's head as the captain looked from him to the Sansheren.

"The kid can stay on board with me if there's a problem," he offered in English.

"No problem," Enrico said as he decided to test just how far being Morgan's adoptee would get him.

"I require transportation to the planet. I must address the beautiful Neadesto immediately," Enrico demanded with far more confidence than he felt.

"I will see to the arrangements myself, most handsome of patrons." With deep bow, the stationer fled the room.

Enrico could see others gathered at the entrance to the chamber, but no one entered for quite some time.

It was the Delta pilot who finally shouldered her way into the large room. "The station administrator Dafsersi has conveyed your reassurances as to the safety of the child. Come, my ship is the fastest." The pilot showed no fear of Amigo.

"There are survivors on board. We have not had food for several days," Enrico waved toward the airlock even as several of the station crew edged into the room.

Their eyes on Amigo, they appeared too frightened to continue.

"Then we should be going. Those old grandmothers will not come any closer until we space." The pilot bared her teeth in the direction of the stationers and was rewarded by their cringes.

"Go on boy, I've dealt with station crews before. They think all us pilot types are insane. Who knows, they might be right." The captain waved Enrico toward the departing Delta pilot with his own tight-lipped grin.

\#

"They have doubled their size in less than a day," Isaac said in Sansheren. "Tell me, do you know why large litters are so uncommon?" Isaac perched on the edge of his lounge watching Neadesto's children eat.

Morgan sat across from him eating fruit, and shrugged before responding. "I never asked. A Sansheren will have a maximum of six children in her life. Perhaps it has to do with my lovely wife's age," Morgan answered casually, and he thought she was more interested in her food than the conversation.

"And how was the beautiful mother?" At Isaac's question, Morgan snorted and almost choked on a bite.

"I would advise you not use that particular compliment again. Your accent is not clear enough. Another might feel obliged to declare a blood feud against your face." Morgan laughed outright at the look of consternation that crossed his face.

"I apologize. I just wanted to know how Neadesto.., How the lovely Neadesto is doing?" Isaac rushed to reassure her of his intentions.

"I know. Sansheren is a language of inflection. Why don't we switch to English?" Morgan followed her own suggestion when speaking the last sentence.

"Tansea has been coaching me, but I doubt I'll ever fully understand the language. It's culturally dependent, I think," Isaac said, and leaned back in his seat.

The children, having finished eating, curled up to sleep.

"You're probably right. My wife Neadesto is recuperating well, and should be up and about by tonight at the latest," Morgan said.

Isaac found himself thinking about how strange it felt to hear Morgan say "my wife" in English.

"I am happy to hear it. Nealoie said Iedonea would travel with us?" Isaac asked, to keep her talking. From the moment he walked into the nursery viewing room, Isaac felt that Morgan wanted to be alone. He kept talking with her because he was concerned the depression that had enveloped her on Wergol was deepening. He tried to speak with Iedonea about it, only to be put off by the busy woman. And he wondered if Sansheren chemistry allowed for depression.

"It is her wish. It would shame her were I to deny her this." Morgan reached for a new piece of fruit and bit into it without looking to identify it.

"Nealoie said that anyone who wanted could fight for you? What's to keep a bunch of freeloaders from camping on your doorstep?" Isaac watched with interest as Morgan grimaced at the flavor of the fruit and then took a second bite.

"Nealoie talks too much. Everyone works, it's another cultural thing," Morgan answered with more than a touch of impatience.

"What of the humans you declared family on Bystocc, or Wergol. Will they be required to work?" Isaac asked, trying to bring the conversation closer to the subject Morgan was ignoring.

"I declared them personal family, they don't have to work. Hopefully, after they understand the honor of their situation, they'll volunteer. Regardless, they will all receive a stipend for the rest of their lives. It is their children who will have to work." Morgan's voice was empty and emotionless.

"And if they don't? I'd never heard a Sansheren word for disowned." Isaac continued to watch Morgan without her noticing.

"Hungry or dead, take your pick," Morgan said, placed the seed from the fruit she was eating down on the table, and sat back on her lounge.

"Oh. I noticed you quit taking the hormones I synthesized." Isaac winced as his statement came out far more blunt than he planned.

"Yes," was Morgan's harsh reply as she adjusted her banners without looking in his direction.

"I know things didn't go the way you planned on Wergol. Sometimes these things take time," Isaac said.

"I had no idea how things were. I had no right to plan for another's behavior or thoughts. It was childish of me," Morgan snapped, and then closed her eyes.

"Maybe if you gave the therapy another chance, you could grow accustomed to it," Isaac said.

#

"I don't want to grow accustomed to it. I want to be myself, and if someone won't accept me, that's their problem," Morgan said, after a long pause. She was thinking about the intense ache, the tears, and the longing she didn't want to give a name to.

"Give it time, and he'll get used to you just the way you are," Isaac offered.

Morgan sat forward with a glare so intense that Isaac broke

224

eye contact first. "Just how would he know 'the way' I am?" Morgan continued to stare at the uncomfortable doctor.

"I meant you, as in 'Morganea,' that's all." He shifted his position and tried to fake a smile.

Morgan refused to release him from her glare.

"You meant something else. What did you tell him?" She was pressing her hands against her legs, she realized, when Isaac tried to find any place to look besides her face. The sense of betrayal she felt creep over her was too painful for him to look at, it seemed, and for a perverse moment she hoped he felt guilty.

"I don't remember exactly. He called you screwed up. I just tried to explain to him all that you had been through. I thought it would help him to understand you better," he finished, and Morgan felt all emotion evaporate.

"Sansheren doctors respect their patients' confidentiality. I see that is still another cultural thing we do not share. You may leave my person now." Morgan slipped into Sansheren with a stilted court accent without being aware of the language shift.

"I… I am sorry," Isaac said moments later before he stood and walked to the door.

Morgan waited until after the door clicked shut to allow the tears to overwhelm her.

Neadesto found her there, still crying, hours later.

"Child, I would listen," Neadesto sat beside Morgan and allowed the young leader to lean into her chest.

"I have been betrayed. Tim had no emotions for me save guilt and pity." Morgan did not try to stifle the tears that flooded up once more.

"Hush now, we will speak of it another time." Neadesto continued to hold Morgan as she stroked her hair and shoulders.

"Isaac told Tim everything. I was foolish to dream he would want me." Morgan fought for composure and lost. It was several minutes before she could speak again.

Neadesto waited. "He is a fool if he does not. Time robs us of familiarity, it makes us strangers to our sisters. You must allow the same time to bring you back together." Neadesto held Morgan's chin, and forced her crying child to meet her eye.

"I love you," Morgan whispered in response.

"Ladies, I bring news of…" the retainer's news was interrupted by a glimpse of the tableau before her.

"If it is truly a crisis, we will be there soon." Neadesto did not look from Morgan as she spoke.

"A human from Bystocc brings news of disaster, my ladies. I will direct her to the House audience chamber," the aide said in a subdued voice as she backed out through the doorway.

"Very well," Morgan said to the closing door.

"I will have the lovely Nealoie bring you a basin and cloth. Enhance your beauty before leaving here; it does no good for a leader to be seen in distress. I will tend to this messenger until you arrive." Neadesto patted Morgan's shoulder and left, leaning over on her cane as she walked.

Morgan fought the tears as she waited for Nealoie. Slowly, she won the battle.

#

"It shames me greatly to kneel before one as beautiful as your lovely person and report the fall of the planet Bystocc." Enrico used his cane to kneel awkwardly and address Neadesto.

"The shame is not yours to bear, handsome stranger." Neadesto gestured for Enrico to stand, but with his head bowed, he did not see.

"I would introduce Enrico, adopted by Morganea, apprenticed to Neavillii, and his brilliant foster child Amigo," the Delta pilot announced from where she knelt beside Enrico.

"In truth? Come, sit with me. We are equals, you and I." Neadesto glanced at Amigo before gesturing once more to the stunned Enrico.

"You jest at my humble expense. I bear dire news, Morganea's planet is lost. He must be contacted at once." Enrico looked up from his bow for a moment to make eye contact with Neadesto, and then returned to the subservient position. From the corner of his eye he could see Amigo as she twisted repeatedly where she sat, in a vain attempt to see everything in the room at once. Hundreds of retainers sat watching the raised dais, though none very close to the child.

"I have been contacted," Morgan said from the doorway behind the platform, and Enrico looked up to stare. She wore none of the orange makeup he remembered, and her face was softer, more feminine than he remembered. Her chest was crossed by seven different banners, each one more impressive than the last, her small breasts gave form and accent to his realization that she was a woman.   "My wife bid you sit with her. Would you insult her so by refusing?" Morgan asked as she walked up behind Neadesto.

Enrico took a deep breath as he watched Morgan place her hand on the old Sansheren leader's shoulder, before moving to claim the more ornate seat that had once been Neadesto's.

"I meant no disrespect, my Lady," Enrico answered Morgan, and struggled to find the right words. "I can only say I was humbled by your beauty," he finished, with a deep bow to Neadesto, and felt a tightening in his throat as he used the compliment Yolunu had taught him for such a breach of protocol, to cover his confusion as his mind questioned everything before him.

"It has been a long time since someone brought a blush to this old face. Your teacher is to be rewarded. What is her name?" Neadesto patted the seat once more and smiled when Enrico levered himself to his feet and climbed the platform steps to sit beside her.

"My teacher is dead, killed when Tadesde forces fired unannounced on her vessel. I would ask that it be recorded that Yolunu died in defense of her House." Enrico held his body straight, refusing to make eye contact with anyone, and focused on a glimmer of light reflecting off of a hinge across the room.

Isaac slumped in his seat with an audible gasp, and Enrico saw Morgan frown at the man before bringing her thoughts back to the news being presented.

"It will so be noted. What other news have you to share?" Iedonea stepped forward and interrupted the silence.

"My master, the brave and courageous Neavillii, fought gallantly to allow me the opportunity to escape. I fear the worst for her, and for everyone left behind." Enrico heard his voice crack as the emotions he'd been holding in threatened to escape.

Neadesto pulled his body toward her, and he focused on the softness of her touch for a moment.

"What is the status of our navy?" Morgan asked the room loudly.

"Seventeen troop transport vessels stand ready to depart.

They await your whim, my Lady." Iedonea bowed to Morgan, a gesture Enrico was unable to interpret.

"The Gulardee stand five thousand strong and anxious for battle, my Lady." An old soldier stood and bowed low.

"I speak for three hundred and seventy-eight fighter pilots; we await your desire, most beautiful of ladies." The Delta pilot who accompanied Enrico stood and bowed with a flourish and a grin.

"Then it is to be war. House against House, until only one remains. See to the arrangements, my friends. I would leave as soon as possible." Morgan gave a shallow bow to the room and the standing commanders before turning and striding to the door.

Enrico watched her departing back until she was out of sight.

"Come, you'll ride in the flagship with me." Iedonea held her hand out to Enrico.

He paused before reaching out with his free hand and using his cane to stand.

Chapter Twenty-Six - Wergol - 2012

"Hey!" Tim didn't turn as he held a shot glass over his head.

Sam exchanged a worried glance with Denise before she moved down the bar in the intoxicated man's direction. Nothing was said between them as she refilled his glass and left the bottle on the counter. He refilled it again before she could walk the short distance back to Sam.

"I spoke with the Choctaw elder who lives down by the depot. He agreed to perform the ceremony. That is, if you don't mind?" Sam looked at Denise, Tim's troubles momentarily forgotten.

"It's not like I can wear white. Sure, a shaman's ceremony would be fun." Denise placed her hand on Sam's as she cast a distracted look back towards their ever-drunker friend.

"He'll snap out of it. Did you see that medic on Seventh today?" It was Sam's turn to reassure Denise.

"What? Oh yeah. He said I was fine for a woman in my condition. When do you think we should tell everyone?" Denise brought her attention back to Sam with a soft smile.

"I'd say today, but how about we just wait until the next time we catch Tim sober?" Sam waved his hand in Tim's direction with a sad laugh.

"Sure," Denise mouthed as she watched Tim up-end the now empty bottle.

"Hey!" He shouted, once more holding up his empty shot glass.

"No more Tim. Go sleep it off upstairs." Sam wheeled his chair over beside Tim and tried to place a hand on his friend's arm to show his concern.

"Fuck you. I don't need this fucking bar. I got money. I got lots of fucking money. The Great fucking Sansheren fucking Houses fucking saw to that. I'm going to go fucking drink somewhere else. So fuck yourself." Tim's voice was a monotone throughout his entire outburst.

"Sleep it off, Tim." Denise moved to grab Tim's arm, only to be shrugged off.

"Let him go, his shadow will keep him out of trouble." Sam shifted his chair and caught Denise's hand before she could follow Tim to the door.

A bannerless Sansheren stood and followed him out of the tavern. She was one of the women who had attacked them before. Morgan, having placed Tim, Denise, and Sam's well-being on their heads, had guaranteed lifetime bodyguards for her childhood friends.

Sam and Denise moved to the bar, and nothing was said as Denise began the routine of cleaning glasses.

"I was hoping Tim would be here." Greg entered the bar unnoticed and now stood next to Sam.

"He decided to go drink somewhere else," Sam said without looking away from Denise.

"Damn. Heard you went to see Doc Hambert. Anything I should be worried about?" Greg shifted his gaze from Sam to Denise with a smile that did not quite replace his frown.

"Yes." Denise kept her eyes on the glass she was washing.

"Yes, I should be worried?" Greg prodded, without changing his expression.

"I asked her to marry me." Sam's eyes dropped to the glass in her hand.

"Congratulations, when's the due date?" Greg slapped Sam on the back with far more force than he intended, and Sam was forced to brace himself against the arms of his chair.

"He asked me before I told him," Denise said and slammed the glass down. The sound of shattering glass brought silence to the rest of the tavern's occupants, and Denise stood glaring at Greg for several seconds as the background volume picked back up to where it had been.

"Let me see your hand," Greg said about the blood that was dripping onto the bar top, and he moved to stand beside Denise. "I'm sorry."

"It's okay," Denise mumbled before running from the room.

\#

"Gregory, it is good to see you again, my friend." The Sansheren that spoke was old; with banners that pronounced her the Twelfth rank Sansadee and the Lady of the House Decado.

Greg did not look up from the meal he and Sam were sharing as he pushed a chair in her general direction. Seven years of war on Bystocc had evolved their relationship from contract owner to trusted friend.

"I have little time. I have come seeking you and your noble leader, Timone. Rumors of war against the spawn Tadesde spread quickly, and my honor requires I be there in person this time." The Sansheren did not accept the proffered chair but knelt at Greg's side. The other patrons in the bar stopped talking to watch, and Greg realized something had changed in their dynamic. Somehow, this new war with Tadesde made him equal or greater than the ruler of a nearly bankrupt House.

"Tim is out getting drunk. As for me, I'm through with war. I've lost too many friends to think it glamorous, my friend." Greg did not make eye contact with Sam as he turned and faced the Sansheren.

"I understand, my friend. Always there must be those who stay behind to guard our families against opportunity and vengeance. There is no dishonor in choosing this role. I will savor the taste of open combat for you, then." The Sansheren stood, bowed, and walked to the door.

"Try the Twin Boars, just down the street. He goes there sometimes," Greg called out to the closing door before pushing his plate away.

#

"Tadalde offer you a commission?" Greg asked Tim as he walked through the bar door less than an hour later.

"Yeah, we ship tonight." Tim crossed the room and accepted the coffee Denise offered him.

"Are you sure they're going to be fighting Tadesde?" Greg asked after he downed his own drink.

"Yeah. Tadalde is hiring anyone who can walk. They want Tadesde bad. Bystocc was recaptured." Tim let the information hang in the air.

"Any word?" Denise asked.

"No. Just a lotta rumors. You coming, man?" Tim did not look at Greg as he threw the question out.

"Sure. Let's go say goodbye to Sam and grab our gear." Greg moved from the bar toward the tavern's back door.

"You go ahead, I'll meet you at the dock." Tim stared into the bottom of his cup for some time before looking up to see both of his friends watching him.

"It's better that way," he said defensively.

"If you don't say goodbye to him, don't you ever think you can come back," Denise said with a glare full of tears.

"He deserves better," Greg said as he walked away from the now silent Tim.

"Yeah, I know," Tim mumbled to Greg's back and followed.

Sam sat at a table in the small back room, working on the components of an unidentified machine. Sweat beaded his forehead and grease streaked his hands and arms.

"Hey, man, we're leaving." Tim shouldered past Greg and walked into the room.

"I know," Sam said without looking up from the pieces he was assembling.

"I just wanted to say, you know, see you later." Tim looked at Sam one last time before spinning and rushing out of the room.

"I thought you were staying," Sam looked up and held Greg with a look that bore none of the accusation his words had.

"I... Someone has to keep him alive," Greg finished.

"Yeah, I know." Sam looked back down at the table and to the part his hands were twisting.

"Hey, don't get married without us man," Greg offered with an uncomfortable laugh. He waited several seconds for response before giving up and turning to go.

"Hey, man, keep it safe," Sam said as the part snapped in his hands.

"Yeah," Greg whispered from the doorway.

Denise stood on the other side of the open door and glared at Greg as he shrugged to her and left. She walked into the room, pulled Sam's chair away from the table, and sat on his lap. They were silent for a long time.

Chapter Twenty-Seven - Space – 2012

Their passage on board the Sansheren transport was nearly uneventful. Tim chose to bunk among the five hundred or so humans who signed on, most only because of his name. Greg accepted the private berth that was offered them, and spent his time polishing his language skills among the Sansheren crew, and visiting Tim to see if the dark humor had left him yet. Days passed, and with each new transit jump the mercenaries grew more skittish, and more spooked. A consensus was building, a group opinion that Tim planned a suicide attack against Tadesde.

"His banner shrinks. I have entertained four this very morning who requested a new leader," Tadalde said in English as she passed a plate of meats to Greg.

"I know. His hatred for Tadesde's overwhelming," Greg said, never looking up from the food before him.

"I would offer an honorable escape to your friend," Tadalde echoed Greg's serious attitude.

"I don't know that he'll take it. He wants her head on a platter," Greg returned, this time looking at the glass of sour fruit juice that passed for Sansheren wine.

"Does my honor dictate that I be forced to sacrifice our friendship to protect his honor from himself?" Tadalde smiled sadly at Greg when he looked up.

"Tell me your thought, my friend," Greg said with no inflection.

"I would offer your services to the Flagship of the House Sheresuan. Humans are in vogue now it seems, and they lead the fashion; their Twelve will appreciate the gesture," Tadalde said deliberately, not wanting to give offense.

"I doubt Tim would agree to play ornamental bodyguard to a Sansheren." Greg gave a disgusted laugh at that thought.

"House Sheresuan will lead the battle and will be first to

ground. Only those onboard her Flagship will have the wonderful opportunity to see Tadesde's demise. I will be there. Think about it, my friend." Tadalde ended her words by passing a new plate to Greg. "My wives did not come; have you anyone to share your bed this night, handsome Gregory?" Tadalde leaned toward her startled human guest and smiled.

"If you offer out of boredom, surely there are those among your people who would be honored to join you this evening," Greg temporized.

"I have found that sleeping with one's underlings can cause troubles among the staff. I will not take offense if you decline without stating a reason." She laughed at his discomfort.

"I do not think I would be capable of what you ask. I'm sorry. But tell me please, why did you offer?" Greg asked with interest, not noticing that this time it was he who leaned closer.

"I admit to wishing to indulge in curiosity. The enthusiasm of your species is often spoken of in the dark." Tadalde reached forward and stroked his bare arm.

"I… I will have to think about it. How many wives do you boast?" Greg asked in Sansheren as he became aware of her proximity and pulled back, trying to cover the movement by reaching for a plate close to him and offering it to her.

"Your grasp of the court tongue improves, my friend. I have been honored by three who have born me children." Tadalde laughed as she accepted the change of subject with the plate.

"I thought you bore your own children?" Greg asked, as much to keep the conversation neutral as he did from confusion.

"It is difficult to explain to another species, it seems. My wives bore children of their flesh for me. I am their father and my claim to them is stronger than that of their mothers. When I finally choose to bear children, I will do so for another."

Greg shook his head to show his confusion.

"The two highest honors one can give another are to bear her children or to die for her, and bear her children." Tadalde toyed with a piece of meat as she tried to marshal her thoughts.

"What keeps someone you do not like from claiming you're the father?" Greg asked, trying to give form to the many questions that he was thinking.

"No one can force another to be a father, it is a title you

embrace with marriage." Tadalde seemed amused at the question, so Greg tried again.

"What is the Sansheren word for bastard, to be born to an unwed mother?" He knew his host's grasp of English at least matched his grasp of Sansheren, but Tadalde shook her head at the word and frowned at its definition.

"There is no word for what you describe. To be born without a father one would emerge from a permanently dead mother, and I have taught you several words for that insult. This is a distasteful subject, I thought we were discussing marriage." Tadalde again leaned forward in an intimate manner as she finished speaking.

"We were, but the subjects of children and marriage seem to be linked." Greg found himself once more trying to maintain a distance from his host and employer.

"Of course they are. The marriage is not finalized until the children are conceived." Tadalde shifted away without losing her focus on Greg's face.

"I thought you had to die to conceive?" Greg moved to lean against the couch that was behind him; he realized his error as Tadalde shifted and laid her head on his now open lap.

"It is the act of trust, in allowing your loved one to kill you that consummates the marriage. The resuscitation team waits outside to revive you." Tadalde reached out and ran a claw tip down the side of the uncomfortable man's neck.

"What about murders?" Greg asked.

"They rarely occur. To kill someone is to inherit all their family, their children, their honor debts, everything. I have not heard of that happening within my lifetime." She continued to stroke his neck, pausing when he swallowed and his adam's apple bobbed.

"So, how do you know the other person wants to have kids, and not just another jump in the sack?" Greg watched warily as Tadalde curled up even closer to him.

"The marriage ceremony is brief, but unmistakable. Five words, 'I would bear your children'."

Tadalde's voice was growing softer, but Greg didn't quite dare to move and look to confirm his hopes. "What about divorce?" he asked, trying to keep the silence from building.

"I've heard humans say 'till death do we part,' this speaks to Sansheren custom as well, but that ties into your question about murder does it not? We could speak of this another time - right now I only ask that you remain until I am asleep. Are you capable of this small favor, old friend?" Her voice was sleep muffled, and Greg didn't bother to respond as he waited for her breathing to deepen.

#

"It's the only real shot you'll have at Tadesde man." Greg sat on Tim's bunk and looked down at his friend.

"Playing honor guard to some furry-assed bitch ain't my idea of a real shot, you dig?" Tim sat up and swung his legs to the edge of the bunk, forcing Greg to stand.

"You say honor as if it is an insult. This is the only shot we got man. I'm taking it. I don't care what you do," he lied.

"Fine, I'll play the part. Hey, let's grab something to eat." Tim stood with Greg.

"Kinda ate with Tadalde. That's how I got us this gig." Greg turned his face away.

"Kinda ate with? Man, you didn't have to whore yourself." Tim yanked him back by his jacket.

"I didn't," Greg growled and jerked free.

"Sure, what'd you do? Discuss battle plans?" Tim snorted with disgust as he moved to cross the empty room.

The other mercenaries assigned to the room were already at the cafeteria, Greg assumed. "No," his terse response. "We discussed marriage customs. Whatever you do, never offer to have a baby for one of them," Greg tried to joke.

"Why not?" Tim stopped moving and held very still.

"That's their marriage ceremony, 'I would bear your children.' That's it. You accept and it's 'until death do us part'." Greg stared at Tim in confusion over his friend's look of panic.

"I need a drink; you have a bottle in your room?" Tim turned away from the door that led to the cafeteria and headed for the room's other exit.

"Yeah, why?" Greg asked to Tim's departing back. He followed him to his own quarters only to have the door slammed and locked in his face.

#

"Your beauty could stand to be enhanced. I fear you will do us both a dishonor with your appearance," Tadalde said in English when she looked up from her desk to see the unshaven and unwashed Tim leaning on Greg's arm. She now pointed to her own washroom with a frown.

"I tried," was Greg's answer to the look she gave him.

"My friend, perhaps you would protect both of our honors if you would enhance your beauty before we dock with the Flagship of the House Sheresuan." Tadalde tried to catch Tim's eye.

"I ain't your friend," he mumbled before shaking off Greg's hand and stumbling toward the indicated room.

"I fear for my standing with the Great House Sheresuan. While they cannot refuse your presence, his behavior may leave them less than appreciative." Tadalde pushed her chair clear from the desk and pointed to an empty chair for Greg.

"He'll be professional, and eventually sober up. I explained this was his only chance to get Tadesde." Greg accepted the chair with a sigh that expressed his concern for his suicidal friend.

"I remember the death of his spouse, but it seems his hatred has grown worse, beyond his control. Now it eats him from within like an unwanted child. What has happened to fuel it?" Tadalde asked while offering Greg a glass of wine.

"He had another lover. She was on Bystocc," Greg said and then took a small sip.

"Many have lost far worse at her hand. But, I understand better, I think. I will warn the Lady of Sheresuan as to his recent grief." Tadalde also sipped her drink.

"Why can't they refuse?" Greg asked after the silence built.

"One cannot refuse a bodyguard. But then, one does not have to feed or clothe an unacceptable guard. There have been many incidents recorded where a guard's only food came from insisting on tasting for poison, and where an unappreciated guard slept in the hallway in front of her chosen master's door." Tadalde's lesson was cut short by muffled shouts from Tim.

"Where's the fucking razor?" he asked, slamming the door open.

"I do not own one. Your down is attractive, why not wear it?" Tadalde offered him a human looking smile.

"Fine. You ready, man?" Tim left the washroom toweling his

wet hair, his wrinkled clothing spotted with moisture.

"I have outfits for both of you," Tadalde lied as she stood and moved to her own vanity. She removed two pairs of pants that belonged to one of her wives. The spouse was a spacer, tall by Sansheren standards. The loose pants looked like they might fit the men.

"Like hell, man. I have battle armor in our quarters. We'll go change and meet you at the aft airlock." Tim cast one last disgusted look at the billowy silk pants and left the room.

Greg shrugged, glad of Tim's reaction, before leaving himself.

When they reached the airlock a short time later, Tim wore solid black. Gone were his slept-in clothes, replaced by first a layer of soft cotton and then by skin tight, flexible black armor. All but his head was protected, and he carried his helmet in hand. Greg wore the same black armor, but one entire leg piece had been replaced with dark blue material. His helmet was also a dark blue. Three other humans, two men and one woman, had suited up and joined them uninvited. Tim was now clean-shaven.

"I don't care how important this bitch is, I won't bow," Tim whispered to Greg as Tadalde approached and the airlock started hissing.

"It would be unforgivable to offer a respect you did not feel. Stand tall, my friend," Tadalde said in English as the hatch opened.

The flagship airlock was open and they moved into it without speaking. When the final sequence was complete, they exited into a large cargo bay that had been converted into barracks for the Sansheren fighters. Many of those present, Greg noticed, bent their knee to Tadalde as she walked past, flanked by her human mercenaries.

"I'm telling you, I ain't gonna bow," Tim said once more to bolster his own determination. They left the cargo bay and moved down the corridor, a short passage that opened into a slightly smaller chamber.

Greg glanced around the room as Tadalde stepped forward and bowed to an old Sansheren woman.

"I am honored by your gift."

Morgan's voice snapped Tim's head up and Greg stared at the person standing behind the Sansheren he assumed to be the head of House Sheresuan. Both he and Tim stepped forward to see her better. She had not been taking the drugs the doctor told them about, Greg thought as he noticed her bare chest. Her small breasts were firm and no longer swollen and tender looking. Something had etched new lines around her eyes, and she no longer looked so young.

Tim took another step forward, bumping several Sansheren retainers out of his way. One hand clenched his helmet, and the other groped about his belt and side, seeking something to cling to, stopping when it found his holstered weapon.

"My Lady!" a bumped retainer said in fear as she watched the human grab a weapon.

Isaac entered the room from the other side and watched as Morgan looked up and froze at the sight of the silent Tim.

Greg, too, felt frozen, unable to move as his lips formed her name.

"They are family," Isaac called out, stopping the retainers who were drawing weapons against what they thought was a threat to Morgan.

"Come on," Morgan said, breaking eye contact with Tim to include the entire party, and turned to leave the room.

"My wife will find you lodgings," Morgan said at the end of the corridor she had fled into.

Tadalde and the humans stood as Morgan closed her door on them. Iedonea came out a moment later and directed them to a large stateroom they were all to share.

"We will make Bystocc orbit before morning. Rest," Iedonea told them before rushing out, Greg assumed to discover what had disturbed Morgan.

#

She found the younger leader crying in her quarters.

"Speak, my niece. I cannot read your face the way you have buried it in the pillow so." Iedonea pulled against the pillow as she spoke.

"He is the family I went searching for. I thought he was safe on Wergol," Morgan said, not giving voice to her personal certainty of defeat.

"He does you great honor in coming to you. Do not shame him by sending him away." Iedonea gave up on removing the pillow and began to caress her shoulders.

"I will not, I cannot. I am too selfish to send him away. I want to be near him so bad." Morgan was aware of how incoherent she sounded. The certainty she felt about her up-and-coming defeat robbed her of any veneer of independence. Right now, she felt like a child and she wanted Tim close. Even if it was in another room on the ship, and even if it meant he would die with her, she wanted him with her. She never noticed when Iedonea left.

#

"You do us a great honor in your presence," Iedonea said in Sansheren, her eyes on Tim as Greg translated.

"I came for Tadesde," Tim answered, and even the Sansheren could hear the pain in his voice.

"As did our beloved, Morgan. She, like you, is focused on the destruction of Tadesde and little else. I fear your unexpected appearance distracted her from the task at hand." Iedonea waved her hand around the command center of the flagship. She had gone from Morgan's quarters to offer a tour of the ship to Tim, Greg, and Tadalde.

"What are your battle plans? How many ships does Tadesde have in orbit? How many bodies can you put on the surface at once?" Tim ripped off a string of questions without waiting for Greg's translation. He moved toward the system display unit and began tracing ships' locations on the holographic globe. Morgan's fleet occupied one small edge of the display and was surrounded by a haze that represented the smaller fighter crafts.

"We detect seven and ten ships to orbit. Tadesde alone uses magnetic mines - for her safety – she is fool," the captain of the flagship stepped up next to Tim and answered in broken but understandable English.

"Or she lays a clever trap," Morgan challenged as she walked into the room.

"Good point. How many troops you plan on beaching?" Tim never looked up from the display as Morgan moved to stand opposite him across the large transparent sphere.

"I brought three thousand Gulardee soldiers-"Morgan said, but Tim's snort silenced her.

"We had over eighty thousand men on the ground at one time, what good is three thousand going to do?" He didn't try to disguise his disgust.

"Our intelligence reports never placed more than ten thousand Tadesde retainers on the ground to your eighty thousand, my friend. The Gulardee soldier is not to be underestimated. And there is a difference between routing a guerilla army and all out orbital war. The planet belongs to whoever controls the gravity well." Tadalde stepped closer and placed a hand on Tim's arm by way of caution.

"In leaving a substantial guard behind us to defend the House Sheresuan, my niece has accomplished two separate goals. First she guarantees that Tadesde cannot seize her other House, a wise precaution when one considers that over half of Tadesde's force is still unaccounted for. Second and far more important I think, she has shamed the other Great Houses into contributing openly to this glorious effort." Iedonea said with a nod to Tadalde and then stopped speaking when she realized Tim was still waiting for the translation of her first words.

Greg spoke slowly as he tried to keep the information in order, pausing to allow Tadalde to fill in the gaps.

Morgan moved to leave before the translation was half finished, only to be stopped at the door when Tadesde's voice flooded the room.

Chapter Twenty-Eight - Bystocc - 2012

"I concede any claim on this miserable rock to you, most beautiful of patrons," Tadesde repeated her first broadcast, and Morgan's communication officer released the speakers with an audible click.

Morgan took a moment to compose herself before she nodded to the captain and then spoke loudly. "You never had a claim on this planet. Your concession is without value. Put my wife Neavillii on now," Morgan said in a stilted court accent as she moved closer to the display unit.

Tadesde's seventeen ships in orbit had more than doubled in number. Thirty seven ships, including two heavy armors, now dotted the display in bright green.

"I will accept your judgment on this, my Lady. If you will give me a day to pull my people off?" Tadesde's voice whined through the communication speakers, and Morgan signaled for the circuit to be broken.

"Fix that," she said as she watched the holographic display.

"It is not mechanical, my Lady. The problem lies within her voice," the communications officer stated with obvious pleasure.

"What is she hiding?" Morgan asked the room in a whisper. "Put me back on. I would speak with my wife now," Morgan said loudly, trying to force the other's hand.

"The Lady Neavillii was murdered by natives. We discovered her children only recently."

Those in the command center winced as her voice grew even more shrill.

"You are stalling for some reason. What is it? My wife is dead, you tell me. Her name will be added to that of the wife of my dearest mate, Timone. Both have fallen at your hand." Morgan never realized that she was staring at Tim as she spoke.

He waited for Greg to whisper a translation to him before looking away from her intense gaze.

Morgan looked to the display again and noticed Tadesde's forces were now surrounded by the tell-tale blurring of smaller fighter craft. Her armada was now double the size of House Sheresuan's fleet.

"We found her children. We have cared for them, fed them, but still you call for war. Your desire to see me dead blinds you to reason." Tadesde's gasp for air could be heard over the communication broadcast.

"I will not let you depart this planet to plot my future destruction. You have given me insults of family, blood, and honor. You will pay for those debts with blood," Morgan said as she watched over fifty vessels begin moving toward her smaller fleet on the edge of the display.

"It is war then. I knew when first we met. Let the record show, I fought you valiantly, whatever the outcome-" Tadesde's piercing whine ended as her fleet picked up speed.

"The records will show that you died without heirs," Morgan said with a confidence she did not feel.

"I do not think she heard you, my niece," Iedonea said with a smile.

"How long until contact?" Morgan asked, and focused on breathing as her fear and panic increased.

"Eight minutes, my Lady. We should assume a position encircled by our freighters and behind our fighters, my Lady." The captain moved to stand beside her bridge crew, awaiting orders.

"No. I will not ask others to take a risk I refuse. We lead," Morgan heard her own voice shout, and leaned forward to grip the railing in front of the display unit.

"Your courage has never been seen, my Lady." Tadalde bowed to Morgan over her bent knee.

Morgan did not see the looks of awe that the Sansheren present gave her, but Tim and Greg did.

"Closing in four minutes," an anonymous crew member called out, and Morgan closed her eyes briefly, to say a prayer to some nameless childhood god.

In doing so, she missed the new blips that formed on the display as the fleets of several planets shrugged off their camouflage and committed to the battle.

"This is the House Medori requesting the honor to fight under your banner. We are fifteen ships strong and ready for battle," a Sansheren voice flooded the room, bringing Morgan's attention back to the holograph before her.

"This is the House Gashere, stating our intention to defend the beautiful Morganea; we are twenty-three ships strong and ready to fight," the second voice prevented anyone from speaking.

"Announcing the Flagship of the royal family of Dreco. It is our honor and privilege to offer the services of the Drecan navy to the Human Morganea. We pledge an alliance for the purpose of destroying Tadesde," the badly accented Sansheren came over the intercom to a stunned silent command room. Two hundred or more medium size blips appeared on the screen as confirmation, haloed by their fighter craft.

"This here is the good ship Montana. Loyal to Morgan, on our own, and loaded for bear." Frank Griffin said in English, and his southern drawl brought a smile to Morgan's face as the system display continued to show new ships coming in behind them and overtaking her older vessels.

"I said my niece was brilliant. And in bringing only a limited force she guaranteed participation of the great Houses. She did not allow her pride in the forces of the House Sheresuan to risk the downfall of Tadesde," Iedonea said, and Morgan noted the smugness in her voice as the command room erupted in cheers. Several of Tadesde's blips had already disappeared from the screen.

#

"It's over." Isaac stood beside her, not touching.

Morgan looked up from the screen and met his eyes. She realized he had seen her fear.

"Get me out of here," she whispered as she felt the threat of tears build. He put his arm around her waist and steered her to the exit.

"Let her go man, just let her go." Greg pulled on the silent Tim's arm as Morgan stumbled from the room.

She never saw the look of shared pain Tim shot her. Neither

244

did she feel the needle Isaac used once they were within her room. She drifted to sleep crying and wishing she were in Tim's arms.

#

"She's crying for you," Isaac said to the chamber of mercenaries waiting for quick passage to the planet.

Greg looked up to see the doctor pinning Tim within an angry gaze.

"You're wrong, man." Tim's voice remained calm; even as he addressed the doctor he didn't surrender his place in the head of the cue waiting to pass through the airlock.

"She cries for her dead wife, perhaps you could share your grief and offer her comfort," Iedonea said after Tadalde translated for her.

It was several seconds longer before Greg finished translating for Tim. "Go to her man, I'll take care of Tadesde." Greg put his hand on his friend's shoulder and pushed him out of line.

Iedonea moved to stand in front of them after Tadalde finished translating. "It would be my honor to take your place in the hunt for the spawn," Iedonea offered, her eyes meeting Tim's.

As Greg translated her words, Tim handed Greg his personal weapon, before leaving the room with a disheartened shrug.

"Come friend, we have a duty to perform." Iedonea waved Greg into the now open airlock.

"I know," Greg said in Sansheren with a feral grin as he followed the old Sansheren into the airlock.

Two of the human mercenaries joined them as did Tadalde. When the airlock cycled, they stepped into a transport vessel. The pilot waved a salute over her shoulder when she recognized Iedonea.

"They should aim for the stomach," Iedonea offered to the mercenaries, who neglected to fasten their safety harnesses and now sat in awkward positions checking and loading weapons.

"We know," Greg answered without his previous smile.

"We're all veterans of the long crusade to defeat Tadesde on this planet," Tadalde said with her own serious expression. She, too, was verifying the readiness of her personal weapon.

"You got a gun?" Greg asked without looking up from Tim's,

which he was loading.

"I had not planned to come; I am ashamed at my lack of preparation." Iedonea bowed her head as she realized her lack of foresight.

"It's a sawed off shotgun. Packs quite a punch so be damn sure of your footing before you pull the trigger. There are six rounds in each magazine, try to keep count. And see if this will fit in your pocket." Greg gave Iedonea a second magazine for the weapon he passed her.

She held the weapon gingerly before unfastening her harness and shifting to shove the magazine into a pocket. The magazine fit, but only just, and she had difficulty sitting back in her seat with its bulk against her leg.

"How does it target?" she asked as she studied it curiously.

"Point and shoot. It does not discriminate. That is the trigger housing; keep your fingers clear until we land." Greg reached out and moved her hand down the pistol grip.

"And it's effective radius?" Iedonea asked, and Greg paused to answer as the craft they were in began to shred atmosphere in its descent.

"Grounding in eight," pilot called over her shoulder.

"Best at short range, the rounds alternate. Tracer, shrapnel, slug, slug, shrapnel, tracer," Greg shouted, to compensate for the increased ship noise as they began skimming over clouds.

"In five," the pilot chanted.

"Keep your friends behind you. It is for crowd control, you know?" Greg grabbed hold of the straps as the craft veered violently.

"One would wonder of the crowds that encouraged the design of such a weapon." Iedonea murmured as she, too, clutched her safety harness.

"And, grounded! The Administration building is straight in front of us, ladies; let's go." The pilot was first out of the craft's airlock bypass hatch; Greg beat her to the ground.

"Clear!" he hissed, and Iedonea dropped down beside him.

Tadalde and the other two mercenaries dropped to the opposite side of the craft using a different auxiliary hatch. The street before them was empty of all except rubble and a few random bodies, and those native Bystocc.

"Call off," Tadalde said softly into her communication unit.

"Second unit, all clear."

"Fifth unit, all clear."

"Sixth unit, all clear."

"Third unit, all clear."

Tadalde made eye contact with Greg under the craft as she waited for unit four to respond.

"Fourth unit, talk to me," Greg whispered.

"Fourth unit, we have multiple surrenders. Request backup," a loud voice answered in English.

"This is unit two; we have people coming out of the building. They are crawling. Thirty, maybe forty surrenders. Also requesting backup."

"This is unit five, we have confirmed surrenders."

"This is unit three here, we need backup for least thirty surrenders."

Greg looked from Tadalde to Iedonea before thumbing his communication unit. "Silence on the line. All units, hold your position and relay requests to orbiting vessels." Greg released the switch and shrugged.

"We're not alone," Iedonea said, pointing to the top of the Administration steps.

A large group of Sansheren were forcing, at gunpoint, several green tinged Sansheren out of the door in front of them. One of the harassed bolted from the group and ran toward their ship. Iedonea growled as she raised her weapon and pulled the trigger. The running woman was blown in half and the tracer shattered against the steps behind. Debris and gore splattered down for several seconds as all but the humans stared in horror.

"Most impressive," Iedonea said.

"I said to make sure your friends were behind you," was Greg's response as he rubbed his most affected ear.

"We surrender!" one of the Sansheren on the steps called out.

"Then drop your weapons," Greg shouted.

"If we do, these carrion eaters will escape," the other replied.

"I demand to be taken to the lovely Arbitrator. Her justice and honor are impeccable," a high-pitched whine echoed the familiar voice.

The one who stepped away from the guns on the stairs was a vibrant emerald green, a shade Greg had never seen on a

Sansheren before. Little hints of orange were all that remained of her original adult markings. The fur had even grown back to cover her forehead.

"Come, Tadesde, I will take you to Morganea, it is witnessed that you voluntarily sought her justice. Come." Iedonea stepped from the side of the craft and leveled her weapon at the former leader.

"She will be just. We are equals, she and I," Tadesde giggled to herself as she moved forward and was chained.

"We would pledge our allegiance to Morganea. We brought her enemies as offering to her beauty," the leader of the captives said rapidly, and her lack of confidence was apparent to all that heard her.

"Morganea will give you justice, whatever you deserve. Shackle the others and bring them here," Iedonea drawled as she handed her weapon to Greg and leaned against the warm craft.

"All units. Forcibly secure any who show symptoms of regression. Press the rest into service." Tadalde released a communication unit with a sigh before kneeling to join Iedonea who now sat on the ground. They both stared at the remains of the Sansheren Iedonea had shot.

Greg leaned against the craft and listened without interrupting.

"Any movement?" Tadalde asked as she finished sitting down.

"No. What could survive such a weapon? I wonder that Tadesde could hold this planet for so long." Iedonea shifted and leaned against the younger leader.

"Such powerful weapons are rare, and well cared for. The one you used belongs to Timone himself." Tadalde brought her arms around Iedonea, and they sat there in silence for some time before Greg sat down beside them.

"Tell me, my friend. What planet created such destruction?" Iedonea nodded to the shotgun Greg handled casually.

"This? This is nothing. Earth, the human home world." Greg set the gun down within the women's easy reach as he shifted to squat on his knees, ignoring the pain in his hip.

"Such a people could conquer the universe, my friend. You scare me." Iedonea met his eyes as she spoke.

"Yeah, well, they would have to get it together first," Greg said before struggling to his feet.

"The pirates are the only species to travel to Earth, and they don't announce themselves, I think," Tadalde said to the silence that followed Greg's departure.

Iedonea drifted into sleep with unpleasant thoughts dancing beyond her reach. Tadalde continued to guard her friend.

Chapter Twenty-Nine - Earth – 1995

The smell of urine woke her. The room was still lit, the glare of the overhead lights painful to her. She lay in the huge bed and listened to the sounds of the giant house: a clock ticking from the stairwell, a cat mewing in some unknown room. She was cold and the bed was still damp beneath her. Lui Moih-Gan rose and left the room in search of a bathroom.

#

"What little flower sings to me?"
She was lying immersed in the near scalding water of a large sunken tub when the door opened, and a male face peeked in and spoke derisively.
"Lui Moih-Gan, what did she sing?" the teen she assumed was her brother taunted from the now open doorway.
"I am pleased to meet you, brother. If you leave, I will get dressed." Her desperate attempt to pull the shower curtain closed seemed to fuel her brother's interest.
"Such a pretty little bird, sweet nectar to my eyes. Sing, sing." He walked into the room and repeated his demand as he tore the curtain from her grasp.
"Please, don't." She crouched into the corner of the tub.
"Now that is music to my ears, little sister. And to think I was worried you would put a crimp in my lifestyle." He laughed as he climbed into the water.
Her gaze darted from his fancy shoes to his face and down his clothed body in fear.
"Such a pretty flower for the plucking, thank you for waiting up for me.   I know we're going to be real good friends," he

whispered in her ear while pinning her body beneath him.

And she felt herself grow faint as the stench of his alcohol laden breath overwhelmed her. But she never passed out, and it was over three hours before he threw her, bruised and bleeding, on to her bed.

The dawn was just beginning to tinge in the sky in sympathy.

Chapter Thirty - Bystocc – 2012

Morgan felt the tears burning in her eyes as she lay perfectly still. The silence of the room was broken by her gasp for air and by another's soft breathing. She was in an adult body, she realized, as the horror of the dream began to fade. A sharp pain in her back brought her attention to the other person present. She was held in someone's arms, propped up with them holding her tight and rocking slowly. The pain was joined by another in her neck as she realized the person holding her was dressed in armor. Flexible but stiff, it poked her in several uncomfortable spots. She opened her eyes, to confirm that it was black. And then suppressed the hope that tried to bloom within her.

"I'm still dreaming," she whispered, hoping for a denial.

"As long as it's better than the last one."

Tim's voice startled her and she shifted to see his face. He let go of her and she felt the ache begin anew.

"I was dreaming about..." she couldn't force herself to give voice to the memory.

"I know," Tim offered and reached out to pull her back into his arms.

She looked up at his face and saw her tears in his eyes.

"My Lady! The carrion born has been captured!" Iedonea threw open the door and shouted with a grin before continuing on her way.

"I should go," Morgan whispered, her eyes drifting to Tim's mouth.

"I know," he answered before kissing each of her eyelids and then her lips.

His tongue lingered in her unprotesting mouth before he pulled away brusquely, stood, and waved her toward the door.

The break in contact left her cold, and she rose without a word and walked from the room.

The corridor was crowded with retainers moving toward the main audience chamber. They all dropped to their knees when they saw Morgan, and she waved them out of her way. She could feel Tim following her as they moved toward the chamber where she had first seen him on board the ship.

Tadesde and several others were crouched within a barricade. Their fur was green, and Morgan wondered briefly as to their fertility; she knew that few regressives bore children.

But to take that risk, Morgan thought with a shudder.

"My Ladee, my Ladee!" Tadesde howled as she dropped to her knees.

The Sansheren present clutched their ears as the voice peaked into a painful range.

"Wee are both Ouosin, you and I. I would honor you, my Ladee!" Tadesde crawled forward, and Morgan noted the ridges that had formed on the captive's back.

The regression was worse than anything she had ever read about, and the thought of fathering death children of the other horrified her.

"She should stand as a warning to indulgent parents. Take her to the zoo on the Shere. All the Great Houses should bear witness to her existence," Morgan said to cover her discomfort, addressing Iedonea who grinned her own response.

"At least keell me! You promised to keell mee! Where is your honor? Keell mee," the voice dropped to a guttural whisper as Tadesde collapsed sobbing on the floor.

Amigo moved from Enrico's side and stood watching as tranquilizer drugs were fired into the regressed leader's back.

"Spontaneous genetic regression. I thought it was just insults, and flowery speech." Isaacs's voice echoed through the room, and he looked about for reassurance.

Tadalde moved to his side and placed her arm on his shoulder. "It is a deep personal fear no one speaks of. I would not be alone this night?"

Her request hung in the air only moments before Isaac draped his arm across her shoulders.

"What of us, my Lady?" Ferseca shouted and Morgan turned to see the old woman's green fur and muzzled face.

"You chose your role in history, accept it," Morgan said as she gestured for the retainers to be drugged.

"Send them all to the home world. Tadesde will need food," Morgan called over her shoulder.

Ferseca's scream followed her into the corridor, and Morgan did not notice that Tim failed to follow her. She made her way to the command center and was joined there by Iedonea.

"She was right," Morgan said, not looking at Iedonea.

"In what? My Lady," Iedonea asked, and Morgan thought she ignored her intent.

"I am as much Ouosin as she. My beloved Neadesto gave me the rank of Twelve but not the right of Eleven," Morgan continued talking as she watched the holograph display without interest.

"Your modesty will be spoken of through the ages, my niece," Iedonea tried to joke.

"I wear a banner that is made a mockery by my lack of experience. How long before the whispers start? It is you who should wear this." Morgan turned to her older friend and began to unfasten the ancient banner Neadesto had given her.

"You're not the first to offer me such honor, but who am I to deny the whim of the great Morganea?" Iedonea again joked as she moved to kneel at Morgan's feet.

"You honor me with your presence," Morgan began the ceremony. "Do not disparage the moment with a false fealty. Stand." Morgan placed her hands on Iedonea's shoulders and lifted; the other made no move to rise.

"It is your presence that honors me, child. I can only hope such bravery is contagious," Iedonea said to begin her own ceremony, and smiled even as her voice choked with emotion.

"It was your bravery I borrowed from," Morgan said as she sank to her own knees.

"Your devotion is beyond measure, I can do no less than bring you closer to myself." Iedonea reached a hand to Morgan's face and was rewarded when the human woman leaned forward and rested her head on the older leader's shoulder.

"Your devotion gave me strength, I can do no less," Morgan paused to take a shaky breath before she continued speaking into Iedonea's ear. "I can do no less than bring you closer to myself," and Morgan whispered the name of the Twelfth rank of the

254

Sansadee to Iedonea. There was a brief pause as the moment built and then Iedonea whispered the name of the Eleventh rank of the Sansadee to her. Both women held the position, the emotions overwhelming them. They were unaware of the small crowd that gathered to watch the double ceremony in awe.

#

"That's it! We just leave? No goodbyes, no nothing?" Greg shouted at Tim's back.

"It's all been said," Tim said without turning. He stood waiting for the airlock to cycle.

Morgan had been on Bystocc for several days before Tadalde had given in to Tim's request, and agreed to grant them passage back to Wergol.

"Maybe, but I ain't said it," Greg stated as he followed his friend into the airlock.

"I sent her a note, invited her to Sam and Denise's wedding. You know how the Sansheren are about marriage and kids. She'll come as soon as her honor lets her leave this rock." Tim pointed out the airlock window as the ship they were in drifted clear of the flagship and offered them a view of the war-damaged planet. The blast craters were easy to spot, and they stood in the airlock for some time as they watched the planet shrink.

"Hey, when you gonna teach me that crap they speak?" Tim hit Greg in the arm as they entered the corridor.

Chapter Thirty One - Bystocc – 2013

"Are you certain?" Morgan sat on a lounge chair, watching three Sansheren children play at stalking each other behind the viewing glass.

"They are the only triplets to be found, my niece," Iedonea said from beside her on a separate lounge.

"When a nursery team comes from Sheresuan we will run the tests. Until then, it comforts me to pretend certainty." Morgan offered Iedonea a half felt smile.

"We have found a group of survivors who claim to have been your nursery team here. They were succored by natives during Tadesde's brief reign. They wish to return to work now." Iedonea did not voice her opinion of the validity of their claim.

"Have they any proof of their claim?" Morgan asked as she stood and gestured for the room's door.

"They have several children with them who have barely passed into the age of reason." Iedonea shielded her eyes as they moved into the brightly lit corridor.

"Indeed. I will grant them audience today." Morgan offered Iedonea her arm as they picked their way through the rubble that decorated the floor of the corridor.

An occasional blood splatter could be seen high up on the walls, and they passed by the few remaining bones of an unidentified, though obviously palatable native as they made their way up to the ground level.

"They will be honored by your personal attention to their case. Tell me, when will we leave to see your family's newborn?" Iedonea cast a side glance at her that Morgan did not see.

"I have duties here to accomplish first," she answered without breaking her pace.

"A leader must balance her duties carefully, lest one aspect of her life becomes neglected," Iedonea seemed to be speaking to the air; Morgan kept walking without pause.

"I do not see Enrico," Morgan said to break the silence that built between them.

The aircar they had traveled in was no longer sitting in the street where they had left it.

"Ah, but I see a shadow. Do you, my niece?" Iedonea asked without pointing to the aircar shadow which betrayed its position above them.

"Yes," Morgan responded as the aircar swooped down silently, mussing their banners with its breeze, and landed in front of them.

"My turn, my turn," Amigo called out from the back seat of the vehicle.

"My turn," Iedonea interrupted as she waited for the grinning Enrico to climb free of the pilot's seat.

"Now you have done it. Her skill and daring are known on twenty planets. The last time she piloted an aircar on Sheresuan, Neadesto entertained claims of accidental regression for weeks." Morgan laughed as she buckled herself in.

"Just unscrupulous cowards trying to enrich their standing by false claims of injury," Iedonea called over her shoulder as she fired the craft's engines and revved them far hotter than was necessary.

"From the head of the clothier's consortium? She was in the craft with you." Morgan's laughing taunts were cut short as Iedonea lifted the craft up and began to wind amongst the buildings at a height that barely cleared the tops of the ground cars as they passed. Their speed built, and soon they were zooming through more rural settings.

"I am told this particular model can circle an average planet in less than a day. Shall we try for dinner on the Southern Continent?" Iedonea brought them into a higher altitude before her question and now did not wait for a response before she threw open the throttle, and the craft shook in protest of the increased demands. The clouds and landscape far below could be seen to move, and Enrico gave up trying to determine their relative speed.

"Um, I would never dream of challenging one so experienced

in the worlds as yourself. But…" Enrico said, and Iedonea allowed his protest to linger as she aimed the nose of the craft at the sky above them and the clear blue began to darken.

"But? I do not think this is the place for flattery my dear. Speak your mind." Iedonea laughed as she once more leveled the craft's altitude.

"This craft may have been equal to your skill when it was built, but it is old and I fear it has not been regularly serviced. Your flying is far more advanced than its ability to fly. I humbly request that we at least return to breathable atmosphere." Enrico swallowed several times while he spoke. The shaking and pinging of protest increased with their altitude.

"Indeed. Has it been so very long, how are we both so old?" Iedonea began to ease the craft back toward the planet. They were now over an ocean, and she could make out the hint of a continent on the horizon.

"You should not protest age, my Lady. It becomes you well," Morgan shouted, over the increased sounds of vehicular distress.

"You speak the truth, my dear. But the ever courteous Enrico spoke a greater truth when he called my attention to this weary vehicle. The air intake regulator just failed. If I were still indulging my childish flying, we would be dead, I fear," Iedonea said as she fought with the controls. A loud hiss grew to dominate all other sounds; it was several moments before the passengers realized the engines were silent.

"I can help," Amigo jumped from her seat and pulled herself forward to cling to the back of Iedonea's seat.

"Climb onto my lap, child. It has been a long time since I glided a craft in, I would appreciate your small muscles and fast reflexes." Iedonea leaned back in her chair as Amigo slid in front of her.

The child braced her feet on either side of the steering column and placed her hands beside Iedonea's.

"This is the test of a real pilot. You watch that monitor; we have to avoid all blue patches. No matter how faint. They're down gusts. Look for the pink ones and we'll try to catch them. The radio seems to have blown out as well," Iedonea finished with an aside to Morgan and Enrico. The craft dropped suddenly, and she returned her complete attention to the controls.

"Sorry," Amigo murmured, but only Iedonea could hear her over the scream of the invading air. Without power for the locks, several hatches were now loose and threatening to tear open.

"They just appear like that. No anticipation will help you sometimes. Let's just try to stay in the pinks and reds." Iedonea pressed her lips to Amigo's head and was distracted to notice that the younger one was already shedding her scalp fur. The loose strands of fine fur floated in her nose and tickled her.

"The global locator shows us just short of the Southern Continent. We should see land soon. Regardless, we will have lost too much altitude before long." Iedonea stopped trying to reassure her passengers and concentrated on the controls again. That, and not sneezing.

"There are no large predators in these waters. Let us just hope the seat floats have been better serviced," Enrico shouted as he found his hand making a familiar path about his body; forehead, stomach, shoulder, shoulder, chin. It was a religious habit he thought broken before his eighth birthday. The memory of the small room, metal floor, silent fountain, and seven other frightened children came to him suddenly. The voice of the nameless priest saying last rites as they waited for their captors echoed from his memory, and he shook his head to exorcize it.

"Where are your flowery words of skill and experience, my friend? I have never crashed a craft yet. Would you foretell such an event now? With land on the horizon?" Iedonea found herself laughing as she forced the controls to obey her desire.

"I have heard human pilots say that any landing you can walk away from is not a crash," Enrico shouted forward, still trying to fight down the memory.

"We are alike then, human and Sansheren pilots. Any landing you can walk away from, I like that." Iedonea pull hard on the steering column and was grateful for Amigo's strength. They turned the craft away from what their screen showed as a looming wall of blue. They banked again, and then found themselves riding upwards on the thermal currents that poured off of the glacial mountain a few miles inland. Clouds enshrouded them, and Iedonea risked freeing a hand from the steering column to tap the global locator they were relying upon.

"The locator shows a city in this direction. Let us see just how close we can come," Iedonea said, her voice low for Amigo only.

They both continued to fight the craft's tendency to drift toward the downdraft just offshore.

"No choice," Amigo grunted as the steering column was once more almost ripped from their hands.

"I know, but never tell your passengers that." Iedonea gave a short laugh as the clouds continued to obscure the city the locator now placed beneath them. The spaceport was marked on the map and they were approaching it rapidly.

As they dropped down further, the clouds cleared and they found themselves fast approaching the vast rectangle of the spaceport. Iedonea risked a hand free of the steering column to activate sullen controls; without electronics they were forced to wait for the hydraulics to cycle the craft's landing gear. In the meantime, the steering column drifted left, and they banked into a steep circle. Seeing the stretch of usable tarmac shrinking fast, Iedonea brought her hand back to the steering column, and she and Amigo wrestled the craft into a violent landing. No one moved for several minutes as the craft skidded sideways to a stop, unencumbered by any remnants of the landing gear.

"Next time I fly," Amigo said fervently, and she scrambled over Iedonea's shoulder and into Enrico's lap.

Enrico held her until her shivering subsided and she looked out of the window.

"Company," Amigo said to her companions. Several natives of Bystocc were approaching the smoking craft cautiously.

"Well, let us see about arranging transportation back to our headquarters," Morgan said in a businesslike manner as she unfastened her harness and released the craft's door.

"Greetings. The beauty of the Arbitrator was understated in the broadcasts we have heard. We are your servants, my Lady." The lead native knelt on the ground and called out in broken Sansheren when Morgan emerged from the car.

"Stand, my friends. Stand," Morgan said as Iedonea accepted Enrico's help climbing out of the craft.

"It would not be fitting for one as worthless as myself to stand with you, my patron." The native continued to kneel as Morgan walked toward it.

"This is your planet. I only have the honor of protecting it." Morgan knelt as she placed her hand on the taller alien's shoulder.

"Your wisdom brings tears to my eyes. We have heard that Tadesde is no more?" the native looked deep into Morgan's eyes as they both stood.

"She is no longer a threat to this world or any other. Come, we require transportation back to my headquarters." Morgan's gesture included the natives and her own party who moved away from the aircar and now stood watching.

"It will be arranged, my Lady. Might I ask when they quit being a danger?" The native pointed at Amigo as the entire party moved toward the buildings at the edge of the square landing field.

"Four, sometimes five years. If there are infants hunting within your city we will be certain to send a nursery team here," Morgan said reassuringly.

The buildings were sunk into the ground, with less than half of a story showing, Iedonea realized.

"There are only three. Children of one that Tadesde killed, we think. The infants are locked within a fortified room. But they want for food." The native continued speaking as it directed them down a gentle slope that led into one of the hangar buildings.

"Have you heard the name of this mother?" Morgan asked as Iedonea and Amigo moved away to inspect the single craft within the hangar.

It was ancient, and technologically it was behind the old Sansheren craft they had arrived in.

"The evidence says that she was your wife, my Lady. We sent an envoy to your headquarters, but no word has come back to us as of yet." The native rushed its words out as Morgan froze and Enrico turned with a hard look.

"Several natives helped me to escape. We were forced to leave Neavillii behind. Dead," Enrico mumbled to no one.

"I know one of those that aided you, she, too, thought the Lady Neavillii was dead. But her name is painted on the door to the cell, I do not know what else to assume-"

Morgan silenced the native by placing her hand upon the other's arm again, reaching up to do so.

"We will send a nursery team back. They can run genetic tests. I thank you." Morgan moved away from the native and joined Iedonea where she stood listening beside the Bystocc aircar.

"I have no skill with this craft," Iedonea said.

"It will be my honor to fly you." A new native moved from the group that followed them from the field. She waved them into the car and began to run a preflight test on it.

"What is our travel time? And can you notify my flagship of our location?" Morgan asked as she struggled to fit her slim form into a seat designed for an even narrower species.

"If speed is required, my Lady, then perhaps it would be best if your flagship sent down a shuttle," the pilot deferred.

"No. I will sleep during the trip, my friend. Thank you for taking us." Morgan leaned back in her seat and closed her eyes.

"I think that I will sleep as well," Iedonea said. With a side grin to Amigo, she climbed aboard as the pilot fired the engines.

#

"We will wait here. I want to talk to the natives that helped me. We can catch the shuttle when it comes down for the infants," Enrico shouted into the craft's open hatch, and secured it without waiting for a response. The Bystocc craft was far louder than the damaged Sansheren craft had been, at any point.

It was Aldera who found him sleeping, curled into a ball with Amigo, in the hangar office late that night. And Aldera who returned from drugging and caging Neavillii's three death children to wake him for the shuttle's arrival. No words were said between the three as they embraced.

Epilogue - Wergol - 2013

Morgan smiled across the ground car cabin as Isaac twisted at his House banner.

He wore it over his shirt as a sash.

"Leave it be, child," Tansea said with a good natured laugh as she reached over and put the banner back where it was before. She also wore the single banner of the House America, as did the car's two other occupants.

Enrico wore an apprentice banner crossed under his House banner.

"When will the drugs take effect?" Tansea asked as she turned her attention to straightening Morgan's banner.

"It can take weeks for the hormone levels to build. I told you to start sooner," Isaac answered as he again twisted at his banner.

"Hush, child," Tansea said as she frowned at Isaac.

"It's okay," Morgan said, meaning the crooked banner as much as her lack of physical development.

"The lead car is slowing," Amigo said from her vantage point in the pilot's seat.

"We're here," Morgan said, and bent to clear the car's door as it opened.

Banessa also exited her car before the door completely opened and now stood waiting for Morgan, holding the tavern door for her.

"Close the fucking door!" was shouted from within as Morgan neared the building. It took her a few steps to realize that the sentence was spoken in a pidgin of Sansheren and English by a very recognizable voice. She stood in the doorway, knowing the sunlight pouring in behind her would give the room's inhabitants trouble identifying her.

Greg, Sam, and a very pregnant Denise were sitting around a single table, playing cards in hand. A fourth card hand lay face down before an empty chair and Morgan looked around before spotting Tim.

"I said, please close the door," Tim growled as he walked from the bar, bottle in hand. He set the bottle on the table amongst his friends and moved toward the still open door.

"With pleasure," Morgan said as she stepped clear of the door, forgetting the entourage that waited behind her.

"Morgan?" Tim mouthed when her voice registered, and she moved from the doorway into the room.

Denise dropped her glass with a gasp and Sam spun his chair around to see behind him.

"Tim?" Morgan whispered in a voice that brought tears to both their eyes.

Tim crossed the remaining distance to stand in front of her, and Morgan did not dare ask for the hug she wanted. Long sleepless nights had convinced her to let things go, to accept anything that came her way and hope that time would bring the rest.

Tim sank to his knees before her. He placed his hands across his chest, in the symbol of fealty appropriate to the head of one's Sansheren House.

Morgan swallowed against the threat of tears and bent to help him stand, only to be stopped by a small sound and a fierce look from Greg.

"I would be honored to bear your children, my Lady," Tim said in clear but heavily accented Sansheren as he brought his eyes to hers.

Morgan found herself sinking to her knees and reaching for him blindly, her tears being more than she could handle.

"Now?" she asked, and her small smile exploded into a fit of cathartic laughter that was joined by Tim's.

The other occupants of the room watched with amusement as Morgan lost her balance laughing and pulled Tim to the floor beside her.

Isaac played out Tim's hand of bridge before they regained control of the laughter that worked to heal them.

"I brought someone for you to meet," Morgan said.

"Amigo," she called and waved the rest of her party to join them at the table. Tears sprung in her eyes anew when Tim barely hesitated before he shifted his chair to sit beside Banessa.

"It is my deepest honor to meet you, my father," Amigo said in clear English as she bowed to Tim.

"Now that's one paternity suit I want to hear all the details about," Greg said with a laugh at Tim's expense.

"I am the daughter of Tadesde, caused by your hands." Amigo kept her head down, and Enrico moved to stand behind her.

"My apprentice saved her life and fostered her. If you wish, the situation can continue," Morgan offered into what she knew would be a tense silence.

"No. Hell no. A kid needs a dad. Hey you know how to play baseball?" Tim reached forward and ruffled Amigos now pale orange head fur.

"Ball? Catch? I can play catch." Amigo looked up into Tim's eyes with unconditional love and Enrico found himself forcing away the jealousy trying to build in his gut.

Morgan reached out to slip her free hand into his with a smile only he noticed.

Thank you for reading.

I have a webcomic:
http://zombpocalypse.cartoonistsleague.org/
https://www.facebook.com/TalesfromtheZombieApocalypse

And you can find me on FaceBook at:
 https://www.facebook.com/cheryceclayton

The artist can be contacted at:

 https://www.facebook.com/pages/JinxMedic-
Studios/154366657980647

www.ingramcontent.com/pod-product-compliance
Lightning Source LLC
Chambersburg PA
CBHW050022180626
46810CB00002B/531